WHAT THE DOCTOR ORDERED

SIERRA ST. JAMES

SALT LAKE CITY, UTAH

To my guy

To all the doctors I've known and still loved
(this is a small group—you know who you are)

Special thanks to Bruno-Baby, aka Dr. Michael Kerr,
who really did tell women he met that he was a janitor

Visit us at deseretbook.com

Library of Congress Cataloging-in-Publication Data

St. James, Sierra, 1966–
What the doctor ordered / Sierra St. James.
p. cm.
ISBN 1-59038-279-X (pbk.)
1. Aunts—Fiction. 2. Idaho—Fiction. 3. Aged women—Fiction.
4. Physicians—Fiction. I. Title.
PS3569.T124W47 2004
813'.54—dc22

2004002843

Printed in the United States of America 54459
Malloy Lithographing, Inc., Ann Arbor, MI

10 9 8 7 6 5 4 3 2

Chapter 1

The topic of conversation at the Baxters' dinner table was insanity. Particularly, whether or not Aunt Bertie belonged in this category. Ellie, as usual, was Aunt Bertie's sole supporter.

"She's eccentric," Ellie said. "That's different from being insane."

"Not very different," her father said.

Ellie ripped a roll in half, sprinkling the tablecloth with crumbs in the process. There was no use arguing about it. In all the time she'd known her parents, they'd never changed their minds about anything. Still, it wasn't a subject Ellie could simply shrug her shoulders about. "You just don't appreciate Aunt Bertie's artistic nature."

"Artistic?" Mckenna leaned back in her chair. "I don't think drawing cartoons counts as art."

"They're sketches," Ellie said. She gave her sister an aloof look, which, as usual, had no effect on Mckenna. It didn't matter that

Ellie was three years older, or a junior in college. Mckenna had just been voted Prom Queen. She didn't listen to commoners anymore.

Ellie's mom spread the butter across her roll in even, measured strokes. "Well, being an artist isn't a ringing endorsement of anyone's sanity. Van Gogh cut off his ear. Picasso spent his time drawing people with three eyes and two noses. He couldn't have been sane."

"Aunt Bertie just sketches things. I don't think she's in danger of cutting off parts of her head." Ellie held her hands out, trying to present her argument in the air. "You just think if someone is different than you, there must be something wrong with them."

Ellie's mom sighed and laid her knife down on the edge of her plate. "Ellie, how often do I have to tell you that your napkin belongs in your lap, not on the table."

"Sorry." Ellie unfolded the cloth and dropped it onto her lap. It slid off her knees and landed on the floor. She bent over, pulled it from underneath the chair legs, and replaced it on her skirt.

When she sat up straight again, Mrs. Baxter sent Ellie a look of silent reprimand, which was just one more reason Ellie didn't visit home more often. Although her parents lived only fifteen minutes away from the New Mexico State campus, the times she made it home for a family dinner were becoming less and less frequent.

She was tired of hearing about all the ways she needed to improve her life and how she'd never find a husband if she didn't learn to cook.

When Ellie finally finished school, got a job, and could afford to get her own place, she was going to use paper plates the entire first year just to spite her mother.

Ellie's mother nibbled at her roll, then set it on her plate. "You don't think we'll have to send Bertie to a nursing home, do you? They're such awful places, and so expensive." She let out a low sigh. "If only she'd been able to have children, someone to take care of her during her declining years."

Ellie let out a sigh of her own. "She's not declining just yet, and she's no more crazy than I am."

Mckenna snorted. Apparently she didn't think much of her sister's sanity, either.

Which figured. Mckenna thought if you wore pink lipstick with a red outfit you were crazy. Wearing shoes that didn't match your belt was evidence of incurable psychosis. She had never understood Ellie. Perhaps none of the family did.

Ellie's father cut his dinner roll into two perfect circles. "Well, are you going to read us Bertie's latest letter or not?"

Ellie slid her chair back and went to the kitchen counter. She riffled through a large bag that held her wallet, keys, lipstick, an array of receipts, loose change, and hair clips. Despite the clutter, it wasn't hard to find Bertie's letter. Bertie always wrote on fuchsia stationery and sent her mail the old-fashioned way. None of those computer emails for Bertie. She didn't trust computers.

Ellie brought the envelope back to the table and sat down. She suddenly wished she hadn't told her family she'd received another letter from her aunt. Now she had to read it, and the contents would do nothing to help prove the case of Bertie's sanity.

"Do we have to hear it?" Mckenna asked. "Aunt Bertie's last letter was all about her gallbladder attack."

Ellie unfolded the stationery. "I thought it was a very creative story. The way she named her gallbladder 'Little Hitler' and referred to the whole attack as the blitzkrieg."

"Yeah, but the cartoon she drew depicting it was gross."

"Sketch," Ellie said.

Ellie's mother put down her fork. "Can we please not discuss Aunt Bertie's medical conditions while we eat?"

Ellie cleared her throat. "Dear One," she read, "I do wish you'd reconsider my offer of coming out this summer. We could find you some exciting summer work, perhaps as a runway model or CIA agent."

Mckenna coughed in a sarcastic way. Her father shook his head. "You know, I think she gets more out of touch with reality every time we hear from her."

"It's called a sense of humor," Ellie said, and read a bit louder. "Besides, there's still the matter of the gentleman friend in my ward. I simply know he's your soul mate, and therefore you must come to Colton and marry him. Just think, you'll be the wife of a rich, charming doctor, able to travel and see the world—"

"Dad's right," Mckenna broke in. "Bertie's crazy."

"—Forget about that silly university. Come lighten your spirit and embrace your future here. It's just what the doctor ordered." Ellie skipped over the next paragraph, in which Aunt Bertie described the beautiful children she was bound to have with the aforementioned doctor and their life of bliss together. She didn't want any more commentary from her sister. Instead she read the last few paragraphs, in which her aunt reported that she was making preparations for Christmas.

"It's May," her father said firmly. "Why would she be getting ready for Christmas?"

Ellie shrugged. "To avoid the holiday crowds. I do the same thing."

Mckenna pushed what was left of her salad around on her plate and raised an eyebrow at Ellie. "You've already done your shopping?"

"It was easy for you. All you're getting is coal."

Mckenna glared at her.

"Is that the whole letter?" Her father pushed his plate away and folded his hands together on the table in a studious way.

"P.S. You asked why I've been signing my letters 'Birdy.' What a silly question. How else should I sign my letters? Hasn't your father ever told you the story behind my name? When I was born my parents thought I looked like such a graceful little bird they decided to name me after one."

"What bird would that have been?" Ellie's mother said. "A swallow? As in, this is all getting very hard to?"

"A cuckoo," Mckenna said.

Her father looked from Ellie to his wife. "You don't think she's actually forgotten her name is Beatrice, do you?"

"She's just joking around," Ellie said. Honestly, how out of touch was her father that Ellie actually had to tell him when his own sister was joking? They had spent their whole childhood together. Didn't he know by now what she was like?

Her father didn't resume eating. He looked silently across the table. "My dad got very odd before he was diagnosed with

Alzheimer's, but he was quite old when his senses started to go, and Bertie is just ten years older than I am—only sixty-five."

"Maybe she's precocious," Mckenna said.

Ellie's mother dabbed the corners of her mouth with a napkin. "Maybe Ellie *should* go out to Colton this summer to make sure everything is fine."

Ellie slipped Bertie's letter back into its envelope and put it in her purse. "You know I can't go. I was just accepted for an internship at KTSM. I start June second."

Her mother shrugged. "That isn't for another month. They still have time to hire someone else."

"I don't want them to hire someone else. Do you realize how hard it is to get an internship at a news station? Half the broadcasting majors hate me for being so lucky, and the other half are kissing up to me in hopes I'll let them drop by the station so they can make small talk with Anthony Ortiz, hunk reporter."

Ellie's mother laid her napkin, already folded, back onto the table. "We're talking about Bertie's health."

"You seriously think something might be wrong with Bertie? Just because of how she signed her name?" Ellie dismissed the idea, and then the next moment felt the fear—the fear of seeing her grandparents' fate repeated.

Her parents exchanged a look of trepidation, and then her father said, "With the history of Alzheimer's in the family, well, we'd all feel better if we knew for sure."

And that was that. Just the word *Alzheimer's* carried the weight of a gavel hitting the table. As far as her parents were concerned,

Ellie's internship was about to fade into the fog of missed opportunities.

"Couldn't Mckenna go to Colton?" Ellie asked. "Aunt Bertie would probably love to get to know her better." She turned to her sister. "You wouldn't mind being a CIA agent for the summer, would you? Maybe Aunt Bertie could even dig up someone for you to marry."

"I don't need a boyfriend. I've got Kirk."

His name caused a momentary thud in Ellie's emotions.

Of course, Mckenna had Kirk. How could Ellie, even for a moment, have forgotten this when Mckenna flaunted the fact every chance she got? She wore the triumph as though it were a tiara.

Mckenna had long since mastered just the right way to tilt her head so her blond hair spilled off her shoulders while she gazed invitingly into a man's eyes. Guys followed her around begging for more of it. Kirk was just the latest in the entourage.

Ellie had no such head-tilting techniques. Her own hair—a mass of auburn curls—had never once lured a man to her. Especially not Kirk. She forced a smile at McKenna, as though the reference to him didn't bother her. "Well, there's still the CIA."

Her mother stood and walked around the table, picking up plates as she spoke. "Ellie, you know you're Bertie's favorite. She keeps asking for you, and it would mean a lot to her if you went out. It's only one summer. You can put up with her for—oh honestly, Ellie, you didn't use your salad fork to eat your salad. Why do you think I put them on the table, if it's not to use them?"

Then again, maybe spending time in Colton, Idaho, for the

summer wasn't a completely bad idea. It meant months without one of these family dinners.

Still, Ellie didn't say the words; she didn't tell her parents she would go, even though she could feel her father's gaze on her, waiting for her to acquiesce. All she could think about was the news station. *Nick and Sophia—First! Live! Local!* She had already imagined herself there with them, chatting around the break table over donuts.

"So, Sophia, how did you get your start in broadcasting?"

Ellie didn't really have to ask. In broadcasting you either started out as an intern or you won the Miss America pageant and your agent landed the job for you.

And Ellie had an internship—an *in* at Channel 9 without ever having to put on a bathing suit or high heels and parade around on stage before a panel of judges.

Ellie's mother took the dishes over to the sink. The silence stretched out. Her father was still waiting.

Bertie didn't have Alzheimer's. She didn't. She'd always been eccentric, and now that she was getting older Ellie's parents were worried. They liked worrying. It gave them an excuse not to enjoy life.

But it wouldn't take the whole summer to prove them wrong. Within a week or two, Ellie should be able to check out the situation and assure her parents.

School let out May fifteenth. Ellie could be to Idaho and back by June first. The people at Channel 9 wouldn't even have to know about her trip.

"Okay, I'll go." Ellie said slowly, "I suppose I always did want to marry a rich, charming doctor and see the world."

Ellie's father smiled. "I'll call Bertie and let her know you're coming."

CHAPTER 2

Ellie grabbed her carry-on case and squeezed into the already-crowded airplane aisle. She stood silently, watching the passengers at the front of the plane. They were taking forever—slowly reaching up into the overhead bins to take out their belongings.

Assisted living facilities. The words kept roaming around her mind, just as they had done during the flight. And the car ride. And ever since her parents had brought up the topic over breakfast. They'd discussed pros and cons as though Ellie weren't sitting right there.

"They do your laundry, your housework, and your meals. Why wouldn't Bertie want to move to one?" Ellie's mother poured a glass of orange juice, then instead of drinking it, held it draped between her fingers.

Her father grunted. "You know how fond she is of that house. She's lived there most of her life."

"Exactly my point. It isn't even her house. Your mother left it to the both of you, and we've just been letting her live there. She ought to have sold it years ago and given you your half of the equity. We're the ones with children to put through college."

Ellie's father stirred a spoonful of honey into his oatmeal, letting a batch of steam escape from his bowl. "It isn't about the money."

"Of course it isn't. Heaven knows it will cost us even more to help her pay for assisted living. Still, I suppose we'll have to do it." She sipped the juice, then set the glass on the table. "How much do you think the house would sell for?"

Ellie stood up and took her dishes to the sink, even though she'd eaten only half of her cereal. She'd been up half the night cleaning out her dorm room and had barely been able to drag herself to her parents' house so they could take her to the airport. Her bowl clanked noisily in the sink as her parents talked about the real estate market in Colton.

Were they seriously considering forcing Bertie out of her home? How could they possibly think that was the right thing to do?

Assisted living. No laundry. No housework. How nice. Like being on vacation. A vacation you never came back from.

She hadn't been quite old enough to grasp the never-coming-back aspect of nursing homes when Grandpa Baxter lived in one. Every time they went to visit him, she had somehow expected they'd round the corner to his room and find him up and about, dressed in the brown slacks and plaid shirt that had been his uniform for so many years. She had walked down the cavernous, white-tiled hallway, ignoring the smell of alcohol and bed pans, reading door numbers until they came to Grandpa's room. But even inside it, they never seemed to find him.

This man—mouth hanging open, fists clenched in contortions by his side—this man wasn't really her grandfather. And he had become less her grandfather every time they visited.

At eleven years old, Ellie never knew what to say to him, never knew how much he understood. When he spoke, his answers came in grunts she couldn't decipher. She'd sit in the room listening to her parents chatter to him while he stared at the dresser in the corner. Drawers for clothes he would never wear. Drawers for belongings he didn't look at. Everything carefully folded and put away. Which of those drawers held his soul? She wanted to take it, shake out the wrinkles, and hand it back to him.

He never came back—was never the grandpa she knew again. Not even for a moment.

* * *

Ellie switched her carry-on bag from one shoulder to the other. The line finally moved, and Ellie pressed forward, trying not to bump the airplane seats with her bag as she walked. In a few minutes she stood at the baggage claim and scanned the crowd. All sorts of people milled around, but none of them was Bertie.

Ellie peered down the corridor. At 5'10", Aunt Bertie was easy to spot, even from a distance. Ellie didn't look for hair color. That changed on a monthly basis. The last Ellie had seen it, Bertie's hair was flaming red, but chances were just as good it would be a frosty blue.

Bertie's wardrobe consisted of vibrantly colored muumuus, and she often wore high heels and chunky jewelry with them. Mckenna called it the Hawaiian hooker look, but Ellie just accepted these things as part of Bertie's larger-than-life personality. People who were larger than life simply didn't wear business tweeds and sensible shoes.

Eventually Ellie's battered old suitcases dropped onto the conveyor belt, and she stacked them on an airport cart. Then she moved away from the conveyor belt to a less crowded space, craning her head to see down the hallway.

Nothing. Should she go in search of her aunt? Call Bertie's home? Stand here until airport security started eyeing her suspiciously?

And then she saw Aunt Bertie.

Her hair was a lavender shade of brown, which complemented her bright purple muumuu very well. Ellie simply hadn't seen her before because she was sitting in a wheelchair.

A wheelchair. In that one moment, Aunt Bertie grew old, the years no longer passing invisibly over her.

Ellie's gaze turned from her aunt to the woman pushing the wheelchair. She was young, perhaps in her late thirties, with short brown hair and a wide smile. She looked back at Ellie, as though she suspected Ellie was the person they were looking for.

Bertie put the question to rest. "Ellie!" she called. "There you are!" and she flung her arms open as though she were presenting the airport to her niece.

Ellie walked to the wheelchair, bent down, and gave her aunt a kiss on the cheek. "Hello, Aunt Bertie."

Bertie held onto Ellie's arm. "Just look at you. You've grown."

"Actually, I think you've shrunk. When did you get the new set of wheels?"

"Oh, this." Bertie shifted in the wheelchair. "I just borrowed this from one of my friends. I'm fine, really. I sprained my ankle a while back, and it still gives me trouble now and again. I figured it would be better to ride than walk through the terminal." She glanced at the woman behind her. "At first I told Claire to push me around in one of those luggage carts, but she thought it would look undignified."

Claire shook her head, then said to Ellie, "I keep telling Bertie she needs to have a doctor look at her ankle but she won't listen to me."

"Claire is my visiting teacher," Bertie said. "It's her job to worry about me—that and bring me cookies once a month."

Ellie reached over and shook Claire's hand. "I'm glad to know Aunt Bertie has someone looking out for her. Thank you."

Claire smiled back at Ellie, but it was a wan smile, as though she didn't feel completely comfortable with the compliment.

Bertie glanced at Ellie's airport cart. "Two little suitcases? Is that all the luggage you brought for the summer—or were you just planning on a shopping spree after you marry John?"

Ellie shifted her purse on her shoulder. She'd only packed for two weeks. "John? Who's that?"

"John Flynn. You know, the gentleman I wrote you about." Bertie twisted in her wheelchair to face Claire. "Didn't I tell you they would make a darling couple?"

"Oh yes," Claire said, turning the wheelchair away from the baggage claim. "Darling."

Ellie couldn't tell if it was sarcasm in Claire's voice. It was probably better not to find out. Ellie pushed her cart, following the other women down the corridor.

"Not only is John a doctor," Bertie went on, "but he gives the most insightful answers in Gospel Doctrine class." Bertie glanced back at Claire. "Don't you think his answers are insightful?"

"I'm in Primary that hour," Claire said.

"Well, he is insightful," Bertie said. "And I told him you're coming for a visit, Ellie." She nodded thoughtfully. "I think he *knows.* Spiritually in-tune people often do."

"Do what?" Ellie asked, hoping she wasn't revealing herself as spiritually off-key.

"Know when they meet their eternal companion." Bertie took a deep, dramatic breath. "I knew on our very first date that my Floyd was the one. When I walked into the room, he was waiting for me by the door, and I just knew—it was almost as clear as if a voice told me—that we were going to do this for the rest of our lives." Bertie laughed and patted the armrest on the wheelchair. "And we did. That poor man had to wait for me all the time. I was continually making us late for something. I guess he's still waiting for me on the other side." She waved one hand across the terminal. "Oh Claire, there's the exit."

Claire had already begun weaving the wheelchair through the crowd toward the door and didn't answer.

Ellie followed after them. "Uh, exactly what did you mean when you said you told John about me?"

Bertie blinked at Ellie as though surprised by her doubt. "I told the entire Sunday School class that my niece was coming to visit for the summer and that you were gorgeous." Bertie twisted in the wheelchair to look at Claire. "Isn't she gorgeous? Won't they have darling children?"

"Darling," Claire said. She pushed the wheelchair through the door and headed across the parking lot.

Ellie followed, keeping one hand on her carry-on so it didn't fall off the cart as she went over the curb. "But you didn't actually tell this guy I was going to have his children or anything, did you?"

"I wouldn't dream of telling him something so personal," Bertie said. "That's your job."

The tenseness left Ellie, and she smiled at herself for being caught up in her aunt's joke. "Right. I'll do that sometime in between the wedding and the shopping spree."

Bertie nodded. "Careful planning is the key to a successful marriage."

Ellie laughed, shook her head, and hoped that when she did meet John, she'd be able to keep a straight face. He might think her odd if she burst into giggles for no apparent reason.

Then again, if the man had a particularly good sense of humor, Ellie would be able to play a trick of her own on Bertie. She'd tell John about her aunt's predictions and then he could pretend to propose to her during Gospel Doctrine class. "He saw me and just knew . . ." she'd tell Bertie in a mystical tone. "Tomorrow we're having invitations printed and then you know what comes next—shopping!"

Better yet, Ellie would write to her parents and tell them the same story, only with more elaborate details. *I find his body piercing most attractive. He says the half-a-dozen studs through his tongue don't hurt at all. At least I think that's what he said. It's hard to understand him when he talks.*

Then she'd go on to tell her parents their new son-in-law was a professional motorcycle rider and tattoo artist—oh wait . . . she couldn't say that. Aunt Bertie had already told them he was a doctor. She'd have to think of some field of doctoring that was particularly embarrassing. *And he says he's more than willing to give everyone free prostate exams at the next family reunion.*

But even that wasn't good enough to pull off the joke. Her parents would probably be more than willing to overlook pierced tongues or prostate exams if it meant having a son-in-law who'd gone through medical school.

As Ellie loaded her bags into the back of Claire's van, she stole a glance at her aunt's foot. "You haven't seen a doctor about your ankle?"

"It's almost better." Bertie pulled herself up from the wheelchair and climbed into the van slowly, but without any limping. "I'm sure it would have healed completely by now if I'd just stayed off of it, but when you're single you can't do that. The trash needs to be taken out whether my ankle feels up to it or not."

Ellie shut the back of the van with a thud, then walked around to the side door. A couple of car seats—and an abundance of crumbs—were crowded in the van, but Ellie was able to find a seat in the middle bench. She leaned forward to talk to her aunt. "Why don't you have John look at it? After all, he's practically family."

Bertie's mouth dropped open as though Ellie had just suggested something scandalous. "I couldn't do that. Why, I'd never be able to look him in the eye again if I had to sit in front of him wearing one of those flimsy hospital gowns."

"I don't think he'd make you disrobe to look at your foot."

Bertie held up her chin. "Doctors *always* make you disrobe. They have a *thing* about naked people."

Claire pulled out of the parking garage while glancing at the map of Spokane that lay between her and Bertie. "I've been telling her to get it x-rayed for the last two months. Now you see what I'm up against."

"Well, we'll have to find a solution," Ellie said. "I know. I'll make sure Bertie's around when John proposes to me. That way he'll already be down on his knees, and I'll just say, 'As long as you're on the floor, would you mind taking a look at my aunt's ankle?'"

Bertie laughed, but Ellie actually considered the idea while they drove. It would be the perfect way to play a joke on her aunt and have Bertie checked at the same time. And it was clear that her foot had to be examined. If Bertie was being unreasonably stubborn about the matter, then Ellie would just have to find a creative way to get it done.

Everything would be so much easier if Dr. Flynn had a sense of humor.

On the two-hour drive from Spokane to Colton, Bertie asked Ellie about her family, her classes at NMSU, and what earthly good a degree in broadcasting would render. They spent a great deal of time on this topic, and it only ended when they pulled into Bertie's driveway. Then Bertie threw up her hands to show she was done trying to make Ellie see logic. "Well, I don't suppose it will matter anyway since you're marrying John."

"That's right. And think of the 'in' I'll have on all the malpractice stories."

Ellie stepped out of the van, surveyed Bertie's house, then unloaded her luggage from the back. Ever since Bertie had moved into Grandma and Grandpa Baxter's old home, she'd kept the outside the same. The small one-story was painted white with green shutters. Rose bushes lined the front porch. Two massive pine trees stood guard on the front lawn, their branches jutting out with jumbles of needles and pine cones.

The porch had always been Bertie's favorite place, and it was home to an assortment of chairs. Over the years the porch furniture had changed. It had seen rocking chairs, a swinging love seat, and even an old overstuffed couch. Now it had pool lounge chairs with tropical print cushions.

The rose bushes, usually kept waist high, were taller this year, as though Bertie hadn't gotten around to pruning them. The lawn looked overgrown, and several weeds peeped out from the shrubbery underneath the window. It wasn't like Bertie to be slipshod about her landscaping, and Ellie was suddenly glad she'd come. Not only was she going to get a doctor to look at her aunt's foot, but she was going to catch Bertie up on all the yard work. She'd also give everything inside and out a thorough cleaning.

As Bertie got out of the van, Ellie put down her suitcases and went to help her aunt walk to the house. Bertie just shooed her away. "I'm fine, dear. I'm always fine at my own house. I know where all the soft spots to fall are."

Ellie watched her aunt's slow progression to the porch steps for a moment, then picked up her suitcases again. She turned to thank Claire for the ride, but the van had already pulled out of the driveway. Ellie gave a wave to Claire that she probably didn't see, then walked up the porch steps and went inside.

The first thing Ellie saw in the living room was a large Christmas tree decked with lights and ornaments. An assortment of presents lay underneath, and on the opposite wall a pine wreath hung above the fireplace. A matching garland was draped across the mantel.

Ellie let her bags slide down onto the carpet. "Don't tell me you've been waiting all of this time to have someone help you put your Christmas stuff away?"

Bertie glanced at the tree, then moved off into the hallway to put her purse in the closet. "Oh no, dear," she called over her shoulder. "I just decided to leave it up."

Ellie picked her suitcases up but didn't move out of the living room. "Why?"

"Christmas is my favorite time of year. You know, everyone so kind and giving. Everyone remembering the birth of Christ." Bertie walked back into the living room without her purse or her shoes. She sat down on the couch, hands crossed on her stomach, and gazed at the tree. "Christmas makes a person feel warm inside. Last year as I was thinking about taking down the tree and feeling sad because it would be another eleven months until I could put it up again, I wondered how many more Christmases I have left." Bertie shook her head. "Whatever the number, it doesn't seem like enough. So I decided I'd make every day Christmas."

"Every day?" The suitcases went down again.

"Just think how wonderful it would be if everyone treated each day like it was Christmas." Bertie's gaze turned to the wall behind the Christmas tree where a portrait of Christ hung. "I can't change the rest of the world, but in my heart, every day it's Christmas."

Ellie looked at the tree again, then at the picture of Christ. Suddenly it seemed so homey, as though the late-May sunshine wasn't waiting outside. It made one want to rush out and build a snowman. "That's sweet," Ellie said. "Although I suppose it makes it hard to decorate for Valentine's Day."

"On Valentine's Day I only turn on the red Christmas lights."

"Well then, you've thought of everything." Ellie reached for her suitcases again, but her aunt waved a hand at the tree.

"Go pick out a present."

"A present?"

"Of course. What's the point of Christmas if you don't get presents?"

Ellie gingerly approached the tree. None of the packages had tags on them, and it somehow felt wrong just to take one. She glanced back up at her aunt and found her sitting with an expectant expression on her face. Finally, Ellie picked up a medium-sized box wrapped in bright green paper.

She took off the bow, unfolded the paper, and held up a box of Hamburger Helper. For a moment she wondered if there was something else inside the box—her parents sometimes did that with gifts, shoved them into odd boxes in order to wrap them better—but Bertie clapped her hands together. "Oh good. You got dinner. Those are always my favorite presents."

Bertie reached over and took the box from Ellie's hand. "It will go nicely with the green beans I unwrapped this morning."

"You put your food under the Christmas tree?" This was not the type of thing that would reassure Ellie's parents about Bertie's mental condition.

"It's not all food. But, well, I find I appreciate things more if I remember that everything we have is a gift."

"But don't you get tired of wrapping things? Doesn't it start feeling pointless?"

Bertie held up the box of Hamburger Helper and scanned the directions. "At my age most of the activities left in life are pointless. I suppose I could take up doing those 1,000-piece puzzles of beach scenes or start watching *Wheel of Fortune,* but I'd rather have Christmas."

"What about your sketching? That's not pointless."

"My hands are getting too shaky to work more than an hour or two a day. Although yesterday I drew some lovely poinsettias."

"All right. December twenty-fifth it is." At least until it was June first, when Ellie had to leave.

Ellie returned to her suitcases and dragged them across the room. "I'll put my stuff away. I'm in the spare bedroom, right?"

Ellie headed that way and heard Bertie call to her, "When you're done unpacking we can sit by the fire and drink eggnog."

When Ellie came out, however, she made dinner. At first Bertie protested, insisting that if she didn't at least help she'd be breaking the hostess code of ethics, but Ellie shooed her out of the kitchen.

Hamburger Helper and green beans weren't exactly gourmet food, but Ellie made up some rice too, and it was a passable meal.

And odd as it seemed, it did make dinner taste better to remember that it had been a gift wrapped in green foil paper only an hour ago.

After Ellie put the dishes into the dishwasher, she poured eggnog into two glasses and brought them out to the living room. Even though it was probably 75 degrees out, Bertie was bent over the fireplace, poking a log and making it sputter small flames. She straightened when Ellie walked over and took the eggnog from her niece's hand. "Very nice. Very nice, dear. Thank you for dinner."

"Tomorrow I'll go to the store and get the ingredients for Mom's chicken casserole."

Bertie shook her head and walked over to the couch. She sunk into it dramatically, but didn't spill her eggnog. "Oh no, I couldn't let you cook two nights in a row."

"You're supposed to be staying off your foot."

"My foot is fine." Bertie patted a place next to her in the couch. "Come sit down, dear. It's time to think about our New Year's resolutions."

Ellie sat down on the couch and stretched her legs out. "But does the New Year ever get here?"

"Nope. That's another advantage to Christmas every day. You can set goals without the guilt that comes when you don't follow them."

"In that case, I resolve to do my homework as soon as I get home from school every night."

Bertie held up her glass as though making a toast. "And I resolve to exercise and eat right." She sipped her eggnog, then leaned over to Ellie. "That's one of my favorite resolutions."

Ellie took a sip of her own eggnog. "I'm going to be more patient with Mckenna."

"And I'm going to take a trip to Tanzania."

Ellie giggled and let her head fall back against the couch cushions. It was easy to relax here, to let the stress of school and home dissolve in the blinking Christmas tree lights. Everything was perfect.

Except for that foot.

Ellie's gaze fell back to her aunt's feet, now decked out in enormous fuzzy pink slippers. "So tell me about John."

"Ah yes, John. He's 6'1", blond, and has broad shoulders and eyes that smolder."

"I trust that's not because his face catches on fire easily."

"He has a very strong face." Bertie gave Ellie's knee a pat. "But here's the bad thing about him. He's divorced."

Ellie took a slow sip of eggnog. "I would think that would be the good thing about him. I mean, imagine the impertinence of trying to set me up with him if he were still married."

"It wasn't his fault. Sister Sneed, who picks me up for Enrichment Night, is his mother's visiting teacher—although she never comes out to church anymore. She's been mad at God since her husband died seventeen years ago. Left her widowed with a one-year-old baby. I can't say I blame her. I'd be mad too. Still, she could come to church just for the social aspect. After all, none of us had anything to do with her husband's heart attack."

"Are we talking about Sister Sneed or John's mother?"

"John's mother. Lauren Flynn. She owns the Pine Top Bed and Breakfast resort up on Cascade slope. Very upscale. Anyway, according to Sister Sneed, John's first wife, Valerie, ran off with a jeweler. Although Sister Trimm, who sits with us in Relief Society, and who helps Lauren with cooking during the tourist season, said that wasn't quite the story. According to Sister Trimm, Valerie just bought so much jewelry that it would have been cheaper for John if she'd run away with a jeweler—but you see, either way it doesn't speak well of her." Bertie nodded in a knowing way. "If you ask me, that's what men get when they marry for looks." She patted Ellie's knee again. "And that's why you're perfect for him."

Ellie nearly choked on her eggnog. "Because I have no looks?"

"No dear, because you have looks *and* substance. That way no matter what he's searching for, he'll find it."

"Oh," Ellie said, and then because she wasn't really interested in a personal exposé on John or her own qualifications for marrying him, she said, "What kind of a doctor did you say he was?"

"I'm not sure. But I think it makes no difference."

"I suppose it does if you're one of his patients."

"When they go to med school they all have to do the same things. You know, cut open people, study corpses, prod around women's bodies like they were trying to find the decoder ring in a box of cereal, that sort of thing. It's the price they pay in order to get their degree. Just try not to think about it when he kisses you."

"Um . . ." Ellie tried to erase this visual image from her mind and concentrate on her aunt's foot again. "So I'll be meeting him in church then?"

"Yes." Once again Bertie's voice took on a conspiratory tone. "Although we could arrange for you to run into him elsewhere sooner."

"Oh? How could we do that?"

"I know about all his haunts in town."

Ellie leaned back and surveyed her aunt. "You haven't been stalking this poor man on my behalf, have you?"

"Of course not." Bertie took a casual sip of her eggnog. "I'm too old to traipse about town spying on eligible men. I sent my friends to do it."

Ellie envisioned a bunch of Relief Society women—purses tucked under their arms, walkie-talkies clutched in their hands, darting in and out of grocery stores and dry cleaning marts following John Flynn as he did his errands. "Exactly what do you mean when you say spying?"

"It's just a figure of speech, dear. My friends occasionally run into him, and his mother and younger sister both live here so of course people talk. In a small town everyone knows things about one another."

"Oh," Ellie said.

"Ricco's, Andre's Steakhouse, Safeway, and the library."

"What?"

"His favorite restaurants are Ricco's and Andre's, he shops at Safeway, and he spends at least one night a week in the library. We have a nice library in Colton. Very up to date. The school children are always doing fund raisers for it. That's where I get all the wrapping paper from." She nodded at the rolls of Christmas gift wrap by the side of the couch. "And of course you'll be seeing him at the Pine Top. I did mentioned that I got you a job interview there tomorrow, didn't I?"

"You didn't." Ellie took another sip of eggnog, trying to wash away a sudden surge of guilt. She ought to tell Bertie she couldn't stay the whole summer, but she couldn't. Not yet.

"You'd be working the front desk. It should be fun, and you'll get to know John's family. Diana is just a few years younger than you. I'm sure you'll be good friends."

Ellie swirled her eggnog in her glass and sighed. "You realize blind dates hardly ever work out. I somehow doubt a blind summer will produce better results. He may not like me at all."

Bertie's eyebrows shot up in surprise, as though such an idea had never occurred to her before. "He'll adore you. I just know it." She finished off the last of her eggnog. "I know it."

CHAPTER 3

After spending the morning mowing the lawn, trimming the rose bushes, and chatting with Bertie far too long, Ellie set off for her interview at the Pine Top resort. She carried with her four large sketches of grazing deer that Bertie had drawn for Lauren.

"She's expecting them," Bertie had said as Ellie slipped her purse onto her shoulder. "She's seen my work around town, and when I called to see if they had any job openings, I mentioned that I'd like to donate them to the Pine Top."

"You bribed her with drawings so she'd give me a job?"

"I consider it advertising. You can consider it part of your dowry."

Ellie tucked the large cardboard portfolio under her arm, then paused at the doorway. "You didn't tell this woman I was going to marry her son, did you?"

"Of course not. I did mention, however, that you came from exceptional genetic stock."

That was the problem with Bertie. You could never be sure she was joking.

Ellie drove up the hill from Bertie's house but instead of finding a resort, found a cemetery. She reread Bertie's directions, this time more carefully.

Oops.

This was the wrong hill entirely. She went back down the hill, staying on the road as it wound through Colton's sparse downtown and then climbed up another hill, a much bigger one this time. The pine trees grew thicker here, with only the hint of a cabin peeking out here and there from the trees.

She glanced at her watch. Hopefully Lauren was not one of those obsessively punctual people who didn't understand that occasionally people got lost while driving.

Finally the trees parted, revealing a two-story wooden lodge that looked as though Paul Bunyan had just come through and put the thing together. As she pulled into the parking lot she noticed wide paved trails leading away from the lodge and a few smaller cabins in the distance, nestled under the trees.

Ellie checked her watch as she stepped from the car. She was only five minutes late. That was practically on time, wasn't it? Or perhaps she should feign that Bertie had given her the wrong time altogether. *Five minutes late?* I thought I was ten minutes early.

Naw. She'd just admit she got lost, promise it wouldn't happen again, and hope Lauren wasn't in a bad mood for the rest of the interview.

With any luck it wouldn't be a long interview, or one where she was supposed to know obscure facts about resorts, like how to work the front desk.

Glass doors led into the lobby, but beyond this one feature, the room was completely rustic. The floor, walls, and ceiling were hewn logs, rich in color. A huge stone fireplace was in the far wall—empty now, but perhaps lit during the winter. Two oversized stuffed couches sat in front of the fireplace. A bear rug lay between them, its face frozen in a growl. Photos of skiers plunging through waves of snow adorned the walls.

Directly in front of the glass doors was a counter, also made of wood, with a granite top. A woman stood behind one of two computers. It was hard to tell how old she was. The wrinkles around her eyes suggested she might be fiftyish, but her trim body and shoulder-length blond hair made her seem younger.

She looked up as Ellie walked over. "Can I help you?"

"I'm Ellie Baxter. I'm here to see Lauren about a job interview."

The woman's brows knit together for a moment and then she seemed to remember. "Oh yes, your aunt called me. You're visiting for the summer, right?"

"Right."

Lauren stepped away from the computer, her gaze slicing up Ellie for inspection.

Ellie blushed under the scrutiny, then remembered the sketches and held out the portfolio. "Bertie asked me to give you these."

Lauren took the portfolio, laid it on the counter, and slipped out the sketches. She flipped through them, sighing happily, and held them up for closer inspection. "These are quite good. Your aunt has such a talent. I've admired her work ever since I saw the pair of bears she drew for the steakhouse."

"I'll tell her you liked them."

Lauren gazed at the pictures for a few more moments then slipped them back into the portfolio. She turned back to Ellie, her expression unreadable. "Now then, about your job. Have you had any experience working at a front desk?"

"No."

"Hmm."

"I'm sure I could learn it."

"I suppose you could." Lauren crossed her arms. "We'll give it a try. Diana can show you how we run things, and if it's too hard for you we can move you to housekeeping."

"I'm sure I'll get the hang of it."

"Good. We'll see you back here tomorrow at 7:00 A.M."

Lauren went to the back room and came back with a tax form. She handed it to Ellie, then gave her a curt good-bye.

Well, so much for any sort of interview. Apparently her job was sealed with those sketches. Ellie tromped back to her car shaking her head and replaying scenes from *Johnny Lingo* in her mind. An eight-cow wife. Suddenly she'd become a four-sketch receptionist.

If working the front desk is too hard for you, we can move you to housekeeping.

For heaven's sake, Ellie was in college. How hard did Lauren think working the front desk was?

Maybe Lauren was just the type of person who thought everyone was incompetent. The first time Ellie answered the phone the wrong way she'd be whisked off to housekeeping and condemned to cleaning bathrooms.

Then again, perhaps it was just Bertie's sketches that made Ellie look incompetent. Of course Lauren wondered about her job skills when her aunt had to bribe employers into hiring her.

From the resort, Ellie drove downtown to run errands. She hadn't meant to look for Dr. Flynn. After all, with Bertie's tendency toward exaggeration, it was entirely possible that he wouldn't be a medical doctor anyway. He might be a troll-ish doctor of philosophy who specialized in vague teachings of Confucius. She wasn't stalking him. She was just running errands.

Bertie had given Ellie a list of things to pick up, and she planned on getting them as quickly as possible and going home. Bertie needed a new drawer handle from the hardware store, Ziploc bags, hand lotion, ginko biloba from the drugstore, and industrial strength snaps from Louie's Vacuum Cleaner and Sewing Machine Shop. Ellie had no idea why Bertie needed industrial strength snaps. Sometimes it was better not to ask Bertie questions.

For example, this morning Ellie had asked Bertie why the mirror in the bathroom was gone and had gotten a whole discourse on the trials of growing old and the pains of lost youth.

Bertie had finished up the lecture with, ". . . and then one day I realized I just wanted to stop reminding myself I wasn't twenty-four any more. I figure as long as I don't have to look at a mirror I can tell myself I'm still young and beautiful."

"But if you have no mirrors . . . I mean, doesn't that make it hard to do your hair and stuff?"

"I've done my hair for more than half a century. I think I have the hang of it by now. Besides," she smiled coyly over at Ellie, "I still have the mirror up in my bathroom in case I need to look at myself for some reason."

"Good." Ellie grabbed her curling iron and headed down the hall in that direction. "Because I've only been doing my hair for two decades—one if you don't count my pigtail stage—and I need—" She stopped short when she reached Bertie's bathroom.

The mirror was still over the sink, but now a large poster of Cindy Crawford, pouting luxuriously for the camera, was duct taped over it. Only the top half inch of the mirror showed.

Ellie stared at the poster a moment without saying anything, then turned as Bertie walked in the bathroom. "And you have Cindy Crawford in here to keep you company because . . . ?"

"Because we all create our own reality—"

"And we all create our own world," Ellie finished. This had been a standard Bertie phrase her aunt repeated every time she drew a landscape or listened to someone complain about life. *You find what you're looking for,* she always said.

Bertie placed herself in front of the poster. She ran her fingers through her bangs as though retouching them and then pouted back at the poster. "Now, whenever I'm feeling old, I come in here and look in my own little magic mirror. It always makes me feel much better. I don't look a day over twenty-four, do I?"

Bertie gave her hair one last pat then turned toward the door. "It's funny—we see everyone else clearly, but have to depend on mirrors to see ourselves. Before mirrors were invented, I suppose everyone just assumed they were beautiful. It seems like a much better system, don't you agree?"

Ellie didn't. It drove her crazy not to be able see herself while she was preparing for a job interview, so she'd taken her curling iron and makeup out to Bertie's Oldsmobile. There she had tried to beautify herself using the rearview mirror. It accomplished the task, but was not something she wanted to do on a daily basis. She had had to go back inside Bertie's house three times to plug in her curling iron to reheat it, and the neighbors who'd been out doing yard work had watched the whole procedure with barely masked curiosity.

It had been a relief to finally leave her spectators. As Ellie had pulled out of the carport, Bertie had called after her, "If you're not home in time for dinner, and want to try one of the restaurants down town, I'll understand. Remember his two favorites are Ricco's and Andre's."

"I'll be home," Ellie had called back.

However, as Ellie put the last of her purchases—a small mirror to hang in her room—into the trunk of the car, she noticed the library across the street and had second thoughts about going home.

She had been meaning to pick up a few books. Besides, her parents were expecting a report on Bertie's condition, and if Ellie emailed them instead of calling, she wouldn't have to listen to one of her mother's diatribes on

a) the correct way to unpack her belongings

b) the correct way to prepare for a job

c) the correct way to evaluate Bertie's mental condition

d) all of the above

And since she would use the library's computer to do her reporting, she wouldn't have to worry about Bertie finding out that Ellie's parents were flipping through assisted living brochures.

Ellie shut the trunk and looked at her watch. The hands read 6:05.

Aunt Bertie wouldn't mind that she wasn't home for dinner. She'd already said as much. Perhaps Bertie's foot was hurting again, and she didn't want to make dinner. This might be her subtle way of telling Ellie not to expect it.

Ellie stopped by a nearby Taco Bell for a chalupa, then went to the library to compose her email.

She registered with the librarian for a temporary library card, logged onto the Internet, then sat in front of the computer, staring at the screen.

How could she truthfully report about Bertie's latest eccentricities without alarming her parents?

Ellie tapped out a few introductory sentences about her flight, her interview at the Pine Top, and the weather. She mentioned that Bertie was having problems with her ankle then added, *Bertie's latest hobby is working on ways to make dinner more gratifying.* No need to mention this included gift wrapping the Hamburger Helper. *She's trying to keep a youthful attitude.* In fact, a Cindy Crawford–like attitude. *Basically, she's the same as she's always been, with a little more holiday cheer.* There was now a four-foot plastic Santa set up in the hallway. *No need to worry about her health. I'll keep you posted about her ankle.*

Ellie hit the send button with a sigh. She'd done her duty by her parents.

With that task accomplished, she went to the fiction section and picked half a dozen paperbacks that seemed interesting. She carried them over to a table to inspect them further.

A tall, blond man with linebacker shoulders sat at the next table over.

Had he been there when she'd come in? If he had, she'd been more preoccupied with her aunt than she thought. She usually noticed men with broad shoulders and striking blue eyes right off.

Notice me, she told him silently.

He continued to stare at his magazine.

It figured. No one ever noticed her. If Mckenna had walked by he would have looked up, smiled, and asked for her phone number before she could even sit down.

That had been Kirk's attitude, hadn't it?

A prick of regret needled her at the thought of him. Perhaps if he'd known how she had felt about him things would have turned out differently. She should have flirted more, learned to toss her hair off her shoulder like Mckenna did.

But it didn't matter now. Kirk and Mckenna were dating.

She opened one of her books and read the opening line. Then read it again. She tried not to imagine Kirk's face bent close to Mckenna's.

Ellie dropped the book back onto the table and picked up a second one. From the corner of her eye she saw Mr. Broad Shoulders shift in his chair and glance around the room.

She tossed her hair off her shoulder in her best Mckenna imitation.

It didn't work. His gaze returned to his magazine.

She sighed and pressed open the book. Books, after all, were likely to be her only entertainment for a while.

Chapter 4

John stared at the medical journal in front of him but didn't read it. His thoughts were still back at the ER. It had been run-of-the-mill at the hospital until noon when some car crash victims came in—among them four-year-old Alissa with severe head trauma. She hadn't been in a booster seat. He could still see her mother standing before him, so distraught she was swaying back and forth with one hand pressed across her reddened face. She kept moaning, "Not my baby, please not my baby . . ."

All he could do for the little girl was relieve as much of the swelling as possible, wait, and hope for the best.

If only she'd been wearing her seat belt.

If only her mother had taken the thirty seconds needed to click it in place.

Ever since he'd left the hospital he'd had the urge to stop every person he saw and tell them, "Buckle up your kids. I don't want to see you swaying back and forth in agony in my ER."

He couldn't do it, of course. They'd think he was crazy.

He flipped the page of his magazine. Why had he gone into medicine anyway? Plumbers didn't have to deal with this kind of thing. Neither did engineers or gas station attendants.

Oh, he remembered the reason he'd so glibly given everyone when he'd applied for medical school: I want to help people. I want to make a difference in the world.

It was during his residency in a Manhattan ER that the truth dawned on him. Somewhere between gang fight victims, HIV cases, and drug addicts faking back injuries so they could get pain killers, he'd lost his idealism. He couldn't make a difference in the world.

What did one say to the twenty-four-year-old cocaine user who came in with heart attack–like symptoms—twice? If the first near fatal experience hadn't woken him up to the dangers of cocaine, what good would a lecture from the doctor do?

And then there were the pregnant fourteen-year-olds. Uninsured, probably without having given a thought to nutrition for all nine months, who sat watching cartoons while they waited to deliver. Cartoons. Girls without the sense or ability to take care of themselves having babies.

Coming home to Colton had really been an attempt to shake off the despair he'd felt in New York. He needed small-town life with its late-night ear infections and trying-to-be-Superman-so-I-jumped-off-the-bunk-bed stitches. He wanted normal life again. He wanted to be near family. And most important, he wanted to live someplace where he'd never bump into his ex-wife.

John tried to shake thoughts of Valerie, to shake the vision of her light blue eyes blinking at him.

Women. So sweet—so charming at first—that you never knew what they were really like until it was too late.

Well, the divorce was final now. After a year of separation, after a year of trying to work things out and hoping Valerie would care enough about the relationship to make a few sacrifices, it was final. His friends all said he was lucky to be out sooner rather than later.

Against his will, Valerie came to his mind again. Valerie home from one of her shopping trips with a diamond pendant draped against her throat.

When he'd reminded her they were still paying off his student loans and that she should have consulted him before buying it, she'd thrown her other packages down on the floor. "If you had one romantic bone in your body I wouldn't have *had* to buy it all. You would have gotten it for me ages ago."

His lack of romance also cost him sapphire earrings and a bright red convertible. A convertible in New York. So practical during those long winter months.

How could he have been so wrong about her? Next time he would be much more careful. If there was a next time.

John flipped through another page of the magazine. Then another. A tall brunette a couple of chairs away from him set one book down on her table and picked up another. Her wavy auburn hair bounced around her shoulders as she shifted in her chair, and for a moment her brown eyes flickered over to where he sat. She seemed to appraise him, letting her gaze rest on him for a second or two longer than was casual. He turned his attention back to the magazine in front of him.

Probably a tourist looking for a vacation fling. Well, he wasn't about to encourage her. He was here to read. All he wanted was privacy.

He glanced at her again. Auburn hair, brown eyes, and flawless pale skin. An attractive combination.

John dragged his gaze away from her and forced himself to focus on the magazine in front of him. Why did God make beautiful women anyway? Attraction based on looks was an entirely unreliable way to find a companion. Everyone knew it was unreliable, and yet who could ignore the magnetism of beauty? In all his wisdom, you'd think God would have come up with a better way.

Dating. Marriage. So important, yet such a gamble.

Back when John was a resident, he'd had a conversation with the other residents on this very matter. They were sitting in the doctors' lounge, trying to summon up the energy to make it through the rest of the shift. Empty coffee cups lay scattered around the room, a Styrofoam testament to their fatigue. John sat on the couch, clutching a concoction of carrot juice, wheat grass, and who knew what else. The lady at the health bar next door swore to its energy-giving ability and he was willing to try it.

The conversation had been going on for some time about girlfriends, specifically the fact that they had a habit of pressuring men for a wedding date. Not one, but six of the men there all swore their girlfriends were pushing the marriage issue.

The two women in the group staunchly defended their sex,

accusing the men of egomania one moment and indecisiveness the next. "You're just afraid to make commitments," one said.

John held up his hand, waving his wedding band. "See, no fear here."

One of the six who felt pressured waved back at John as though dismissing him. "You married someone you'd known less than a year. Is that fearlessness or stupidity?"

John didn't have time to answer. The women both spoke at once, loudly defending John, which just went to show how foolish residents were.

Bruno, who was so newly an attending doctor that he still hung around the residents, sat next to John on the couch. He remained quiet for the debate, but after it was over and everyone was heading back out onto the floor, he took a last sip from his cup and said, "This is why I'm a janitor."

"What?" John asked.

"A janitor. When I meet women at nightclubs and they ask me what I do for a living, I tell them I'm a janitor. If they're still interested, I know they like *me* and not my paycheck." Bruno stood, stretching, the coffee cup still gripped in one hand. "You'd be surprised how many women take off after hearing I'm a janitor. Sort of makes you angry on behalf of all the cleaning people of the world."

Bruno walked to the garbage can, picking up some of the littered Styrofoam cups as he went. "Look, I'm straightening the lounge, so hey, the janitor story isn't even a lie."

When John moved away from New York, Bruno was still single. But then, so was John.

I'm a janitor. That's what he should have told Valerie when they'd met.

"John, good to see you!" A voice boomed out across the rows of library tables. Half a dozen people looked up and watched as Bishop Whiting strode across the library toward John. "Are you catching up on your reading or just gathering dust in here?"

Not just Bishop Whiting's voice, but everything about him seemed oversized, including a stomach that stretched the endurance of his suit. Bishop Whiting was never without a suit, as though even on a Tuesday, he was still on duty as leader of the ward.

"I try to get some reading in now and then," John said, his voice low.

Bishop Whiting didn't turn down his volume. "They keeping you busy at the hospital?"

"Too busy, unfortunately." John tried not to think about the little girl—silent in a room full of noisy equipment, her small form hardly taking up any space on the hospital bed.

Bishop Whiting smiled and patted John's shoulder in a farewell gesture. "See you on Sunday; don't let them work you too hard."

"I'll try."

The bishop gave a parting wave, then headed to the door. Turning back to the table, John noticed the brunette had slid into the chair next to him.

She smiled, and he saw that her eyes weren't really brown. They were brownish green—khaki—with little flecks of gold. He should have guessed they'd be something exotic. Beautiful women always had flair.

"Hi." The woman brushed an auburn curl behind her ear and leaned closer to him. "I'm sorry to bother you, it's just that I couldn't help but overhear your conversation."

"You and half the library." His joke earned him another smile. "He's a nice man. Just a little loud."

There was a moment's silence, and he could tell she was debating what to say next. "So . . . you work at the hospital?"

Well. This one didn't beat around the bush. Next she'd be asking to see his W-2 forms. Exactly what tax bracket did you have to be in to get a date with this woman? "Yes, I do."

"Are you a doctor, then?"

And could he afford to decorate that bungalow in the Bahamas she wanted?

Her lips turned upward into a smile, and her eyes glowed as she looked at him. Such pretty eyes. Eyes a man could just stare into and contemplate so many things.

"I'm a janitor," he said. "Well, at least I'm a janitor until I can start selling my paintings. Then I'll be an artist."

"Oh." The smile froze on her face. So predictable. Now she'd come up with an excuse to end this conversation and be off in search of a man wearing Calvin Klein cologne and a Rolex watch.

He cocked his head at her, raising his eyebrow at her sudden discomfort. "I take it you're not an art lover?"

"It's not that." A blush stole into her cheeks. "I just thought you might be someone I knew. If you were a doctor, I mean. Well, I mean, I haven't actually met him yet, that's why I was introducing myself." She stopped talking and the blush deepened. "It's a long story, but um, good luck with your art." She pushed her chair back from the table too quickly to be graceful. Sending him one last apologetic look, she murmured, "I need to be going."

Mmm hmm. It figured.

She thought he was someone she hadn't met yet. That had to be the most pathetic excuse to ditch a person he'd ever heard.

He watched her walk up to the checkout counter, shaking his head as his eyes followed her slim figure. Pity it had to be that way. But still, still, he'd probably just saved himself from a lot of problems.

* * *

Ellie flung open the car door and slid into the driver's seat, throwing her books onto the passenger side. She shut the car door with a thud.

She thought he was someone she hadn't met yet.

That had to be the most pathetic explanation she'd ever given in her life. Why hadn't she asked him right off if his last name was Flynn? Why was it that when she was nervous she just babbled incomprehensible explanations that made her look like she was auditioning for the role of village idiot? Of course he wasn't the John she was looking for. The man in the library had been incredibly good looking. If Dr. Flynn had been that handsome Bertie would have mentioned it.

He's single, he's a doctor, and oh by the way, he's so good looking women intentionally injure themselves just to see him.

So of course it hadn't been him, and why hadn't she considered the possibility that there might be more than one John working at the hospital? There were probably half a dozen men named John wandering the halls at any given moment.

This was the type of thing that was bound to happen when parents insisted on calling their children a name that was already used by a major portion of the population. It wasn't Ellie's fault at all. If she ever did have children, she was going to name them after obscure Greek mythological figures.

The only saving grace of the meeting was that she had been able to stop talking before blurting out that she'd mistaken him for the stranger she was destined to marry.

Ellie pulled out of the parking lot.

First lesson of the summer learned: Don't strike up conversations with men you know nothing about. Even if they're good looking. Especially if they're good looking.

At least she was only going to be here for a couple of weeks. What were the chances she'd ever run into that guy again?

CHAPTER 5

The next morning as Ellie left for work, Bertie followed her to the door, kneading a blob of white putty eraser as she spoke. "Maybe John will stop by to see his family today. If you're not home for dinner, I'll understand."

"I'll be home for dinner."

"That's what you said last night."

"And I came home."

"But you didn't eat much, and you blushed when I asked you whether you'd run into John."

Despite herself, Ellie blushed again. She should have told Bertie last night about her episode with janitor John, but she'd been hoping to banish the memory as quickly as possible. And besides, if she'd told Bertie about the mix-up, it would undoubtedly lead to endless teasing at future family reunions and references to how Ellie thought Pine Sol was an aphrodisiac. *Hey Ellie, what perfume are you wearing? Could it be love potion number 409?*

"I'll be home," Ellie said.

"Don't worry." Bertie smiled as she stood on the doorstep. "I remember what it's like to be young and in love."

* * *

When Ellie walked into the bed and breakfast, she recognized Diana right away. She looked like a younger version of her mother, Lauren. Her shoulder-length blond hair was pulled back in a stiff braid, except for the few wisps that had escaped and fallen into her face. She was pretty now, and would most likely be gorgeous later. She glanced up at Ellie. "Can I help you?"

"I hope so. You're supposed to teach to me how to work a front desk."

"You're the new girl?" Diana's brows drew together as she surveyed Ellie. "Have you ever worked registration?"

"No, but I've checked into hotels before. It's the same thing but in reverse, right?"

"Not quite."

Diana showed Ellie the door that led to the back room and around to the front desk counter. Once she was there, Diana went into a litany of explanations which included the check-in list, the check-out list, cabin key protocol, how to transfer telephone calls, how to set up wake-up calls, how to page housekeeping or security, how to take phone reservations and enter them into the computer, how to print out upcoming reservations, and where to file the hard copies of everything.

"These are important phone numbers," Diana said, holding up a slim leather book. "Everything from poison control to cabs to restaurants." She put the leather book down by the phone and slipped out a stack of paper from a shelf by the computers. "These are the maps of the cabins. After you check in a guest and give him a key, you circle the guest's cabin number on the sheet, then explain how to get there. Sometimes guests are dropped off at the lobby and don't have cars. In that case you offer to take them up in the guest cart. I'll show you how to work that later. It's really just an oversized golf cart. Are you remembering all of this?"

"Um, most of it." Or at least some of it.

"It takes a little while to get everything down, but in a couple of weeks you'll be an old pro."

In a couple of weeks she'd be gone. Ellie felt a twinge of guilt at the thought. By the time she learned the job she'd be handing in her resignation. They were wasting time training her, and perhaps she should save everyone the trouble and just quit now. But how could she? How could she explain that she was staying only long enough to assure her parents that Bertie was sane, healthy, and capable of taking care of herself?

Ellie followed Diana around the small area by the front desk, trying to repeat the information she'd just learned. Diana smiled and nodded when Ellie got something right. Diana seemed easy going and nice. After a short time the two were talking together as though they'd known each other for years instead of minutes.

It occurred to Ellie that she might ask Diana if her brother was the type of man she could enlist in her attempts to get Bertie's ankle examined.

While the two were sorting and stacking restaurant coupons for the housekeeping staff to leave in the cabins, Ellie broached the subject.

"My aunt knows your brother. She really likes him. She says he gives insightful answers in Gospel Doctrine."

Diana snorted. "I bet he does. He's always giving me gospel insights at home."

Diana's tone was prickly, and suddenly Ellie was afraid to push the topic, but she had to say something. She settled for a benign, "Really?"

"Yes, really. He just loves to tell me everything I do wrong. You know, like missing church because I work on Sunday." She shrugged. "He knows the weekends are our busiest time."

"You don't get Sundays off?"

"I do every once in a while, and then John is over at the house dragging me out of bed to go with him. He says he's coming over for Mom's homemade breakfast, but I don't buy that. I've tasted her pancakes."

Again, Ellie didn't know what to say. This time she chose, "Oh?"

Diana leaned up against the counter, tilting her head so that her braid slid onto her shoulder. "It's not that I don't like church. I just like sleeping in more. I guess I won't get to do much of that this summer. You probably want Sundays off, don't you?"

Only for the next two weeks. Ellie looked at the restaurant coupons instead of Diana. "For a little while." She wanted to change the subject before Diana could ask her what "a little while" meant. "So, what kind of doctor is your brother?"

"A thorough one. Don't ever get him started about the dangers of tanning. That's another one of those insights he loves to share with me."

"I meant what field of medicine."

"He works in the ER."

Ellie's head snapped up. This was the first piece of good news she'd had in her quest for a doctor. "Then he would know something about ankles, wouldn't he?"

"I suppose. What do you want to know?"

"My aunt hurt hers awhile back and refuses to see a doctor about it. I thought she might be willing to have John take a look at it since she likes him so much, but I wouldn't want to ask him if it would make him feel uncomfortable. I mean, I don't know how he feels about giving advice without an appointment."

"Well, he gives *me* advice all the time without an appointment. In fact, you can ask him for advice and tell him to put it on my account. I can give away some of my advice-time with him."

"So you think I should ask him?"

"Sure. He's basically a nice guy, just a little overprotective." Diana took a pen from the counter and turned over one of the coupons. "Like he could make a living at it. He puts the 'pro' in overprotective." She scribbled a number on the coupon, then handed it to Ellie. "That's his phone number. He's working the day shift now so you should be able to catch him home in the evening."

Ellie folded the paper and slipped it into her pocket. "Thanks. Maybe I'll give him a call."

They sorted and stacked the last of the restaurant coupons, then Diana placed them in the housekeeping box. Just as she did, a light blue van pulled up in front of the resort. Painted onto its side were the words *Tour Store.* Diana caught her breath and clutched the edge of the counter.

"It's the hunkmobile."

"The hunkmobile?"

She tapped her fingers against the countertop. "Please let it be Andrew. Please let it be Andrew . . . "

A young man stepped from the driver's side of the van, and suddenly the term *hunkmobile* became clear. He was tall, tan, and looked like a giant red S would be found on his chest if he ripped off his T-shirt.

"It's Andrew," Diana said.

Ellie didn't have time to ask who Andrew was before he pushed open the front door and strode up to the front desk. "Hey, Diana."

She smiled back at him calmly. "Hi, Andrew."

"I'm here to pick up the . . . " He took a piece of paper from his pocket and unfolded it, ". . . the Turleys. Do you want to let them know I'm here?"

"Sure." Diana ran one finger along the phone list until she located the name, then picked up the receiver to call their cabin. She nodded over at Ellie as she did. "This is Ellie, Mom's latest front desk slave. Ellie, this is Andrew. He lures tourists up the mountainside and tries to kill them by putting them on bikes and sending them off steep inclines."

"Hey, don't blame me for any injuries. Everybody signs a waiver before they go up."

"Mrs. Turley?" Diana's voice took on a professional tone as she spoke into the phone. "The biking tour van is at the lobby waiting for you. Mmm hmm. I'll tell him."

She hung up the phone and leaned back against the counter.

"Mrs. Turley says she can't wait to come out and see you in your tight shorts, Bikerboy."

Andrew turned to Ellie. "Can you believe the grief this girl gives me? I'm providing a service for her guests."

"Yeah, yeah," Diana said. "You charm little old ladies into paying large sums of money to spend the afternoon with you."

He smiled. "And I'm coming back tomorrow to take them canoeing on the lake."

"What? No hang gliding?"

"Hey, I keep telling my boss we should offer hang gliding, but he refuses. The man worries too much about people crashing into the ground and then suing him for everything he owns. He really shouldn't be so concerned. It's not like he owns anything good anyway."

Andrew talked for a few more minutes about hang gliding while Diana gazed up at him, her elbow on the countertop and her chin resting in her hand. Finally Andrew turned and looked out the front windows at a group of women walking down the trail toward the lobby. "There are the Turleys. Gotta go."

Then without another word he strolled outside to greet his customers. Diana kept her gaze on him. She watched as he opened the door of the van, helped the women into the van, and then drove off.

"So," Ellie said. "You've got a thing for Andrew, huh?"

"What?" Diana straightened up and turned her attention to the key drawer. "Not at all. I mean, he's a friend and everything, but I already have a boyfriend." She opened the drawer and her finger ran over the key slots, checking to see which keys were still out. "His name is Chris, and we've been going out for almost a year. We're . . . " Her finger stopped. "Why do you ask? Do you think Andrew likes me?"

"Well, I was just wondering why you said, 'Please let it be Andrew' when the van pulled up."

"I said that out loud, didn't I?" Diana returned her attention to the drawer. "I've got to stop doing that sort of thing."

Ellie took a batch of faxed reservation slips to the front desk. Diana had shown her how to type in reservations, and it had seemed easy at the time. Now she looked at the computer screen, trying to remember the procedure. "So you have a thing for Andrew but you shouldn't?"

"Of course I shouldn't. I have a boyfriend already. And besides, Andrew doesn't know I exist."

"It looked to me like he knew you existed."

Diana turned from the drawer. "Really? You think so?"

"Well, he wasn't trying to impress *me* with his hang gliding stories."

Diana didn't answer, and Ellie was too busy trying to remember how to work the reservation screen to continue the conversation. Several minutes later she turned to ask Diana a question and found her still staring blankly into the key drawer.

"Diana, how do I make sure the Shumways get a cabin that sleeps six?" Ellie asked.

"I liked Andrew my entire junior year, but he was going out with Crystal Markland. By the time he broke up with her I was going out with Daniel Singer. Then when I dumped Daniel, he'd already started dating Suzanne. We've never both been available at the same time. But he broke up with Suzanne about a month ago, and I have to wonder . . . "

"What would happen if you both were free?"

"Yeah."

Just like Ellie and Kirk. Friends all through high school. When he got back from his mission things were supposed to be different. She'd *planned* that they were going to be different, anyway. She'd planned late nights strolls while the stars glowed overhead and picnics out in the white sand dunes near Alamagordo.

She hadn't planned that after his homecoming talk in sacrament meeting, he'd stare at Mckenna with admiration and say, "Wow, you've really grown up."

Ellie should have said something to him before then. He had been home for two weeks before he gave that talk. Two weeks. She'd had him all to herself and never once hinted that she wanted to be more than friends.

She had told herself she was letting him readjust, but that wasn't it at all. It had been plain, simple fear.

Diana let out a sigh. "My timing just never seems to be right. Still . . . I just . . . you know . . . I mean," she held up one hand. "He's *Andrew.*"

Oddly enough, it made perfect sense to Ellie. "But you have a boyfriend."

Diana's eyebrows came down. "And I care about Chris."

"But not enough to keep you from daydreaming about Andrew?"

Diana slid the key drawer shut. "How do you know when it's time to break up with someone? I mean, Chris is just comfortable.

In fact, he's the living embodiment of my comfort zone. When I'm with him I feel secure. But when I see Andrew, somehow 'secure' doesn't seem good enough anymore." She let out another sigh, her eyes staring at the parking lot. "I bet when Andrew kisses a girl, her toes spontaneously ignite."

"So what are you going to do?"

Diana's lips pressed together. "What can I do about it? I'm dating Chris."

"Is it fair for you to date Chris when you want some other guy to ignite your toes?"

Her shoulders rose and fell. "But what if I break up with Chris and then Andrew doesn't care?"

And that was the real question. The question that had kept Ellie silent for those two weeks last February. What if she had told Kirk how she felt and he didn't care? Or worse yet, what if she'd seen the panic in his eyes that meant she'd lost his friendship too?

"Are you dating Chris because you want to be with him, or because you're afraid to tell Andrew how you feel?"

Diana bit her lip. She turned her back to the parking lot and folded her arms as though she were cold. "But I have no idea, I mean, I don't know what I would say to Andrew. How would I get his attention? I was in orchestra the entire four years of high school, and he played varsity football and basketball. He's a totally unrepentant jock. A hesitant smile spread across Diana's lips. "And at the same time he's a really nice guy. Like this one day during our sophomore year—a bunch of varsity football players were picking on Eugene Baker in the hallway. They knocked his books out of his hands and pushed him until he tripped. Andrew walked up and told them to stop it. Those guys were all on the team with Andrew and probably gave him a lot of grief about it, but he still helped Eugene pick up his books. How could a girl not fall for a guy like that?" She tilted her head and lifted her shoulders. "But I can't just tell him how I feel. What if he rejects me?"

"What if you never let him know how you feel? You'll wonder the rest of your life what would happen if you had done something?"

"You're right." She nodded, gulped, then shook her head. "I can't say anything to him."

"Embrace your fear, Diana, and you may get to embrace Andrew too." Ellie said the words to Diana, but knew she was saying them to herself, too. She needed to talk to Kirk. When she got home to New Mexico she would.

Guests began to trickle in, checking in or out, and Diana and Ellie didn't have time to say anything else about the subject.

Around noon a large group from a writer's convention came in. They formed two lines—the one in front of Diana moved quickly, while the one in front of Ellie moved considerably slower as she struggled to remember the check-in procedure.

"Let's see," Ellie told one less-than-patient man. "I had you fill out the check-in information. I took your credit card. I circled your cabin on the map and then gave it to you. You're all set."

"You didn't give me my key."

"Oh, yes. The key." Ellie reached into the key drawer. "What was your cabin number again?"

"Eighteen. You should remember the number because it took you that many minutes to find it on the map."

"Sorry. I'm new at this."

The man tapped his thumb against the counter. "Please tell me it won't take you eighteen minutes to find the key."

"Here it is. No wait. This is cabin eighty-one's key put in the wrong spot. Or maybe not. Diana, is there a cabin eighty-one?"

"Just give me the stupid key. I'll bring it back if it doesn't work." He grabbed the key and turned around to leave before Diana replied that no, there wasn't a cabin 81.

Ellie tried not to hold the man's rudeness against him, just as she forgave all the people who stood in her line for a few minutes and then defected to Diana's line. If Ellie had been in their place she probably would have done the same thing.

By the end of the shift she'd checked in sixteen people, changed rooms for two unhappy guests, called housekeeping about a clogged sink, transferred eleven calls—only routing two of them to the lodge restaurant by mistake—and taken four messages. Her feet hurt from standing so long.

The worst moment was when a soft-spoken older woman came back to the front desk claiming her key wouldn't unlock her cabin. Diana couldn't leave Ellie to man the front desk alone, so Diana called Gus, the security guard, to go out with the woman and try to remedy the problem.

Several minutes later Gus came back to the lobby chuckling. He slid the map in front of Ellie and pointed to the box she'd circled, "Next time you're giving directions you might want to be more careful. You sent the poor woman to the grounds shed."

Ellie stared down at the map. "Oops. Sorry."

From behind her, Diana laughed. "It's a good thing the key

didn't fit. I mean, we're supposed to provide rustic decor, but not *that* rustic."

Gus pointed to little slashes on the map. "These are benches along the walking trails. Try not to check anyone into them."

Ellie pulled the map away from him. "Well, the grounds shed is close to cabin 23 and really, the map makers should have known better than to put it on the map."

Gus and Diana were too busy laughing to respond.

It was going to be a long two weeks.

Chapter 6

In the car heading home, Ellie kicked off her shoes and drove barefoot. Every once in a while she fingered the restaurant coupon in her pocket. She couldn't call Dr. Flynn yet. It was only a little after three and Diana said he worked till the evening.

Somehow she wasn't nearly as eager to call him now as she had been when she was talking to Diana about it. John Flynn didn't know Ellie, and to just call him up out of the blue and ask for a favor . . .

Embrace your fear. It had been an easy enough thing to tell Diana, and here Ellie didn't even want to make a phone call.

As she pulled up to Bertie's house she surveyed the lawn. It looked much better now that it had been weeded and mowed, but it emphasized how shabby the porch was. Would a good cleaning be enough, or would she have to repaint it? Did she have time? She climbed out of the car and walked inside, laying her purse on a little table by the door. She fingered John's phone number for another moment, then took it out of her pocket and dropped it next to her purse. "I'm home!"

A muffled moan came from the back of the house.

"Aunt Bertie?" she called.

No answer. She walked down the hallway, and then ran as the moan increased in volume.

She flung open her aunt's door and took several steps into the room. "Aunt Bertie?"

The sound stopped, and from behind the bed came the call, "I'm over here."

Ellie took tentative steps toward her aunt's large, four-poster bed, as though someone or something might jump out and grab her. Was this a joke? Perhaps a new fad of her aunt's? Was she about to tell Ellie that everyone practiced ritual moaning before yoga these days, and behind the bed was the most appropriate place for it?

Ellie crawled on top of the bed and peered over the side. Bertie was lying sideways on the floor, pressed between the side of the bed and the wall.

"Aunt Bertie, what are you doing down there?"

"I fell and now I'm stuck."

Ellie's stomach lurched. "Are you all right?" She slid off the bed and tried to push one end away from the wall. At first the bed remained steadily in place, but then it creaked and gave way.

"Of course I'm not all right. If I was all right I wouldn't have been lying here pinned to the wall half the afternoon." As the bed moved further away, Bertie rolled from her side to her stomach. "Ow."

"Ow what? What's hurt?" Ellie leaned over her aunt, somehow

afraid to touch her. Should she try to help Bertie move or just call the paramedics?

"My ankle. I twisted it again. And my arm. I landed wrong and now I can't feel it. It *is* still there, isn't it?"

"Everything is still there."

Slowly, carefully, and with a fair amount of pulling, Ellie helped her aunt to her feet. Together they hobbled out of the room and down the hallway.

"Ow," Bertie said at every other step.

"How did this happen?"

"I moved the bed away from the wall to vacuum the baseboards a while ago and never got around to moving it back. Ow. Too heavy. Ow. Today when I was taking a nap I must have rolled over the wrong way. Ow. Suddenly, there I was on the floor with the quilt pressed against my face. I need to sit down and rest."

"You need to see a doctor, and I'm taking you. You may have broken something."

"Yes, and if I rest for a few minutes, I'll be able to tell you what. Right now everything hurts." Bertie paused momentarily and lifted her muumuu to inspect her ankle. "Dear heavens, look at my leg! It's swollen up like an elephant. I must have—no wait, both of my legs are huge. Good grief, I've gained more weight than I thought."

Ellie tugged at her aunt, moving her to the doorway. "Would you stop joking around. How am I going to know if you're really hurt if you won't be serious?"

"I am serious. I'm going to have cut back on the eggnog and peanut brittle. Ow. That will be my next New Year's resolution."

Ellie helped Bertie to the car, then jogged back to the house to retrieve their purses. Grabbing them, she raced back out to the car. She drove toward the hospital quickly, glad she'd seen it while running errands, because Bertie didn't even try to offer directions. Instead, she sat limply in the passenger side, her lavender-brown hair disheveled, her head tilted back against the headrest. She winced over every bump in the road.

If only I had made her see a doctor sooner, Ellie thought, and then realized it wouldn't have mattered. This fall had nothing to do with the last, and the only silver lining in it all was that Bertie was finally agreeing to let a doctor look at her.

Bertie gripped the door handle as they bumped over some railroad tracks. "No matter what they say, I won't have surgery. I don't trust doctors."

"You don't trust them? You're trying to marry me to one."

"Yes, well, marrying one is fine, but you shouldn't trust someone who enjoys cutting people open, should you?"

Ellie tried to follow the logic, then decided she ought to concentrate on traffic.

"And don't let them put me on life support. If it's my turn to go, just let me go."

"I'll remember that."

When they arrived at the hospital, Ellie helped her aunt across the parking lot, shouldering her 5'10" frame the best she could. She hoped they wouldn't both fall somewhere during the trek. Why didn't the hospital have wheelchairs located in the parking lot? This was, after all, the way to the emergency room, which meant that only hurt people came here. What was the point of having a hospital if people couldn't make it across the parking lot?

Together the two hobbled into the waiting room, and Bertie collapsed into the nearest chair. The room, thankfully, was almost empty. Besides a mother and fussing baby in one corner, the only other occupant was an elderly gentleman who held an ice pack on his shoulder. At least the wait wouldn't be too long.

Ellie picked up the admitting forms from the front desk then returned to her aunt with them.

Bertie filled out a few of the spaces then handed the clipboard back to Ellie. She put one hand to her temple and shut her eyes. "Could you finish filling it out for me, Dear? My head is throbbing."

"But your insurance information—"

"My Medicare card is in my wallet." Bertie leaned back into the chair, resting her head against the wall.

Ellie took a pen to the form. *Address.* It was a good thing Ellie knew it by heart. It wasn't written anywhere in Bertie's wallet. *Birthday.* April first. You couldn't forget that birthday. *Social Security number.* It was probably somewhere on the Medicare card. Her hands trembled as she turned the card over, the full impact of the accident suddenly hitting her.

What if Ellie hadn't been there? What if she'd stayed home for the summer? What if this fall had happened after she left? How long would Bertie have been stuck behind her bed? Who would have found her?

The numbers blurred together on Bertie's insurance card and

Ellie couldn't read them. How could she leave on June first? Who would look after Bertie?

She reached over and gave her aunt's hand a squeeze. "I'm going to stay here all summer."

"I know, Dear."

"And I think we should get you one of those medical alert bracelets."

"Perhaps."

"And a cell phone for when you're out."

"Those things are just a bother."

"We'll get you one anyway."

While Ellie finished filling out the form, the triage nurse brought out a wheelchair to Bertie. Ellie stood to go with them, but the nurse smiled and motioned for her to sit down again. "Finish the form and then we'll call you back." She wheeled Bertie through the foyer doors into the back room.

A few minutes later Ellie returned the form to the front desk. Then waited. And waited. And waited. The room smelled of disinfectant, and the fluorescent lights hummed annoyingly.

Wasn't Bertie supposed to come back out after seeing the triage nurse? Could it be more serious than Ellie thought? She'd only worried about broken bones, but perhaps Bertie had sustained some internal injury. Could you get those from falling off a bed?

The mother with the baby was called into the treatment rooms. So was the older gentleman.

At last a nurse appeared at the door and beckoned for Ellie to follow. She walked through the swinging double doors into a large room. Cloth partitions for the patient beds hung on one side of the room and a nurses' station stood on the other. Boxes were stacked around the nurses' desk, and hospital equipment—all sorts of unrecognizable machines with tubes growing out of them—crowded what was left of the room.

The nurse led Ellie along the cloth partition and pulled back one of the curtains. Bertie lay propped up in the bed, wearing a hospital gown and a stern frown. "See, I told you they'd make me take off my clothes. They like you naked." She nodded pointedly at the nurse. "It makes one wonder what they do in their spare time."

The nurse forced a smile. "The doctor will be with you in a minute," she said, and then tugged the curtain closed.

Ellie sat on the foot of the bed. "What did they tell you about your ankle and your arm?"

"Oh, they don't tell you anything. They just ask you a bunch of questions. One would think this was school and not a hospital—What's your name? What's your birthdate?" She held one hand out to Ellie. "Didn't you write all of that down outside?"

"Yes."

Bertie folded her arms tightly across her chest. "Besides, a woman never tells her age. It's impertinent to ask."

The curtain slid open, and a tall man wearing scrubs stepped inside. His blond hair was mussed, and a shadow of stubble grew on his jawline. Even though he looked down at the clipboard he carried and not at Ellie; still, she knew his eyes were blue. She'd recognized him at once. It was John from the library.

He spoke mechanically. "I'm Dr. Flynn, and I hear you're Bertie's niece?" It was then he looked up at Ellie. His eyes narrowed as though he recognized her but couldn't place her.

She stood, walked to him, and held out her hand. "Yes, I'm Ellie Baxter."

John hesitated, then shook her hand.

"I'm glad to know this hospital is so generous in its promotions. To think that just yesterday you were a janitor."

And then John's face colored. He remembered.

He lowered his voice, and one hand mussed his hair further. "Miss Baxter, I apologize for that conversation, but this is really not the time or place to discuss it." His gaze darted to Bertie and then back to the clipboard. "I need to talk to you about your aunt's diagnosis."

"What are you going to do about my leg?" Bertie called over. "And my arm—it was quite numb for a while. That can't be normal."

Ellie folded her arms and kept her voice low. "You apologize but don't offer any explanation? You tell strangers that you're a janitor for the fun of it, is that it?"

"No, of course not. It's just that when you came up to me—" He held up one hand, as though to fend off the questioning. "Look, I don't have time to talk about this right now. I need to ask you some questions about your aunt's injuries."

"I can't hear you over there," Bertie called. "Are you talking about my leg or just flirting?"

Ellie blushed, then felt worse for doing so. She didn't flirt with strangers, but he wasn't likely to believe that now. He thought she was the type that hit on men in libraries. Why else would he have told Ellie he was a janitor instead of admitting he was a doctor? He had wanted to get rid of her. Plain and simple.

John tapped one finger on the clipboard then called over to Bertie, "I'm going to have a word with your niece, then we'll come back in and talk with you."

John motioned for Ellie to walk through the curtains. She followed him back behind the nurses' station. When he at last stopped, he looked back at his clipboard. "Your aunt's arm is fine, and the X rays didn't show any breaks in her ankle. She has mild swelling and needs to stay off of it until the swelling goes down. Ice packs for the next twenty-four hours will help."

"All right."

"Did she hit her head during her fall?"

"I don't think so. She didn't say she did."

"How long has she been disoriented?"

"Disoriented? Is she disoriented?" Ellie clutched at the buttons on her shirt, as though next he'd pronounce something fatal.

"She says today's date is December twenty-fifth and she's twenty-four years old."

Ellie released her buttons. "Oh, that. She says those sort of things all the time. I mean, just in a joking sort of way." Ellie shrugged. "You know."

John raised an eyebrow at her. "No, I don't know, Miss Baxter. Patients don't generally joke around with their doctors in the emergency room."

"She didn't really mean it. She just thinks it's impertinent to ask a woman her age."

"And today is Christmas because?"

"Oh, well that's just because . . . " Ellie didn't answer. He was not going to understand about the Christmas tree or the gift-wrapped Hamburger Helper. "Aunt Bertie is eccentric. She's an artist, like Van Gogh or Picasso, only we don't think she'll cut off pieces of her head."

This was not helping.

John gave her a long stare. "So you're saying she's been disoriented for quite some time?"

"No. I mean, yes—she's always been eccentric. Aunt Bertie thinks we all create our own reality. In her reality she'd like to look twenty-four and have every day be Christmas. That's not really so odd, is it?"

"Yes, Miss Baxter, it really is." He lifted the top sheet of his clipboard and began writing on the second sheet. "Many conditions affect cognitive reasoning. I'd like her to have a CAT scan to rule out the most obvious ones. The nearest hospital with that equipment is in Spokane. I can call them and—"

"Just like that? You're branding her crazy because she likes Christmas?"

He held the clipboard down. "Miss Baxter, I like Christmas too, but I know the difference between May and December."

"Maybe, but you don't know the difference between a janitor and a doctor."

Instead of anger, a smile turned up the corners of his lips. "I suppose I deserve that. I should have never told you I was a janitor, but we're talking about your aunt. Do you know if she has any episodes of paranoia, depression, or if she's ever heard voices?"

"She isn't schizophrenic. Go back, ask her the questions again, and let her know she needs to answer seriously this time."

He sighed, as though it was unbearable how she was making his job harder like this, but he strode back toward Bertie's partition.

They Bertie found still propped up in bed, her arms crossed over her gown. "There you two are. I was afraid you'd gotten so wrapped up in each other that you'd completely forgotten me."

"We were discussing your case," John said. "I want to ask you a few questions again."

"And answer them seriously," Ellie added, "So that Dr. Flynn doesn't think you're crazy."

John shot her a sharp look, but then put back on his patience-for-the-patient doctor-smile. "Can you tell me your name?"

Bertie humphed. "You keep asking my name, and I'm the one who's crazy? I go to church with you every week. You know my name."

"Today's date then. What is today?"

She paused, as though really having to think about it. "It's Wednesday because Enrichment Night is tonight, and Sister Sneed called to see if I needed a ride. I told her no, which is a good thing now since I won't be up to it."

"And is it Christmas today?"

"In my heart, or on the calendar?"

"On the calendar."

"No, the calendar doesn't care anything at all about an old woman's wishes. The calendar goes on being May."

Ellie shot him a triumphant look. *See, Aunt Bertie is just fine. Christmas is in her heart, and May is on the calendar.* Doctors just worried too much. And they didn't understand. At least this man didn't understand. He was probably in the same category as her parents. A salad-fork-for-the-salad type of man.

John stared for another moment at Bertie as though trying to see her neurons fire. "I'd still like to have a CAT scan done to rule out problems."

"No, I don't think so," Bertie said. "I've never been fond of cats. I don't want a scan."

John did not smile. "There are no cats involved in a CAT scan. It stands for computerized axial tomography."

"I know what a CAT scan is," Bertie said. "It's where they put you in tube and play music through ear phones so you won't think about the fact that you're lying in something the same size as a coffin—except a CAT scan costs more and isn't lined with velvet." Bertie tugged at the covers, pulling the blanket further up her chest. "Well, I don't want to lie like that unless all my friends are going to come visit me and tell a congregation what a wonderful person I was."

John wrote something on his clipboard. "You're thinking of an MRI. CAT scans are quicker, and only your head is involved. It's a simple procedure."

Bertie shook her head. "It's unnecessary."

"I really recommend you have one," John said.

"She doesn't want one," Ellie said.

Ellie could see the muscles around John's jaw tighten. "All right, then. You're not required to take my advice." He turned to Ellie. "I'd like you to keep an eye on your aunt for the next twenty-four hours. If you see any signs of a concussion, any more signs of amnesia or delirium, bring her back in."

Any *more* signs.

Ellie picked up Bertie's muumuu and handed it to her. "If we have another problem, I'll contact her regular doctor."

"You should do that anyway. He should know about this episode."

"Fine." The word wasn't an agreement. It was simply a way to end the conversation. She didn't care what he thought. In fact, Bertie was right about doctors. You couldn't trust somebody who enjoyed cutting into people.

Chapter 7

The rest of the shift was uneventful. A broken arm, an IV for a pregnant woman suffering from hyperemesis, and an iron poisoning watch for a child who got into a bottle of multivitamins. John even had time to check on Alissa in the critical condition wing. She'd improved enough that everyone was hopeful. A good day. Nothing stressful, which was how he liked his shift, except that it gave him lots of time to relive Bertie's visit. Or rather, Ellie's visit. Ellie with her khaki eyes staring at him coldly.

A janitor. It was a stupid thing to have told her. He should have realized that he'd run into her again. This wasn't New York, where Bruno could meet women at nightclubs and judge their monetary interests without repercussions. This was Colton, Idaho, where the entire town shopped in three grocery stores.

He should have known.

Still, it was better this way. Now he knew Ellie considered artists and janitors below her. If they hadn't met in the library first, when she'd come in here today—when he'd pulled back the curtain to Bertie's room and seen Ellie there—well, he would've had a hard time concentrating on Bertie's problems, which was ironic, because he was still having a hard time concentrating on Bertie's problems. He tried to banish auburn curls and khaki eyes from his mind.

Bertie.

He was thinking about Bertie.

Despite Ellie's assurances that Bertie was fine, it was hard to believe Bertie was joking when she came into the emergency room. This was not the place for humor, nor was it a spot where people waxed philosophical on the necessity of calendars.

And besides, over the years, after seeing his first few thousand patients, he'd developed a sense about them, an intuition for when things were not quite right. Something was not right about Bertie Goodwin.

Ellie said Bertie was this way before her fall, which ruled out recent head trauma as the cause. It could be the result of a past stroke in which she had received permanent damage to a portion of her brain. Or perhaps hydrocephalus or Alzheimer's. It could even be a tumor, which meant every day might be critical in making a diagnosis.

He should have pushed more for the CAT scan. Then at least they'd know what it wasn't.

John ran one hand through his hair, a habit of frustration. What information did he have to work with? As if he were flipping through a patient's chart, he tried to bring up scenes of Bertie at church. What did her behavior reveal? Bertie usually sat in the front of the Gospel Doctrine class with the other elderly women. It was easier for them to hear up there. Sometimes the comments from that area were interesting or helpful, at other times off the wall. He couldn't remember who gave which answers, but he would pay attention now. He should have been paying attention all along. As high priest group leader he was supposed to know who needed help.

He'd been so busy with work, church, helping his mom with the resort, and turning the rundown house he'd bought when he moved here into someplace livable . . . and there he was, giving the same I-have-no-time excuse he always heard during PPIs.

Most of his time as high priest group leader had been spent reminding the brethren to do their home teaching, checking up to see whether they'd done their home teaching, and trying to arrange interviews where he could chastise them for not doing their home teaching. He didn't give the brethren any slack, and he wasn't about to give himself any. He'd have to do better.

First he'd check in with Bertie's home teachers and see what they knew about her. Who had Bertie?

His hand went through his hair again. Clark and Carlson.

Good old twenty-percent Clark and Carlson. They wouldn't be any help. Well, John would change that. He'd assign himself as Bertie's home teacher. That way he'd be able to keep an eye on her and check for any telling behavior. Besides, when he became her home teacher, perhaps she'd trust him enough to follow his medical advice.

When John got home there were three messages on his answering machine. All from his mother. The first message insisted he call her immediately. The second insisted that instead of calling, he should come to her house to talk. The third told him to call before he left so she would know he was on his way. The emergency that caused this crisis: Diana had broken up with her boyfriend.

While dialing his mother, John put away the groceries he'd picked up on the way home. No point in making something for dinner now. Apparently this was an event that required an immediate family council. He would undoubtedly be subjected to a lot of female emotions and crying.

His mother picked up the phone on the second ring. "Thank goodness you're home. You need to come over and talk to Diana."

"And what am I supposed to say to her?"

"Something. You can't just stand by and do nothing while she makes the biggest mistake of her life."

"How do you know it's a mistake?"

His mother gasped. "How can you say such a thing? Don't you like Chris?"

"Sure, I like Chris, but I'm not the one who has to date him. If Diana doesn't like him anymore, what am I supposed to do about it?"

His mother's words came over the line in a clipped staccato rhythm. "She still likes him, she just doesn't know it. She's—she's infatuated with Andrew, and so she's making this horrible mistake."

"Andrew?" The name brought pricks of displeasure to the back of his neck.

"Yes, Andrew. The guy who rents biking equipment at the Tour Store."

"Does she even know him?"

"No, which is why it's the biggest mistake of her life, and why you need to—" his mother's voice broke off, and then she said, "I think I just heard her go down the stairs." A silence punctuated by footsteps followed, and then he heard his mother yelling, "Where do you think you're going?"

Even from a distance John heard his sister's reply. "Out!"

"I didn't say you could go anywhere," his mother yelled back.

"I'm eighteen and you can't tell me what to do!"

"You're still living under my roof, young lady!"

The slam of a door reverberated over the line, then John's mother came back on the phone, sounding breathless. "She left, just walked out of here. That's it. I'm grounding her. For a month. For a year. Until she's thirty."

He let out a sigh as he put away the last of the groceries. "I'm on my way over now."

* * *

Ellie didn't sleep well that night. According to the nurse's instructions, Ellie had to check Bertie every two hours for signs of a concussion. After the first two times Ellie came into Bertie's room with a flashlight to make sure Bertie's pupils were still dilating, Bertie grabbed the flashlight out of her hands and said, "If you thought I was crazy before, you should see how I'll act if you come in here and shine that thing in my eyes again."

"I'm supposed to be checking on you, and I never thought you were crazy, just the hospital staff did. Honestly Aunt Bertie, why in the world did you tell them it was Christmas?"

Bertie ran a hand through her mop of lavender hair. "Hospitals are frightening. They're where people go to die. I was sitting there on that awful bed, smelling that hospital-sanitized-death smell, and they asked me what the date was. Well, when your mind is crowded by thoughts of impending doom it's hard to remember those kind of details." She straightened the collar of her flannel nightgown, fixing a button that had come undone. "To tell you the truth, I'm still not sure what the date is. When you sit home every day you lose track. I just figure it's a number under thirty."

"It's May twenty-first."

"Young people know the date because they have things to do. When you get old . . . " Bertie sighed wearily and lay back down, pulling the covers up to her chest as she did. "Young people just don't understand what it's like to grow old."

"You're not *that* old."

"I'm old enough that I can get stuck on the side of my bed—and don't you dare tell a soul what happened yesterday." She slid her hand across the sheets, smoothing out the wrinkles. "Stuck like a pair of forgotten socks! It's bad enough that my future nephew-in-law knows about it."

"Um, about your future nephew-in-law—"

"Oh, I'm sure you have all sorts of things to tell me about him—how mysterious the color of his eyes is and how endearing his dimples are, but I'm tired and need my sleep."

Yes, it could wait until morning. Then she'd tell Bertie that John wasn't going to ever ask her out on a date. And even if he did, she'd turn him down. Gleefully.

A janitor. Honestly.

Ellie put the flashlight on Bertie's nightstand, mumbled, "Good-night," then padded back to her bedroom.

How much should she divulge to her aunt about the meeting in the library? Bertie might wonder why Ellie was avoiding John at church—and she was going to avoid him—then when she told Bertie about their first meeting . . .

Ellie's job.

The thought made her stop, midway to bed.

She couldn't tell Bertie that John had lied to ditch her. Bertie would be horribly offended, tell everyone she knew what a jerk he was, and thus make the people Ellie worked with—John's family—hate her.

The best thing to do was to pretend the library never happened. And never talk about John at work. And hope she never came within twelve feet of him for the rest of the summer.

Crawling into bed, she pulled the covers up to her shoulders. She would have to call the news station and let them know she couldn't take the job after all. They wouldn't mind. It wouldn't be a heartbreak for them. They'd just call up one of the other students they'd interviewed and offer the job to them.

Someone would be thrilled. Someone's prayers would be answered. Not Ellie's.

She turned on the mattress, hauling half the covers with her as she moved. So much for seeing Kirk in two weeks. She wouldn't be able to tell him how she felt for months. By then it might be too late.

It didn't matter. Ellie had to stay and make sure Bertie was all right.

Ellie lay as still as she could, hoping it would trick her body into sleep, but it didn't. Her mind had already turned the pages of the calendar, was already fretting about the fall. Bertie would still need someone to watch after her then.

But not a nursing home. Not assisted living. Nothing extreme. Just someone to phone her every day. Someone to stop by every once in a while to look under the hood of her car, to pull weeds, and to sing Christmas carols with her.

Did her home teachers know she needed help? Judging by the state Bertie's lawn was in when Ellie came, probably not.

On Sunday Ellie would find her home teachers, have a talk with them, and explain the situation. If they promised to check up on Bertie, to look out for her, then perhaps Ellie could leave after the summer without much worry after all.

* * *

John had spent a good portion of the night with his mother, and now as he pulled himself out of bed his head felt as if it were weighed down with bricks. He stumbled into the kitchen, put bread in the toaster, and poured himself a glass of orange juice. He usually got up at 5:00 A.M. to make his shift at 6:00. Today he'd given himself an extra fifteen minutes of sleep. It didn't help.

It had taken John the better part of two hours to calm his mother last night. For fifteen minutes she vented her anger as she called all of Diana's friends trying to find her. Lauren finally found her at Jill's. Diana was over there watching videos and wasn't coming home until she'd seen every single *Star Wars* movie made. Twice. She was eighteen years old and she didn't have to come home. Ever.

Lauren slammed down the phone, paced a pathway on the

kitchen floor, and waved one hand in the air to emphasize each of her points.

How could Diana just stomp out of the house without even a word as to where she was going, then sass off to her mother on the phone that way? Such disrespect! Such defiance! Well, she could just live over at Jill's if she wasn't willing to obey the rules of the house. Diana had been given everything—everything! A home, a job, food, clothing, all the love a parent could possibly give a child. Did John remember how Lauren used to carry Diana everywhere she went when she was a little girl?

Yes, he remembered.

Lauren's knees had never been the same after that, but did she complain? No she did not.

Did he remember how Diana was afraid to go to school and so Lauren had volunteered every day in the kindergarten class until Diana felt comfortable?

He'd been on his mission then, but he remembered her writing about it.

She'd been a single mother, struggling to make the resort work without a husband's help. It had been a sacrifice—a sacrifice—to go into that school and help the children make construction-paper butterflies, but she had done it for Diana, and now this was the thanks she got.

For a full hour he listened to his mother go on like that.

Then the anger left and she sunk into tears. *Her baby. Her baby had just walked out of the house and she had only been trying to help Diana. She cared about Diana. Of course she didn't want her daughter to make the wrong choice when it came to relationships. The wrong choice could be so painful. John knew all about that.*

Oh yes, he knew.

What if Diana did something rash? What if Andrew was the type who just used women? He probably was. He looked like the type.

John didn't say anything about that point. By law he couldn't. And yet he could suddenly see Suzanne lying on the hospital bed as clearly as he saw his mother in front of him.

How long ago had she come into the ER? A few weeks?

John knew Suzanne had been Andrew's girlfriend. He'd seen the two of them around town—Suzanne with her long brown hair and short shorts, platform sandals and half-a-dozen earrings in her ears. She always carried a soda in one hand, always wore a smile. When her mother had brought her into the ER at noon, she'd been in sweats, her hair tangled, no jewelry, no smile. She laid passively on the hospital bed, an IV line hooked up to her left arm. Her eyes were glassy and her skin pale.

Suzanne's mother sat in the chair next to the hospital bed. "She hasn't been able to keep anything down for a week, and I'm really getting worried about her. At first I thought it was the flu, but it just won't go away, and now I'm wondering if it could be some sort of parasite or infection."

He nodded and looked down at the nurse's notes. Suzanne had been feeling ill for two weeks and it had grown progressively worse. She was thirsty all the time but couldn't keep liquids down. Classic signs of dehydration. Well, the IV should take care of that temporarily. She hadn't been out of the country or drunk any impure water that she was aware of. No other injuries. No allergies. She was sexually active, but always used birth control. Her last menses had been three weeks ago, which meant the nausea shouldn't be a symptom of a pregnancy, and yet he'd better be sure. Sometimes a pregnant woman spotted a bit and thought it was a period.

He looked at her date of birth. Eighteen years old. Not really a woman at all. She was still a child, and he was going to have to tell her she needed a pregnancy test.

He put the clipboard down and palpated her stomach, looking for any tenderness that might indicate appendix problems. "Any pain here?"

"Just nausea," she said. "Everything smells horrible."

"Have any aches or pain?"

She nodded. "My ribs hurt, but I think that's from throwing up so much."

"How about your chest?"

"Yeah, my chest feels really sore."

"You say your last period was three weeks ago. Was it lighter than usual?"

Suzanne's mother leaned toward John, her voice low. "She isn't pregnant. I made a point of discussing birth control with Suzanne when she began dating. She's always been protected. I buy her the stuff myself."

He didn't have time to reply. Suzanne struggled to prop herself up on the bed. "Yes, it was really light." She looked from her mother to John, her face growing even paler. "Am I pregnant?"

Five minutes and one test answered the question.

Suzanne lay on the bed, knees drawn up, head buried in her

arms, the IV line pulled tight. Her mother sat beside her on the bed, stroking her hair while they both cried.

"She and her boyfriend broke up a month ago," her mother said weekly. "And now this. I don't understand how it happened. She was always protected."

He picked up a prescription pad so he didn't have to look at them anymore, so he wouldn't say any of the things he wanted to. He scribbled down an order for Phenergan. "Only abstinence is 100 percent effective. She should also be tested for STDs. I can give her something in her drip for the nausea and a prescription to take home. You should make an appointment with an obstetrician as soon as possible."

The mother gripped the prescription in her hand. "STDs? You mean a test for AIDS?"

"I mean tests for all of them. Seventy-five percent of sexually active people have some kind of sexually transmitted disease. Some STDs have no symptoms initially but can cause problems down the line."

"But she's so young."

"People twenty-five and younger account for two-thirds of all STD cases."

He tore out another prescription paper. "I'm going to give you the number of American Pregnancy Helpline." Then wrote 1–888–80-WOMAN. "It can put you in touch with pregnancy resource centers. I'll also give you the number for Heartbeat CareNet International. It's a support group." He had the number memorized from his years in New York. 1–800–395–4357.

The mother was still clutching the prescription slips when he left the room.

She was protected.

Exactly what had that mother been thinking?

* * *

Now his own mother sat before him discussing the possibility of Andrew and Diana. Together.

Over his dead body.

"Andrew listens to that screechy gangster music," Lauren said. "I've heard it playing in the tour van when he's driven up, and I don't trust boys who listen to rap. Rap stars are always out killing people. And what do any of us really know about Andrew anyway?" She sniffed and took one of the napkins from the napkin holder to wipe the mascara streaks from under her eyes. "He probably smokes, and drinks, and uses all sorts of illegal drugs. Simultaneously. He's probably a full-blown crack addict."

"Probably not. It would be hard to maintain a habit while negotiating mountain bikes at high speeds."

"You just don't like Chris, do you?"

"I like Chris, Mom."

She sniffed and crumpled up the napkin. "Well, you need to talk to Diana about it. She listens to you."

"No she doesn't."

"You're like a father to her."

"I know. That's why she doesn't listen to me."

Lauren reached out and put one hand on his arm. "Go over to Jill's and talk to her, John. You tell her that she's being selfish, immature, and"—Lauren sniffed, then shook her head. "No, perhaps we'd better wait until she's cooled down. Come to the resort tomorrow. I'll have some handyman things for you to do, and Diana can take you round to the rooms. You tell her no good will ever come of her hanging around that crack addict Andrew."

John sighed and finished off the rest of his cocoa.

"And if that doesn't work," she went on, "you can go rough up Andrew and tell him he'd better stay away from Diana."

Well, he would talk to Diana. He'd find out what in the world she was thinking, that is *if* she was thinking and not just letting herself be steered by wild teenage hormones.

And if talking didn't work he'd enroll her in summer school. In some small, predominantly female country.

He had tomorrow off. He'd go over to the resort and talk to her then.

Chapter 8

When Ellie stumbled into the kitchen for breakfast, Bertie was already at the table, cereal bowl pushed aside and notebook paper in front of her. Scrawled across the top of the paper were these words: *One hundred reasons not to clean.*

Ellie took a bowl from the cupboard, plunked it down at the table, and poured Shredded Wheat for herself. "You're giving up cleaning?"

"Trying to, Dear. I figure if a person can come up with a hundred reasons not to do something, she's justified in not doing it. The only problem is there are some very compelling reasons *to* clean." She flipped over to a second piece of paper and held it up for Ellie. Across the top it read, *The Case for Cleaning,* and on the space directly below it were the words, *Who wants to look at a dirty toilet?* Below that were the words, *My slippers will stick to the kitchen floor after a few weeks.*

Ellie nodded. "I see. Very compelling."

"But then again, we're talking about my safety. If I hadn't vacuumed those baseboards I never would have gotten stuck on the side of my bed."

"Perhaps you should just get a lighter bed."

"Yes, but it would be so much more gratifying to give up cleaning altogether. I could tack this list to my door and then when people came to visit and thought, 'Why would a person choose to live this way?' Well, they'd see the list and know."

"I can do the cleaning while I'm here."

Bertie waved off the suggestion, then stood and took her bowl to the sink. "I won't have you spending your summer being my maid. You have things to do—a job to work at and a man to marry. Speaking of your job, you never told me how things went yesterday."

"I accidentally checked someone into a shed."

"I see."

"People avoided standing in my line so I didn't have to help them."

"Oh, dear."

"As I left, Sister Flynn mentioned that housekeeping jobs weren't quite so complicated." Ellie poured the milk over her cereal. "Just think, I'll be able to tell my friends I spent my summer with my head hovering over a toilet, and all without becoming drunk or pregnant."

Bertie sat back down at the table and picked up her list. "You're definitely not going to work in housekeeping. You do enough of that here. If she tries to move you there, apply elsewhere. Get a different job."

Ellie shook her head as she swallowed a bite of cereal. "I'm a broadcasting major. I don't know what I'm qualified to do in Colton."

"Call the Chamber of Commerce and see."

Ellie didn't reply.

"You're a bright and talented girl," Bertie went on. "Pick something out, then go in and talk to the manager. Emphasize your qualifications. Then don't leave until he's penciled you in on the work schedule."

"Or arrested me for trespassing."

"No, no. We'll have none of that. Your parents would never forgive me if I got you arrested, and besides, mug shots are dreadful things. I've never seen one yet that wasn't horrid."

Ellie would have asked Bertie just how many mug shots she'd seen, but by then her aunt was giving her a motivational lecture on the power of positive attitude and finding the right job. She ended her speech with: "Of course, maybe you're worrying about nothing. It will probably go perfectly today."

* * *

After a half an hour of work Ellie finally had the check-in system down. Welcome. Map. Key. All with a smile. No one defected from her line today. She even remembered how to get from the check-in computer screen to the check-out computer screen without erasing all the information she'd just typed in.

She felt, well, almost competent.

Diana half-heartedly greeted the guests and did her tasks silently, only speaking when Ellie asked questions. Then a little after 1:00, cabin 21 called the front desk to say they were running late and if the bike tour guide got to the lobby before they did, would the front desk please tell him they'd be out as soon as possible?

Diana cheered up considerably after that.

"He's coming," she breathed out as she paced the narrow walkway behind the front desk. "He's coming and waiting here. This is the perfect time for me to mention that I broke up with Chris."

"You broke up with Chris?"

"Yes. Last night. I mean, I couldn't very well hit on Andrew while I was still going out with Chris." She stopped pacing. "And I am going to hit on him. I'm going to embrace my fear. I'm going to . . . " She bit a fingernail and then turned to face Ellie. "Exactly what am I going to do?"

"Talk with him? Flirt with him?"

"I already do that. Every girl who knows him does that. I have to do something more."

"Ask him out?"

"Yes," Diana said, and then just as quickly added, "No. If he turned me down I'd never be able to face him again, and with my job that would be a bad thing. Just imagine me running into the bathroom every time he walked through the doors."

Ellie scanned the check-in list to see how many guest were still arriving. "Why don't you ask him to something really casual? You can tell him you're showing me around and invite him to come along too."

Diana snapped her fingers. "That's great. Except I don't want him to think I'm setting him up with you, so I'll tell him to bring along a friend for you. It'll be sort of like a double date."

"Right. That'll be fun. As long as Andrew has nice friends." Ellie put the check-in list back on the counter. "Does he have nice friends?"

"All the guys at the Tour Store are really great. I'll tell him to bring one of them." Diana sighed, then tapped her fingers together as though she was clapping very quietly. "I'm going to do this. I'm really going to do this."

The hunkmobile pulled up. Andrew got out of the driver's seat and walked toward the building.

"I'm not going to do this," Diana said.

Ellie shook her head and laughed as she typed.

"I don't know what to ask him out to. Besides, he doesn't know I've broken up with Chris. I can't ask him out when he thinks I still have a boyfriend."

"So tell him."

"How am I going to work that into casual conversation?"

Andrew opened the door and smiled at them.

Ellie lowered her voice to a whisper. "If you don't ask him out, I'll ask him out for you and that will be more embarrassing for you."

As Andrew walked to the font desk, Diana stood beside Ellie, the smile frozen on her face. Andrew took a piece of paper from his pocket, unfolded it, and read it. "I'm here to pick up the Richardsons."

Ellie smiled back at him. "They just called the front desk. They'll be here in a few minutes."

Diana didn't move. The smile remained fixed on her lips.

Andrew looked from her to Ellie, and no one spoke for a moment. Finally he said, "So, how's it going?"

When Diana didn't say anything, Ellie said, "Fine. Everything's going fine. Well, except that Diana feels a little blue. She just broke up with Chris."

"I did," Diana added.

"That's always the pits," Andrew said.

"I've been telling her she needs to get out and be with people, and since I'm new to town I need someone to show me around the social life. We were just talking about doing something." Ellie turned and nodded at Diana. "What was it you were suggesting that we go to?"

Diana gulped and tapped her fingers against the counter. "Um . . . the ward social," Diana said.

The ward social? It wouldn't have been Ellie's first choice in the town's social-life category. She had been thinking more along the lines of dinner and a movie, but Ellie couldn't suggest anything different. Diana was plunging along with the conversation, her nervousness giving her words rapid-fire speed. "It's this dinner we're having on Saturday. I mean, my church is having it, and Ellie and I will both be going, and well, it'll be really fun. And I know you're not a member of my church or anything, but it's not really a churchy thing where you read scriptures or hear a sermon or anything. It's just sort of a social thing because, you know, Mormons love to cook and sit around and eat. Not that I'm saying we're a religion of bingers. Because we're not. We're really healthy, and you may have heard of the Word of Wisdom and how we don't smoke or drink or do drugs or anything. I know you're a very healthy person yourself. Anyway, it would be great if you could come."

"To the dinner?"

"Yes, to the dinner. Saturday at 6:00. And you could bring a friend and we could all sit together."

He shrugged. "Saturday night . . . I think I'm free. How much does it cost?"

"It's free," Diana said, and then with a laugh, added, "It's free. You're free. See how nicely that works out?"

Andrew shrugged. "Sounds good."

A man walked toward the lobby and Ellie picked up the registration printout in case he was checking in. No point in distracting Diana when she was on a roll. As Ellie moved to the key drawer the man swung open the doors and she saw who it was.

John Flynn.

* * *

As he walked into the lobby, John spotted Andrew standing by the front counter and Diana leaning across the counter toward him, so many stars in her eyes her face could have qualified as a galaxy.

His little sister wasn't wasting any time at all.

And he'd better not waste any time either. Infatuation was a shortcut to stupidity. She needed to start thinking about what she was doing before it was too—Ellie Baxter. Ellie was standing next to Diana, smiling in that forced way you smile at people you'd rather not see.

What was she doing here?

Well, he knew what she was doing here. She was wearing a

polo shirt with the Pine Top logo embroidered across the top and standing behind the front counter. It was obvious that she worked here, and now every time he came in and saw her he'd feel like a jerk all over because he'd lied to her about being a janitor.

Why had fate done this to him? What's more, why had his mother done this to him?

"Ellie," he choked out. "I didn't know you worked here."

Another stiff smile. "It's only my second day."

Diana glanced at Ellie, "Oh, then you called him already?"

"We talked," she said.

He wasn't sure exactly what this exchange meant, but he didn't want to press the point. He didn't want to say anything more to Ellie than he had to.

Diana glanced between Ellie and him, taking in his discomfort. He'd be grilled about it later unless he avoided being alone with Diana until she'd forgotten about this whole—Dang. He'd come here to talk to Diana, hadn't he?

He sighed in defeat. Better get on with it. The talk with Diana in which he was going to save her from making stupid mistakes. "Um, Diana, Mom had some things for me to do in a few of the cabins. You want to take me around?"

Diana didn't take her eyes off of Andrew. "I'll just give you the keys and you can let yourself in."

"It's stuff that takes two people to do. I need your help."

"I can't leave the front desk unmanned," Diana said.

Or leave the man at the front desk, apparently. "Ellie will still be here," he said.

"And she's too inexperienced to work alone. Yesterday she tried to check someone into the grounds shed." Diana pulled the master key out of the drawer and handed it to Ellie. "Here. You go with my brother. You really should see the cabins and the facilities, anyway. That way you'll be able to give more informed directions. John, show her around."

Ellie gripped the key in her hand as though she'd just been handed a jail sentence, but she walked through the back room and out the door to come with him.

Well, that was the end of the argument. Diana wasn't about to leave Andrew, and any more insisting from John that she do so would only manage to insult Ellie. He'd already done enough of that.

A janitor. He could kick himself.

He continued to hold his hand out to his sister. "The cart key?"

Diana took another key from the drawer and tossed it to him. "Show her how to work the guest cart while you're at it." Then Diana turned back to Andrew with an oblivious smile.

John walked across the lobby, and Ellie walked beside him, but not close beside him. He stopped at the supply closet, pulling out a curtain rod and a drain, along with an orange caddy that housed an assortment of nails, screws, and tools. Then he strode to the front door, pushing it open with his shoulder because his hands were full. "The carts are this way."

She followed him outside. Neither spoke as they walked around the side of the building where half a dozen beige carts were lined up in the parking lot. Housekeeping, grounds crew, and security all had their own carts, but the front desk's cart was a mammoth thing that could squeeze in six guests and their luggage. He put the tools in the back, then sat in the driver's seat. She climbed in next to him and folded her arms as though it were cold.

He inserted the key and turned on the engine. "This is how the guest cart works. You push the lever forward for forward and backward for backward. Did you catch all that?"

She nodded without smiling.

"I'll let you drive on the way back to get the hang of it."

She didn't say anything.

He drove the cart through the parking lot to the wide trails that led to the cabins. The cart's hum and a number of ever-present bird calls were the only noises in the silence.

"So how is your aunt this morning?"

Ellie looked at the passing scenery and not at him. "Fine. Maybe a little tired because I woke her up during the night, but besides that I think she's her usual self."

"Has she called her regular doctor yet?"

"I'm sure she'll get around to it today."

"Make sure she does."

More silence. The smell of pine was as thick as fog. The trees stood so tall on this mountain that the sky seemed dark green instead of blue. He pointed things out as he drove. "Those are cabins one through four up there. That's the road that leads to the tennis courts. The indoor pool is over there."

Still silence. Ellie wasn't going to make this easy on him. He shifted in his seat, gripping the steering wheel harder than he should have. "Listen, about the library. I'm sorry for telling you I was a janitor. It's sort of long story, and I don't want to bore you with the details of my life, or why I said it; the important thing is I regret saying it. Really. I'm sorry. I'm generally painfully honest. You may find that hard to believe after I tell you the next thing."

He pulled up in front of a cabin with a 25 hanging over the front door, stopped the cart, and took out the key. "I don't have anything to do that actually requires two people. Just a drain to switch out and a curtain rod to put up. I only told Diana I needed her help because I wanted to talk to her."

Ellie tilted her head at him. "Why didn't you just tell her you wanted to speak with her, then?"

He stepped out of the cart, hefting his supplies from the back, then they walked up to the cabin's front porch. "Because I didn't want her to think I came up here to give her a lecture," he said. "Besides, I wanted to talk to her about Andrew and he was standing right there."

"Oh, Andrew." She said the word knowingly.

John unlocked the front door. "What do you mean, 'Oh, Andrew'?"

She walked into the cabin, peered into the side bedroom, then slowly turned around in the living room, taking it in. "I thought these were supposed to sleep four."

"They do. The couch folds out. Cabins one through ten sleep six because they have two bedrooms. And what do you know about Andrew?"

"She just asked him out. It was so cute."

"She asked him out?"

"Yeah. She was so nervous, she would have chickened out if I hadn't forced her into it." Ellie sat down on the couch as though testing it. "He said yes."

John tossed the curtain rod down on the living room floor, but kept hold of an orange caddy. "You *forced* her into it?"

"I didn't twist her arm, I just told him Diana and I were going out because she wanted to show me around. I gave her a reason to do it."

"Great. Just great." He walked past her into the bathroom, ripping the packaging off the new drain as he went. "And where will the three of you be going?"

She stood and followed him to the bathroom, then leaned against the doorway and watched him take off the water trap on the pipes. "The four of us. Andrew is bringing a friend from the Tour Store so we can double to the ward social."

"The ward social?"

"It wouldn't have been my first choice either, but Diana seemed pretty determined in the matter."

John hit the pipe from below to release the drain, pulled it up, then tossed it in the garbage can. He dropped the new drain into the sink and pushed it with his fingers until the fit was snug. "All right. I'll let Diana go to the ward social with him, but in the future please don't force Diana into any more dates."

Ellie's arms folded and her eyebrows shot up. "You'll *let* Diana go to the ward social with him?"

"Against my better judgment, I might add, but I don't suppose she can get into much trouble in the cultural hall." He gave the drain a final inspection, opening and closing it while the water ran. "Besides, once Bishop Whiting gets out the karaoke machine and does his Frankie Vallie impersonation, Andrew is likely to bolt from the church and not come within a mile radius of Diana again. That will be for the best."

Ellie raised an eyebrow. "Well, I guess we'll see."

"I guess we will. I wouldn't miss the social for the world now."

He left the bathroom, walked to the front room, and picked up the curtain rod. She left the doorway and plopped down on the couch to wait for him. She put her elbow on the arm and rested her head in her hand. Her hair fell over her arm, its curls giving her a disheveled and inviting look.

He turned and surveyed the window. It wasn't nearly as beautiful a view, but it was considerably safer to gaze at.

Every cabin had a window that looked out onto the porch and each was equipped with heavy light-blocking curtains. This curtain hung limply to one side. He pushed it aside for examination, his fingers running along the length of the rod. The bracket holding the curtain rod had snapped and pulled loose from the wall on one side, but the rod itself was fine. He pried the bracket the rest of the way off and threw it into the caddy. Then he got a new one out and screwed it to the wall with the electric drill. He couldn't see Ellie, but he knew she was behind him, watching silently, her hand entwined in her auburn hair. Such shiny hair. It was probably as soft as silk.

Man, he'd been single too long.

Once the new screws were in the wall, he reattached the curtain rod, then pulled the rope and watched the curtains swing back and forth as they moved across the window.

"A doctor, a janitor, and a fix-it man too," Ellie said from behind him. "I'm impressed."

"Don't be. I learned out of necessity. I was the resort's after-hours handyman all through high school. It was one of the main reasons I went to college. I wanted to do something besides snaking toilets and replacing light bulbs." He picked up the tools and extra curtain rod and they both walked to the door. "Of course, that strategy didn't really work. I'm an M.D. and my mother still has me up here fixing things."

"It's sweet that you help out. Or do you just help out when you want an excuse to lecture Diana?"

They walked to the cart and he climbed into the passenger side, then handed her the key. "I only lecture Diana when I think she's acting irresponsible or silly or not thinking clearly. Or, as in this case, all three."

Ellie turned the key and the cart sputtered to life. It lurched forward, then she found the reverse and backed the cart onto the road. "Why don't you like Andrew?"

"You're going the wrong direction." He nodded at the road behind them. "The lobby is that way."

"Oh." She swung the cart around in a wide arc, running off the road and crushing grass and pine needles as she did. "They ought to have the roads marked."

"They do." He pointed to a nearby totem pole of wooden signs, each with a destination and an arrow.

"Okay. I would have noticed that eventually." She took the cart back onto the road, bumping it over gravel, which spit angrily from underneath the wheels of the cart. "I'm just nervous because you're watching everything I do." The wind picked up some of Ellie's curls, making them flutter in the sunlight. He watched that, too.

"So why don't you like Andrew?" she asked again.

"He's not right for Diana. They have different values."

"People can change their values."

She said this so glibly, like a person could change his soul as easy as changing socks. Well, Ellie was too young to have seen much of the real world. She hadn't discovered yet that most people never changed. Not their values, not their habits, and never their pasts.

"What do you really know about Andrew?" he asked.

"I know that Diana likes him."

"That isn't much."

"It's enough for Diana."

"I shouldn't have expected a different answer from you. You're going out with one of Andrew's friends who you've never even met. For all you know the guy is wanted in four states."

Ellie laughed, and it sounded like music. "Diana calls you overprotective. I'm beginning to see what she means."

"I'm not overprotective. I'm reasonable."

"Do you think it's reasonable never to take a chance on people?"

The road divided up ahead, and she squinted, trying to read the signs.

He saved her the trouble. "The road circles around the resort so either way will bring you to the lobby."

She didn't veer one way or the other. He watched the fork draw nearer and gripped his arm rest. "But if you drive straight ahead you'll hit several trees."

She swung right, and the cart careened in that direction. "I see the trees. I just hadn't decided which way to go. And you didn't answer my question."

"Sorry, I got a little distracted when my life flashed before my eyes."

She turned her head, appraising him, and at the same time looking sad and sultry and not at all like she was paying attention to driving. "You don't believe in taking chances with people, do you?"

"I'm letting you drive the guest cart, aren't I?"

"You know what I mean."

She turned her attention back to the road, which was a good thing since she'd nearly driven off it again. The wheels protested with a low grind as they went over gravel. She straightened the cart out, then grinned sheepishly at him. "You don't have to say it. I'll concentrate on the raod. I'm a good driver, really. I've never even gotten a ticket."

Right. He knew her type. She had probably been pulled over half a dozen times but every time a policeman looked into those big, innocent eyes he somehow let her go with a warning.

Men lost all sense of reason when they were around beautiful women.

But he wasn't going to act that way.

She drove silently until she reached the parking spot at the side of the lobby. Once there she pulled the cart into the spot with lurching plunges, then turned off the cart.

"I just haven't gotten the hang of this yet," she said.

He smiled back at her. "I'm sure it won't take you long, and besides, if all the guests suddenly volunteer to walk to their cabins, it will give them a good cardiovascular workout."

She swatted him then stepped out of the cart.

The sports van had left the parking lot, which meant that Andrew was gone, but there was no point in trying to talk to Diana now. Not with Ellie, Miss Take-a-Chance-on-People, working beside her at the front desk. He'd wait until later. He'd go over to his mom's for dinner and help Diana with the dishes afterwards. No point sticking around the resort any longer. Still, he hesitated to leave. He stood for a moment longer, watching Ellie walk back into the lobby.

Yep, he'd definitely been single too long.

Chapter 9

Bertie stood in front of an easel in her bedroom, dotting wildflowers into a forest landscape and then painting over them again because they weren't right. Her frown deepened as Ellie told her of the ward social plans. "You're going out with a stranger?"

"Only to help Diana out. She was too shy to ask Andrew to do something by herself."

"It's all very good of you to help out Diana, but what does John think of it?"

Ellie leaned against the door frame, watching the flowers come and go. "He was actually up at the resort today, and we talked about it. He's not pleased. For some reason he doesn't like Andrew."

Bertie huffed and dabbed a darker green onto the tips of the trees. "I doubt he likes the idea of you going off with a stranger, even if it is to help his sister."

"I doubt he cares about that."

"Is that what he told you? He said those words?"

Ellie shifted her position on the door frame. "No, actually he told me I was behaving recklessly."

"I'd say so. Toying with his affections that way."

"You mean John's or the stranger's?"

"Don't think that I don't plan on meeting him."

Ellie knit her eyebrows together. Somehow it felt as though she and Bertie were having two different conversations. "Meeting who?"

"The stranger. When he comes to pick you up, I intend to get a full accounting of his intentions, his salary, and his medical history."

"Aunt Bertie . . . "

"And if he can't beat John's credentials—"here she waved the paintbrush at her niece, "and I'm telling you right now I don't consider that a likely possibility—then he won't be encouraged to ask for a second date."

"Aunt Bertie, you really don't need to do that."

She stabbed more paint onto the canvas. "I owe it to your parents."

Ellie rolled her eyes, then went into the kitchen to make dinner. If at all possible she'd meet her date at the church.

Ellie had Friday off from the resort. She spent the day washing windows and cleaning Bertie's carpet. In between chores she took Bertie's cordless phone into her bedroom, locked the door, and made herself call Channel 9.

She reached the personnel department and explained the situation the best she could.

"So you see, I need to take care of my aunt this summer, and I won't be able to come back for the internship . . . "

"Thank you for calling," a crisp-sounding woman replied. "I'll pass along the message. I hope your aunt is all right."

The woman hadn't tried to talk Ellie out of her decision. Of course she hadn't. Ellie was only an intern. Or, well—she had almost been an intern. Now she was only a mildly capable check-in clerk.

After Ellie hung up the phone she cried for ten minutes.

Finally she wiped the tears off her face and went into the kitchen to make lunch. Bertie was already there, making egg salad sandwiches, smashing the eggs as though she had a vendetta against them. Ellie sunk down into a kitchen chair wordlessly.

"You're having second thoughts, aren't you?" Bertie asked.

"What?"

"You regret your decision now."

Ellie felt her face flush. "Of course not." After processing the conversation she added, "What decision are you talking about?"

"Deciding to go out with that stranger. It doesn't seem like such a good idea now, does it?"

Ellie didn't reply. It was better not to.

"Well, you'll just have to give John a little extra attention at the ward social. That will make everything better." Bertie walked to the table and placed Ellie's sandwich in front of her. "I'll do what I can to help."

"No, Aunt Bertie. Really, you don't need to help."

Bertie didn't reply, but she smiled as she bit into her sandwich.

* * *

Ellie and Diana both worked Saturday morning. Because it was the busiest time for checking in and out, and because Ellie still wasn't very efficient, a woman named Theresa also worked the shift. Theresa had hair like an iron kettle, hands as big and rough as a farm hand, and a voice like an army sergeant. She made Ellie even more jumpy. Theresa was constantly checking up on her work and pointing out all the ways she needed to improve.

"You typed the guest's address as Pheonix, Arizona. It's spelled P-H-O-E-N-I-X, not P-H-E-O-N-I-X."

"Well it should be spelled P-H-E-O-N-I-X. Since when did an O make a long E sound?"

Ellie barely got to talk to Diana, and when things slowed down long enough that they could take a break to file paperwork the news wasn't good.

"I don't actually know if Andrew is coming to pick either of us up, or whether we're all going together, or whether his friend is planning on picking you up separately and then meeting us at the church."

Ellie took the keys that housekeeping had returned from the cabins and sorted them into the key drawer. "What do you mean you don't know? Didn't you arrange all of that with him?"

"Well, I meant to, but I was so flustered, and then the Richardsons came up and he had to leave. But I'm sure he won't leave us hanging. He probably just wanted to get it all planned out with his friend. I'm sure he'll let us know sometime today. Maybe he's going to stop by today."

He didn't stop by.

When their shift ended at 3:00, they still hadn't heard from him.

"Maybe he said he'd meet us there," Diana said as they walked out of the lobby together. "Did he say that? I can't remember. I was in a sort of dazed shock during the whole conversation."

"Call him when you get home and then call me." Ellie paused to take a scrap of paper and a pen from her purse. "Here's my phone number."

Diana took the paper, but looked at it skeptically. "Shouldn't he be the one to call me?"

"Ideally, yes."

"Will it look like I'm pushy if I call him?"

"No, it will look like you want to know what's going on." They walked to the parking lot, but Ellie hesitated before heading off for her car. "If it's all the same to you, I'd rather meet my date at the church. Since I don't know anything about him, it just seems better not to give him Bertie's address."

Diana tucked the paper with Ellie's phone number into her purse. "Yeah, I know. My brother gave me the Safety in Dating lecture last night. According to him, if anything bad happens to you it will be my fault, and it will eat away at my conscience until I die a tormented soul."

"Your brother worries a lot, doesn't he?"

"It comes from being an ER doctor. He's used to seeing the worst outcome of every scenario."

Ellie suddenly wanted to ask Diana more about John. She wanted to know what he did in his free time, what sort of things made him smile, and what it had been like to grow up with a brother with piercing blue eyes and linebacker shoulders. What was John like when he wasn't worrying—when he was neither a big brother nor a doctor?

Instead Ellie got her car keys out of her purse. "Give me a call as soon as you find out something."

"All right. If Andrew hasn't called me by the time I put my pie in the oven I'll call you."

Ellie stopped walking. "You're making a pie for this?"

"Yeah. I figured it would be the most impressive dessert to bring." She glanced down at her watch. "I'd better hurry or it won't be done in time."

"We're supposed to bring something to this?"

Diana blinked at her. "Didn't you know?" Then she waved a hand in dismissal. "Just stop by the store and buy some cookies or something. It doesn't matter if they're not homemade. Once you put them on the table no one knows who brought them."

Great. Diana was going to be the girl who baked fresh pies, while Ellie would be remembered for bringing Oreos to the ward social. What a wonderful first impression that would be.

"I'll figure out something," Ellie said.

It was now 3:15. By the time she made it to the store, picked out something to make, and drove back to Bertie's, it would be at least 4:00, perhaps 4:30 depending on how quickly she could find things in the grocery store. The ward social started at 6:00. She wasn't sure how long it took to drive to the church. If it took 15 minutes, that meant she'd have a little over an hour to both get ready and prepare something. What could she prepare and cook in under an hour?

She asked this question again as she paced the aisles at the grocery store. Was it better to just buy a cake in a Safeway container or risk trying to make one of her own?

A cake might not have time to cool down before it she was supposed to frost it. Frozen cookie dough might work, but she'd never used it before. Did the cookies taste store bought?

Brownie mix. That was good. You added oil and eggs and shoved the thing in the oven. Best of all, it was hard to tell whether brownies were made from scratch or not.

She paid for a box, then hurried home. It was 4:15 when she pulled up to Bertie's house. She'd have plenty of time to make them.

Bertie sat outside on the porch with two elderly women, playing cards and sipping lemonade from tall tumblers. One wore a straw hat with an apricot ribbon around the brim that matched the color of her sundress. Her middle was thick, but the arms and legs that poked out of her dress were spindly thin. The other woman was so large she seemed to be spilling out onto her chair. Her polyester blue dress flowed around her shapelessly.

Bertie was dressed up in a crisp pink muumuu, her lavender hair teased into place, fuchsia lipstick carefully applied to her mouth. It was clear she was ready to go, and it occurred to Ellie that Bertie probably had a dessert made and waiting in the kitchen. Ellie had rushed to the store for no reason.

"There you are, Dear," Bertie called to her. "Come and meet my friends, Lucille and Margaret." With a grand wave in Ellie's direction, she said, "This is my niece Ellie."

Ellie waved at them, feeling a bit silly for carrying a brownie mix. She walked up the steps fingering the box. “I bought this in case we needed to bake something for the ward social.”

“That’s sweet of you, Dear, but Margaret made a side dish of stewed tomatoes, and I thought we’d just say it was from all of us.”

“Stewed tomatoes?”

The large woman smiled as she put down three cards on the table. “From my garden last summer. I always get so many tomatoes I don’t know what to do with them.”

“I thought we were supposed to bring desserts.”

“But everyone will be bringing those,” Margaret said, “and they never have any interesting side dishes at these things. It’s always just salad and rolls.”

Ellie smiled, gripping the box harder. Now she was about to be known as the girl who brought nothing to the ward social but someone else’s stewed tomatoes. She edged toward the door. “I’m sure everyone will really love the tomatoes, but you know, as long as I have this box of brownies, I might as well make it up.”

“Do you see what I mean?” Bertie leaned toward her friends but waved her cards at Ellie. “She’s always working. If she’s not at the resort, she’s here cleaning my house or doing my yard work. I’m going to start calling her CinderEllie.”

Lucille took a sip of her lemonade, daintily holding the straw. “But wouldn’t that make you the wicked stepmother, Bertie?”

“That’s what I feel like,” Bertie said. “Watching her trim the bushes and wash the windows when I know she’d rather be out with a prince. Yesterday she told me she wanted to paint my porch. Can you imagine?”

“Don’t worry about the porch,” Margaret said to Ellie. “It’s a fine enough place for us. Youth is fleeting. Go to every ball you can. Spend your summers dancing with Prince Charming."

Ellie scanned the directions for the brownies, mentally cataloging every ingredient and kitchen utensil she would need. "Prince Charming can do without me for a while. The porch needs work and Bertie's supposed to stay off her foot as much as possible. Besides, I think paint coveralls suit me better than ball gowns."

Lucille stirred her lemonade with her straw, her voice soft and melodramatic. "But how will Prince Charming find you without your glass slippers?"

"Well, I suppose if he were really charming, he'd help me paint the porch instead of bothering the neighbors about their foot sizes."

Bertie picked up a card and discarded another. "I'm sure he'll help out if he can, Dear, but you know he's awfully busy at the hospital. Sister Simmons says the doctors there work ten-hour shifts."

Oh. So they were talking about *that* Prince Charming. Honestly, didn't Bertie know any other single men? The way she had fixated on John Flynn, you'd think *Bertie* was in love with him.

"Ten-hour shifts." Margaret shook her head. "Such a long time."

"A hard worker," Lucille added.

"Were you able to talk to him today?" Bertie asked.

"No, he didn't stop by the resort."

Bertie laid down a trio of cards. "Well, I can't say I'm surprised after you accepted a date with someone else. I'm sure he's still quite angry about that."

"I doubt it," Ellie said.

Margaret clucked her tongue and shook her head in a knowing manner. "It sounds like someone is fighting."

Lucille nodded in agreement. "The course of young love never did run smoothly."

"I don't think Dr. Flynn and I are destined to live happily ever after," Ellie said, and then, because she knew she ought to give Bertie a reason for such a pronouncement, added, "He didn't treat you nicely enough when he examined your ankle. I found it utterly uncharming."

Bertie took a sip of lemonade. "It's good to have high standards where men are concerned, Dear, but if you're too exacting you'll wind up an old maid."

"I think I'm a little young to worry about that."

Lucille and Margaret exchanged looks. "Today's young women think they have all the time in the world to get married. Just think of poor Joan Hickman." All three women nodded in a sad, knowing sort of way. "She waited and waited, and now she's at least twenty-eight."

Margaret waved a finger in Ellie's direction. "If I were you, I'd snatch up John as soon as he asks."

"Yes, well, I'll worry about that when he proposes." Which was only likely to happen if some natural disaster wiped out the rest of the female population. Ellie opened the screen door and stepped inside before she had to endure any more dating advice. "I'm going to start the brownies."

"Are you sure you have time? The social starts in an hour and a half and we have to stop by Margaret's house to get the stewed tomatoes," Bertie called to her, and then added in an overly sweet voice, "You don't mind that we go with you and your date, do you? None of us drives well at night."

Ellie stepped back out on the porch. "You want to come with my date and me?" She waved one hand in front of her as though this would show Bertie the impossibility of the situation. "I haven't even spoken to him yet."

"If he's a nice young man he won't mind taking us. I know John wouldn't mind."

Margaret nodded in agreement. "During the winter when the roads are slick, the high priest group always makes sure we have rides to and from church."

Ellie stood on the porch for a moment longer, staring at the group. She couldn't tell them no. Bertie knew she couldn't tell them no, and that's why Bertie had set out to purposely sabotage Ellie's date.

Only it wouldn't be as easy for Bertie as she imagined. Ellie answered back with a smile of her own. "I still don't know what the arrangements are for tonight, but I told Diana that I wanted to meet my date at the church. So it shouldn't be a problem for me to drive you all down there."

"Good," Bertie said. "We'll want to leave early to get good seats."

"Oh, yes," Lucille put in. "We want to make sure we get the cushioned seats they use in Relief Society, not those hard plastic things they keep in the Young Women's room."

Bertie nodded as though the matter was decided. "Can you be ready in an hour?"

"Forty-five minutes," Margaret said. "Remember we have to stop by my house for the tomatoes."

"We'll leave as soon as the brownies are done," Ellie said, and rushed into the house before the three woman could worry themselves into leaving immediately.

She had just finished tossing the brownie pan into the oven when Diana called.

Her voice came over the line breathless and worried. "I can't get ahold of Andrew, and I don't know what to do."

"He isn't at home?"

"No. I've called twice and couldn't even get an answering machine. Do you think he's standing me up? Did he just decide he doesn't want to go out with me?"

Ellie set the timer on the oven, pushing the buttons while she spoke. "What exactly did he tell you when you talked about it on Thursday?"

"He said he'd come, and he said he'd bring a friend from the Tour Store."

"That's it?"

There was a pause on the line and then Diana added, "As he was leaving with the Richardsons he said, 'See you on Saturday.'"

"But he didn't ask for directions to your house or your phone number or anything?"

"Um, no."

"Well, it sounds like he was planning on meeting us at the church then."

Another pause.

"But what if I go to the church and then he comes here? He'll think I stood him up."

"Leave a note on the door explaining that you weren't sure of the arrangements and tell him where you are."

A heavy sigh. "All right. I'll see you there."

CHAPTER 10

Despite Ellie's best attempts at speed, they made it to the church only five minutes early, partially because Bertie and her friends had to critique Ellie's appearance. ("Your hair would look nice up. Why don't you try it that way?") And partially because once Ellie was driving, the three older women got so busy talking that they kept forgetting to tell Ellie which streets to turn on until she'd passed them.

But when they arrived there were plenty of seats left. In fact, there were several by John. A dozen round tables were set up in the middle of the room, and he was just sitting down at an empty one. After Ellie and Margaret dropped off their dishes at a side table, Bertie took hold of Ellie's arm and pulled her in John's direction. "Look, Dear, John's saving a spot for us. Very charming, I'd say."

"But I . . . " She was supposed to meet Diana and Andrew and Andrew's friend. Only a survey of the room showed that none of them was there. Not even Diana. "I suppose I could go over and say hello to him. Just until the others arrive."

Ellie walked toward his table, her three chaperones close at hand.

"Here. Sit here," Bertie pointed at the seat next to John.

What else could she do? It would be rude to protest. She sat down with a stiff smile. "Hello, Dr. Flynn."

"*Brother* Flynn," Margaret said.

"*John,*" Bertie said.

"Hello," he said back. "How is your ankle doing, Bertie?"

"I'm hobbling around well enough. Luckily Ellie is here to take care of me. She's such good help. Cooking and cleaning. She'll make someone a wonderful wife someday."

Ellie scanned the room often. *Please let Diana show up so I don't have to sit here any longer.*

"She made brownies for the social," Lucille said. "You know, it's so hard to find young women who'll cook and clean these days. Nowadays they all want careers."

"How very nice," John said; but Ellie wasn't sure whether he meant, how nice it was that she cooked and cleaned, or how nice it was that most young women were out busy with their careers instead of here bothering him.

John's cell phone rang, and he pulled it from his pocket. Looking first at the caller ID, he sighed and clicked the phone on.

Bertie, Margaret, and Lucille began talking to each other, but Ellie couldn't help but hear his conversation.

"No, he's still not here."

A pause.

"How would I know where he is? I didn't ask him out."

Another pause. "Well, you might as well just come to the church. The social is about to start."

Still another pause. "Yes, she's here, but she's with her aunt."

He held the phone away from his mouth for a moment and looked at Ellie. "Diana wants to know if you've heard from your date."

Ellie shook her head.

"She hasn't heard anything. Yeah, I know, if he comes I'll call you."

He clicked off the phone and slid it back into his pocket. His gaze turned to Ellie. "You know, real matchmakers probably arrange these details when they set people up."

"I couldn't arrange any details. I was off hanging curtains with you."

"Maybe Andrew got wind of the karaoke entertainment and had second thoughts."

But just then Andrew walked through the cultural hall doors. He wore a pair of tan Dockers, and a crisp maroon shirt, which somehow transformed him from a biker boy to an utterly handsome male. He looked to be the perfect date for Diana, except for one thing. He was standing next to a tall blond woman in a halter top and jean skirt.

Andrew slipped his hand around her waist as he glanced around the room.

"Well," John said with raised eyebrows. "Andrew's here. Do you suppose I should call Diana now?"

"I don't understand," Ellie said.

"Apparently you should have been a bit more specific when you asked Andrew to bring a friend to this."

Ellie shut her eyes and groaned. In her mind she replayed the conversation with Andrew—tried to remember exactly what Diana had said when she gushingly asked him to come to the social. Had she asked him out on a date, or had she simply asked him to come?

Diana had told him about the dinner and then said, "It would be great if you could come. You could bring a friend, and we could all sit together."

Oh dear.

Poor Diana.

"Call her," Ellie said. "Tell her not to come. She isn't going to want to be here."

John took the phone from his pocket, chuckling while he punched in the numbers.

While John spoke to his sister, Bertie, Lucille, and Margaret suddenly noticed Andrew walking about the room. They all craned around in their seats to stare at him. "He's brought another girl with him?" Bertie gasped. "When he was supposed to be here with Diana?"

"The impertinence," Lucille said.

"I don't think he should have any of my stewed tomatoes," Margaret said. "And I'm not afraid to tell him so."

Bertie nodded solemnly at her niece. "He's definitely not a gentleman. I don't think you should go out with his friend after all."

"Nor do I," John said, and then laughed again as he slipped the phone back into his pocket.

"Whenever your date shows up, you just tell him that you're

not interested," Bertie said. "And you stay sitting right here by John. By us." Then she tsked tsked some more under her breath.

Andrew caught sight of Ellie, smiled, and waved at her.

Ellie smiled back, then still smiling, hissed out to the other ladies, "Don't say anything to him about the date. Just stay quiet."

Andrew and the woman strolled up to the table. "Hey Ellie, the food looks great. Thanks for inviting us."

"Any time," Ellie answered in what she hoped was a perfectly normal voice.

"This is my friend, Madison. She works the cash register at the Tour Store." He then nodded toward the table. "Ellie is one of the front desk girls at the Pine Top, and that's John. His mom owns the resort."

Andrew looked at the older woman expectantly so Ellie quickly put in, "This is my Aunt Bertie, and her friends Margaret and Lucille."

Lucille smiled and mouthed a hello.

Bertie humphed.

Margaret only nodded and said, "Don't eat the stewed tomatoes."

"Thanks for the tip," Andrew said, and sat down. Madison took the chair beside him.

Andrew looked around the room. "Where's Diana?"

"I just talked to her on the phone," John said. "It turns out she can't make it after all. She's feeling unwell."

Bertie, Lucille, and Margaret all tsk tsked some more.

Ellie checked her watch. 6:05.

It was going to be a long, uncomfortable night.

* * *

Eventually dinner was served. Lasagna, salad, and rolls. And John hadn't been joking when he'd mentioned the karaoke machine. Apparently it was a regular fixture at the ward socials, and Bishop Whiting kept calling members up to sing. It didn't leave much opportunity for conversation at the table—thankfully. Ellie wasn't sure how many more of John's sideways, gloating barbs, or Bertie's don't-you-think-it-would-be-a-good-idea-to-marry-my-niece speeches she could take. Before any of them had finished their lasagna, Lucille actually went to the dessert table, brought back some of Ellie's brownies, and made John eat one.

"Aren't these good?" Lucille said nibbling on one herself. "Such a wonderful cook."

Madison broke one in half, handed part to Andrew, and took a bite of what was left. "Mmm. Really good. What's your recipe?"

So much for Ellie's image as any sort of cook. "They're from a mix. Betty Crocker, I think."

Bertie gave John a nod. "But she could make them from scratch if she wanted to."

It was painful sitting here next to him. Painful because he knew how she'd blundered her setup of Andrew and Diana, and painful because Bertie's hints were getting less and less subtle.

It was as though Bertie thought Ellie couldn't attract a man without some sort of promise of cooking and cleaning thrown into the package.

John probably didn't need a public relations team to get a date. All he had to do was look at a woman with those blue eyes and raise that square jaw and tousle that blond hair and . . . what had she been thinking?

Bishop Whiting took the microphone from the latest singer then peered out in the audience to claim his next victim.

"This song is a duet, so we need a couple." His gaze landed on Ellie's table. "John, why don't you bring Ellie up here."

Ellie stared at the man open-mouthed. How had he even known her name? She had assumed that being a stranger to nearly everyone here, she would be exempt from making a fool of herself.

"Go on." Bertie nudged her arm. "He's calling you up. John will show you where the stairs are."

Ellie stood and numbly followed John out of the cultural hall and through the door that held the stairs. Once on stage, Bishop Whiting handed both John and Ellie microphones. "You're going to be Sonny and Cher for us—and I guess I don't have to tell you guys to have a little Chastity." He laughed, his belly pushing in and out as he did. "Get it? Sonny and Cher's daughter is named Chastity."

Before either of them could respond, the music started and the words flashed across a small television screen that sat above the karaoke machine.

They say we're young and we don't know . . .

It took Ellie halfway through the first verse to figure out which lines she was supposed to be singing and which ones were John's. Plus she was blushing too badly to look at John's, and how could you really sing the words, "Babe. I got you, Babe," in any way that sounded good?

He didn't seem flustered at all. He even swayed a bit while he sang, which made her look stiff standing up there clutching her microphone. She tried to sway, but was afraid she'd lose her balance and topple off the stage.

The song ended, as did any chance Ellie had for appearing dignified in Bertie's ward.

Bishop Whiting came back and, before taking the microphone, he put his hands on Ellie's and John's shoulders. "Let's hear it for these two babes."

A stream of polite clapping—from people who were just glad it hadn't been them up on the stage—filled the room.

Ellie smiled back at the audience through clenched teeth. *Yes, thank you for this opportunity. I couldn't be more mortified.*

"We're glad to have you visiting here, Ellie," Bishop Whiting went on. "Bertie can use the company and so can John."

No, I was wrong. I could be more mortified.

Bishop Whiting then called up the next victim, and Ellie trudged off stage. John followed.

When they got back into the hallway he said, "Not only do you cook and clean, but you sing too. What a multi-talented woman you are."

"Sing? Please. I haven't misplaced so many notes since I was in junior high passing them back and forth to my best friend." She bent down and got a drink from the fountain, trying to erase the shakiness in her voice.

Instead of going back into the cultural hall, John leaned up against the wall and waited for her. "During dinner I asked Bertie if she's seen her regular doctor, and she brushed off the question. I'd like you to talk to her about it. Make the appointment for her if you have to. If she's having episodes where her cognitive reasoning is affected, something serious—even life threatening—could be the cause."

Ellie straightened from the drinking fountain and wiped a stray drop of water from her chin. "Bertie is fine."

"No more odd behavior?"

Ellie laughed, because he obviously didn't know her aunt very well.

"What?" he asked.

"She wears muumuus, costume jewelry, and dies her hair purple. What odd behavior should I be on the lookout for?"

He leaned toward her. "You know what I mean."

"She's fine." Having him stand so close was disconcerting, and she fiddled with the drinking fountain handle because she didn't know what to do with her hands. "Although, she is getting older, and I worry about her being alone all the time. She'll need help taking care of her house in the fall, and I could use some help painting her porch before I go. Who's the high priest group leader in this ward? I'd like to know who her home teachers are."

"Oh. That would be me and me."

"You?" She didn't mean for it to come out as an accusation, but it did.

"I put myself on her route this week. I know she didn't have the most reliable home teachers before so—"

He didn't finish his sentence. The cultural hall door opened and Margaret walked into the hallway. As she made her way toward the stage door she said, "I loved your song. You two make the cutest couple, really."

Neither Ellie nor John said anything as she passed by, and she went through the door to the stage, swishing it closed behind her. John stared at the door for a moment. "Do you get the impression people think we're a couple? You know, Bishop Whiting's comments and now Margaret . . ."

"Maybe because we sat together at dinner."

"That doesn't seem enough to cause speculation."

No it didn't, which meant Aunt Bertie must have been telling lots of people about her marital predictions.

How nice.

Well, Ellie was not about to fill him in on those. He already thought Bertie was crazy.

Ellie shrugged and tried to look thoughtful. "Margaret said we made a cute couple. Bishop Whiting said you could use some female company. It sounds like people are just desperate to set you up. Do you have a habit of chasing women off, or is it only women who approach you in libraries?"

"I said I was sorry about that."

"But you never told me why you did it."

He ran one hand across his hair, the muscles in his arms flexing as he lifted his arm and then relaxed it again. His gaze flashed over at her, and once again she was caught up in the color of his eyes.

This wasn't a man who looked like he'd ever be desperate to be set up.

He leaned toward her in a silent appeal for understanding. "I've just known too many women who cared more about my M.D. than my personality. So when you came up to me in the library and asked me if I was a doctor, I figured I'd see if you'd still be interested in me if you thought I was a poor struggling artist. As you recall, you couldn't get away from me fast enough when you thought I was a janitor."

"Oh. I see. You're calling me a gold digger, is that it?"

"For all you knew, I could have been a really good artist. The next Renoir. You didn't stick around long enough to find out."

"That's because I was trying to find a doctor for my aunt."

"Of course. Most people do that in the library. Why hadn't I thought of that?"

She crossed her arms. "Okay. Don't believe me. Apparently you have some issues with honesty, anyway. But for your information, I wasn't hitting on you. I don't plan to hit on you, and I don't care that you're a doctor. You'd be more interesting to me as an artist because at least then you might come up with some attractive ideas for painting my aunt's porch. I'm just visiting here for a little while, not scouting around for a man."

He held both hands up as though to fend off the force of her words. "All right. Sorry. I've misjudged you again. I guess I've grown jaded as to people's motivations. Really, I'm sorry."

As he said the last sentence, the door to the cultural hall swung open again and this time Lucille walked through. Instead of continuing on to the stage, she stopped by Ellie and John. "You're apologizing? Does that mean you've made up?"

John shot Ellie a questioning look. She could tell he was wondering how many people knew about the library incident. "I hope so," he said slowly.

"Good. I thought it was such a shame when I heard you were fighting." Lucille patted his arm, her fingers frail and shaky as they lay against his skin. "We were talking with Ellie before dinner, and I could tell how much you meant to her. She called you her Prince Charming. Said she wanted you by her side while she painted Bertie's porch. You're going to help her with that, aren't you?"

He smiled stiffly in Ellie's direction. "Yes. She just mentioned it to me."

"Good. Well, I've got to go sing now. Hope they give me a Celine Dion song. I just love her. See you two later." She shuffled off to the stage door, pushing it open with more force than Ellie thought her capable of.

John folded his arms. "Prince Charming? We made up? What was that all about?"

"Oh that." Yes that. How did one explain *that?* Ellie fiddled with the drinking fountain handle again, creating spurts of water. "Well, you see, before dinner Aunt Bertie was calling me CinderEllie, and we were talking about Prince Charming. I thought we were talking about Prince Charming in a general sort of way, and they thought we were talking about Prince Charming in a specific way. Specifically in a *you* sort of way. It's just a misunderstanding, really. I'll clear it up with them on the way home."

"Uh-huh." He narrowed his eyes at her as though reconsidering her potential as a gold digger. "Why did they think you were talking about me in a Prince Charming sort of way?"

"I don't know. But it wasn't because I was hitting on you in the library."

The stage door swung open and this time Margaret walked out. "I hear you two made up. That's just wonderful. We wouldn't want Ellie to wind up an old maid like Joan Hickman."

John nodded at her. "Uh-huh."

"Let me help you with the door," Ellie told Margaret, then quickly made her retreat into the cultural hall before John could say anything else.

Chapter 11

Ellie did a lot of steering wheel gripping on the way home. She tried, in a gentle manner, to explain her single status to Bertie and her friends. "John and I are not a couple. To be a couple you have to date, and John's never asked me out."

"He's helping you paint the porch," Bertie said.

"That's not a date because I asked him to do it."

"It's all right for women to ask men out," Margaret said. "We're very modern here."

"Well, okay, but painting the porch is still not a date because John's doing it as Bertie's home teacher."

"He's not my home teacher," Bertie said.

"He is now. He put you on his route. He's worried about you because he's a doctor, and he wants to make sure you're all right."

"He was never worried about me before you came to Colton," Bertie said.

"He isn't worried about *me,*" Lucille said, "and I get arthritis something terrible."

"Do you think he'd take a look at my bad knee?" Margaret added. "I could come over sometime when he's visiting Ellie."

"He isn't going to visit me," Ellie said.

"Of course he is, Dear. You just said he made himself our home teacher."

Margaret went on to describe her knee, her symptoms, and all the doctors who'd ever looked at it, while Ellie drove and mumbled under her breath, "We're *not* a couple. We're really *not.*"

* * *

John stayed after dinner to help put away chairs and tables. Then he stopped by his mom's house to try and cheer up Diana while pretending he wasn't smug and happy that Andrew had showed up with another woman.

Diana was safe from Andrew. Hopefully permanently.

By the time he got home it was 9:00. Enough time to go over the home teaching numbers for last month before he turned in. He'd have to remember to find Brother Clark and Brother Carlson tomorrow at church and tell them he'd changed their assignment. He walked to his desk singing, "I got you, Babe."

Ellie had looked so sweet standing there, trying to pretend she wasn't nervous while simultaneously twisting the microphone cord around her finger so many times he nearly had to stop mid-chorus to warn her about the dangers of tourniquets.

He opened the file cabinet and flipped through folders until he got to the one marked home teaching routes.

"I got you, Ellie."

And then he realized what he was singing—that he had actually said the words out loud. His hands froze on the folder.

Not this again. Definitely not. His divorce had been final only a couple of months. There was no way he was even going to think about getting involved with someone new. In fact, he wasn't even going to think about thinking about it.

He sat down at the desk, opened the file, and spread it smooth. He was going to sit here and figure out what changes to make. And he wasn't going to picture Ellie's face. Or the curve of her lips. Or her khaki eyes.

Ellie might be a pre-Valerie, after all. And he didn't need that. Again.

As he thought of the divorce the familiar sting of anger engulfed him. *I did everything I could to make Valerie happy. I've a list of times and places I sacrificed for her. None of it mattered.*

He spread the sheets of home teaching routes in front of him. It was time to forget Valerie, to go on with his life, to shake off this anger that shadowed him. The marriage had cost him time, energy, and money. Did it have to cost him his peace too?

He tried to bring himself out of this mood, to force forgiveness by using the only method that had ever worked. He made himself remember that Valerie used to be different. Like reviewing old videos, he willed himself to see her.

Valerie cheering from the audience as he received his diploma. Valerie, looking radiant on their wedding day. Valerie home from a shopping trip with a pink ruffled baby dress. When she'd shown it to him, he'd dropped his water glass on the kitchen floor and stood open-mouthed among a hundred slivers of glass.

"You're pregnant?"

"No. Of course not. I just bought it for *someday.*"

And then the most painful image of all. The one of him holding Valerie while the doctor explained to them that *someday* would never happen. Valerie couldn't have children.

In a way he'd always blamed himself for that. He was a doctor. He was supposed to be able to fix things. Or at least be able to fill the void left in her heart. He had tried.

"We can always adopt," he told her when he caught her throwing every baby item she'd ever purchased into the bathroom trash.

"It wouldn't really be our child," she said.

"Yes, it would. Of course it would." He had taken her hands and tried to pull her out of the bathroom. "The baby would be sealed to us in the temple. God will make it our child."

"God?" She threw clothes and ribboned headbands onto the floor. A rattle rolled behind the toilet, making a tiny clinking sound, and everything stared up at him pathetically. Laughing and crying together, Valerie leaned up against the wall for support, so drunk with emotion he was afraid she'd slide down onto the floor.

"This is all God's fault. God made my body this way, and I'm supposed to ask him to make a stranger's child my own? He'll give babies to teenagers and heroine addicts. He'll give them to women who'll have abortions without a second thought, but he won't give one to me. Why should I ask God for anything? I don't want anything from him, and I don't want someone else's child."

She didn't slide down to the floor. She stormed out of the bathroom, then out of the apartment, slamming doors behind her as she went.

Perhaps he should have gone after her. He didn't. He picked up all the baby things off the floor and out of the trash so she wouldn't have to see them later. Tiny, pastel stuffed animals, bibs, and a seemingly endless supply of baby outfits. After they were bagged up, he drove them to a women's shelter. He gave everything to a smiling woman at the front desk, who told him over and over how much they appreciated his donation.

Well, he hadn't given them everything. He kept one item. The first pink dress Valerie had shown him. He'd saved it knowing one day she would change her mind about adoption. One day they'd put the dress on their daughter and all the wounds they felt now would be healed.

He still had that dress somewhere. It was stuck in a box in his closet because she had never changed her mind about adoption. After that day she wouldn't discuss it. She insisted she had changed her mind about having children. They would cramp her style.

That was her new goal: living in style. Shopping had been her favorite entertainment before, and it became an obsession now.

She racked up charges on credit cards he didn't know existed.

She took their tithing money and used it for a downpayment on her convertible.

And then the anger was back, reciting the offenses, adding up the charges against her more faithfully than the bill collectors had.

He had to let go of this. He knew that. He just didn't know how.

* * *

Ellie's parents called that night. They hadn't heard from her since her first email and they wanted to know how she was doing. They missed her.

But they didn't ask about her beyond checking to see whether she'd found a job yet. Their questions were all about Bertie.

Did Bertie seem as lucid as she'd always been?

Yes.

Was she able to take care of herself?

Yes.

Was she forgetting things?

Ellie couldn't remember.

Ellie, please be serious.

Her parents then moved on to questions about Bertie's ankle, and Ellie told them, in measured words, that Bertie had fallen. She'd seen a doctor. It was just a mild sprain. Bertie needed to stay off of it for a few weeks and it would be fine.

"She's falling now," her mother said, as though the end was very near. "We definitely can't let her live by herself if she's falling."

Bertie wasn't *falling.* It wasn't like she was staggering around the house grabbing onto objects for support. Only Ellie couldn't say this because her aunt was sitting on the couch across from her working on the reasons-not-to-clean list. Instead Ellie held the phone a little ways a way from her mouth. "Aunt Bertie, Mom and Dad are worried about you living alone. What are your thoughts on remarriage?"

"Tell them I'm holding out for a movie star this time. Sean Connery or Harrison Ford. Maybe Tristan McKellips. Do you think he's too young for me?"

Into the phone Ellie said, "Bertie's considering remarrying a younger man. I'm all for it."

"Ellie," her mother snapped, "we are trying to find out how

well your aunt is. Did you talk to her doctor? Was he worried about a reoccurrence? Is he aware that she lives alone? Perhaps you should have told him she's not always in the best frame of mind."

"It's sweet of you to worry about her, but her doctor is also her home teacher, so I'm sure he'll take good care of her once I leave. He's um, a nice guy—" for Bertie she added, "a real prince. He's coming over to help me paint her porch . . ." she held the phone away again. "What color did you decide on, Aunt Bertie?"

"Either chartreuse or magenta."

"Bertie still hasn't decided on the color."

"Did I hear her say chartreuse?" Ellie's father asked.

"She's not *really* going to paint it chartreuse."

Bertie nodded. "Right now I'm leaning toward the magenta."

There was silence on the line. Then Ellie's father said, "Can we have the name and number of Bertie's doctor?"

"I don't know it right off hand."

"Find out. We'll wait."

Ellie held the phone down, then pressed the mute button with more force than necessary. She looked at her aunt without speaking.

"What is it, Dear?"

"They're worried about you. They want John's phone number."

"They worry too much." Bertie wrote something on her list with a flourish, and it was clear she had no intention of giving out John's phone number. Then a slow smile crept over her features. "But perhaps they're more worried about you than me, Dear. Perhaps they want to talk to John and make sure his intentions are honorable. Here, let me talk to them."

She took the phone from Ellie's hand, pushing the mute button so Ellie's parents could hear again.

"I know how parents worry about their children," she said. "It's quite understandable, but really, John is a fine man. Completely trustworthy. I wouldn't let Ellie go out with him if he wasn't. I love her like she was my own daughter, and I'll make sure she behaves in ways that would make you proud. Why, just the other day I told her she had better not get arrested while she's here or you'd both be quite angry."

Bertie paused for a moment, nodding into the phone, while Ellie shook her head.

"What was she doing? Well, I don't remember right off hand, but the point is, Ellie won't be arrested while I'm watching after her. Now you two stop worrying, and take care. I don't want to run up your phone bill anymore. Good-bye."

Bertie replaced the receiver with a smile. "See, I told you I'd take care of it. Now they won't worry at all."

* * *

John didn't see Bertie in sacrament meeting, but he knew where she'd be in Gospel Doctrine class: up front with the other elderly women. He'd try to sit somewhere close to her so he could observe her behavior.

Back in medical school his neurology professor said he learned half of everything he needed to know about patients by watching them walk across his office. John would pay careful attention to Bertie and see if her gait was even and symmetrical. He'd check to see if she drifted, signaling a weakness on one side.

When he went in to Gospel Doctrine class, Bertie and Ellie

were already sitting together in the front. As he walked down the aisle, Bertie turned and waved at him.

"Yoo-hoo, John, we're saving a seat for you."

Well, you couldn't get closer than that.

Half the classroom turned and watched him walk up and take the seat next to Ellie. He nodded a hello to both women. Ellie returned his greeting but then sat stiffly facing forward and wouldn't look at him.

Fine. She didn't have to look at him. He didn't mind being ignored. And besides, this way he could sneak sideways glances at her without being noticed.

Her hair fell across her shoulders in shiny auburn waves, and flecks of green sparkled in her eyes. A touch of maroon on her lips contrasted with her pale skin. Bertie had been calling her CinderEllie. Well, she didn't look like he'd ever imagined Cinderella. Along with the cinders, Cinderella probably had a look of perpetual tolerance mixed with oppression on her face. Ellie looked . . . well, Ellie looked . . .

Ellie looked over at him.

"About painting," he said, "I was just wondering when you needed my help with that?"

"I work Tuesday through Saturday next week."

"Great. I'm off Monday. We can do it then. I'll talk to my companion and get back to you."

Bertie leaned over across Ellie and patted John on the knee. "I want to let you know I wholeheartedly approve of your being my new home teacher. In fact, I've been anticipating it for quite some time."

"I'm glad to hear it."

"Well, I have some things to discuss with . . ." Bertie glanced around the room, ". . . sister Rohner, so I'll just go back and sit with her and leave you two alone."

A pillar of subtly, she wasn't. Bertie left her scriptures on the seat next to Ellie, probably so no one could sit there, then walked back several rows. Her gait was a bit wobbly, but that could have been caused by her fall.

Bertie sat down by Sister Rohner, whispering something to her and looking back where Ellie and John sat.

John turned his attention back to Ellie, but he still felt Bertie and Sister Rohner discussing him.

"So, I take it you didn't clear up that little prince matter with your aunt and her friends."

"Well, I tried to, but somehow they didn't believe me. They either think *you're* so wonderful that I should be drawn to you, or that *I'm* so wonderful you shouldn't be able to resist me. I'm not sure which, but one of us should feel complimented."

"I'll leave the compliment on your door. I'm sure men find you irresistible."

She ran a finger over her scriptures, tracing the letter B over and over again, as though she hadn't heard his compliment. Perhaps she was just too used to them to take particular note when they came. "I'm sorry Bertie keeps making us sit together. I'll talk to her again."

The teacher came in, and Ellie turned her attention to him, which shouldn't have disappointed John but somehow did.

* * *

That day while Ellie and Bertie were unwrapping lunch, Ellie brought up the matter of John, explaining that she didn't really have time to develop a relationship this summer, and that he probably wasn't her type anyway.

Bertie's only comment was, "Are you trying to convince me or yourself?"'

Ellie rolled her eyes. "Oh, obviously myself, because I could never convince *you* of anything. Honestly, Aunt Bertie, John and I barely know each other."

"Don't wait around for love, Ellie. Take action. *Carpe Diem.* You never know if you'll have the chance tomorrow."

"But—"

"I'm older and wiser and therefore you have to listen to me. Seize the day. Leap before looking. Forget the bird in your hand and grab the two in the bush before they fly off to greener pastures, because the grass isn't greener over the fence. It's lush and blooming with clover right here." She stood up, grasped a can of soup, and hobbled toward the kitchen. "That stopped making sense two analogies ago, but you get the idea."

Yes, Ellie got the idea. Bertie wanted her to act with John the way she hadn't with Kirk.

She tried to think of Kirk, to see his face, but could only see John. Blue eyes. Broad shoulders. Mussed hair.

Strange. Once she'd thought of him, it was a very hard image to banish.

On Monday morning Ellie's mother called. After Ellie spent a considerable amount of time convincing her that she hadn't been and never would be in danger of arrest, her mother turned the topic to Bertie.

"Are there any adult care facilities in Colton? Could you look into it? Your father is checking to see what Medicare will cover. Of course Bertie could move out here and be closer to family, but she's always been so fond of Idaho."

"She doesn't need adult care."

Her mother's voice took on a sympathetic tone, a tone that somehow made Ellie angrier than when her mother had just been cold about it all. "Bertie has been losing her grasp on reality for some time, and now she's falling. This is the same thing that happened to Grandpa Baxter. We need to think about the best way to help Bertie."

"Bertie isn't Grandpa Baxter. Look, Dr. Flynn is coming over in a couple of hours to help me paint the porch. If you talk to him, if he tells you Bertie isn't senile, that she's perfectly capable of taking care of herself, will you just forget about the whole nursing home business?"

There was a long pause on the phone. "I think it would be a good idea to talk to Bertie's doctor and see what his professional opinion is."

"Good," Ellie said. "I'll have him call you when Bertie isn't around."

"Good," her mother said.

And it would be good, just as long as Ellie could convince John to say the right things.

Chapter 12

When John and his companion, an older gentleman who introduced himself as Brother Cromwell, walked up on the porch, Ellie was ready for them. She had the whole afternoon planned. She sent Bertie and Brother Cromwell off to the hardware store to pick up the paint while she and John did the sanding and taping. Ellie knew Bertie would take her time about it. She'd want to leave Ellie and John alone together for as long as possible. Fine. This was one time Bertie's scheming would work to Ellie's advantage. It would give her plenty of time to explain the situation to John and have him call her parents to reassure them.

Only, how was she going to bring up the subject? *Could you do me a favor, John? You see, my parents are both humorless and heartless, and they want to put Aunt Bertie away . . .*

While Ellie clipped paper onto the electric sander, John walked around, surveying the porch. He rubbed a thumb against a patch of peeling paint on the banister. "This isn't a lead-based paint, is it?"

"What?"

"Lead-based paint is poisonous. We wouldn't want to sand it and breath in the fumes. Do you know if this porch was painted before the 1970s?"

Ellie shrugged. "My grandpa built the porch before he got sick, about fifteen years ago."

"It should be okay then." John walked over to the stairs, stepping up and down them with a heavy gait.

"What are you doing?" Ellie asked.

He turned and stomped back up the stairs, each footstep making a sharp, smacking sound. "I'm checking to see if the floor needs repairs. Sometimes these older porchs have wood damage. Water rot. Termites. That sort of thing. I wouldn't want Bertie to step through the floor."

His footsteps smacked down the stairs again. This time as he strode up the stairs she noticed the way his leg muscles filled out his worn blue jeans.

She probably shouldn't pay attention to those types of details. She waited for him to quit stomping, then said, "Do you always do that?"

He didn't look up at her. "Do what?"

"Think like a doctor. I mean, are you going check the ladder to see if it's sturdy, and then insist I don't step on the top rung?"

"You mean the rung with the warning label that says, 'Absolutely, positively, if you value your life, do not step on this rung'?"

"Yes, that one."

He crossed his arms over his chest. "Do you know how many people I've seen in the ER who've fallen off ladders?"

"See, you're doing it again."

He grunted, then walked across the porch, apparently satisfied it was safe. "People pay me a lot of money to give them advice, but if it makes you feel any better, I won't charge you for any instructions I give today."

He held out his hand for the sander, but she didn't give it to him. As soon as he turned it on, it would be too noisy to talk. Instead she fiddled with the sander cord. "Actually, I *was* hoping to get some of your advice today. It's about Bertie. And my parents." But that was the wrong place to start. She needed to go back almost a decade and a half ago. Back to Grandpa Baxter. "You see, Bertie's father had Alzheimer's. Grandma Baxter took care of him until he started getting up in the middle of the night and doing things. He'd leave the water running or the stove turned on. She had to hide the car keys so he wouldn't drive off. Everyone was worried he'd hurt himself. They sent him to a nursing home."

Ellie looked down at her hand. The sander's cord was tangled around her fingers. She hadn't even realized she'd been twisting it as she spoke, and now she tried to shake her hand free of it. "I suppose you've been to nursing homes before."

"In med school they have you do a rotation in geriatrics."

"Then you know what horrible places nursing homes are."

"Not *all* of them are horrible. Many of them are loving and caring places."

"They aren't real homes. They're where you put people to forget about them."

He shook his head. "The only people who do that are those who don't care about their families to begin with."

"Well, my parents don't care. Not really. Not like I do. And they . . . " Somehow she couldn't bring herself to say it. How could she admit what her parents were discussing?

He finished the sentence for her. "They think Bertie should live in a home?"

"Because she fell, and because they don't understand her. They think since she's eccentric there must be something wrong with her mind. But if you could talk to my parents, if you could reassure them that she's really all right, then they'd stop worrying."

He took the sander from her hand, unwrapping the cord from where she'd rewrapped it around her finger. "You're going to cut off your blood circulation if you keep doing that."

"You'll talk to them, won't you?"

"Ellie." He drew out the word, making it sound like a sigh.

"Why can't you?"

"I'm not sure Bertie *is* all right. She acted strangely when she came into the ER, and she refused to have any of the tests I recommended to rule out problems. If I recall right, you discouraged her from following my recommendations."

Ellie held out both of her hands in front of her, pleading with him. "She got the month right. She told you it was May and not December."

"Ellie."

"She's always been different."

"Yes, but Ellie, I'm not sure that's a reassuring indicator of good mental health."

"Fine. Be that way." She walked over to the chair where the rolls of tape sat, ripped open the package, pulled off a section, and then realized she didn't know where to put it. Exactly what were they taping off? Weren't they painting everything? She wasn't going to ask him about it. She'd just walk around the porch until she found something to put tape on.

She went to the back section of the porch and looked from the floor to the banister.

"It's for the electrical outlets and the door and window frames," he said.

"I knew that." She walked to the door and ran the tape along the side molding to protect it from stray paint. She waited to hear the sound of the sander going, but didn't. Instead, she heard his footsteps and then he stood next to her.

"Ellie, what if something really is wrong with your aunt—a tumor, maybe. Wouldn't you want her to get help? What's the harm in having a few tests to make sure she's well?"

Ellie didn't answer, just ran another piece of tape across the top of the door.

"If she has a family history of Alzheimer's," John went on, "then it's imperative she be checked for that. Early diagnosis can make a world of difference."

Still no answer.

"I can schedule a neurological exam, memory, and cognitive tests here, but I'd also like her to have a CAT scan in Spokane. Can you drive her there?"

"And exactly how am I supposed to tell her about these appointments? 'By the way, Aunt Bertie, your home teachers and your family all think you're crazy. We're taking you in to see what's wrong with you.'" Ellie ripped off a final piece of tape and attached it to the door with shaky hands. "I'm not doing it. There's nothing wrong with her. I've always been eccentric and no one thinks I have Alzheimer's."

"Ellie."

"Stop Ellie-ing me."

"You're not thinking about what's best for Bertie."

"Yes I am. She's fine." There was no cure for Alzheimer's, so she had to be fine. Ellie refused to think of Bertie as just another doorway in a cavernous hallway, the smell of bedpans and alcohol everywhere. The smell of death everywhere. She wouldn't see Bertie propped up in bed, being spoon-fed by someone who didn't care about her, who didn't know how wonderful she was. "She doesn't forget things." Ellie added, as though this was proof. "She always knows who I am."

"Does she have mood swings or show poor judgment?"

"No."

"Does she ever have difficulty speaking?"

"No."

"Problems with incontinence?"

"That's not something we discuss on a regular basis, so I wouldn't know."

"Any odd or inappropriate behavior—like putting on her clothes backwards?"

"Of course not." Bertie didn't do *that.* There were other things though, that John was not going to understand. The Christmas tree in the living room, for example.

Ellie glanced over at the windows in the front of the house. The drapes were drawn—they were always drawn—but through the crack in the curtains, she could see the outline of pine needles.

"Maybe I'm just worrying too much," John said. "But that's my job. And now that I'm Bertie's home teacher, it's my job to keep an eye on her."

"Of course. I'm sure once you get to know her better, you'll realize she's just fine." Ellie picked up one of the drop cloths from the porch, walked to the window, and held the canvas against it. "Perfectly normal."

She leaned against the window, clutching the drop cloth with one hand while she struggled to get tape off the roll with her other hand.

John cocked his head at her. "What are you doing?"

"I just washed this window. I don't want to get paint splatters on it."

"We'll use a brush around the trim. The window should be fine."

"You never can be too careful." She tore off two large pieces of tape and stuck them to the heavy fabric, smacking them on the window to make sure they'd stick. Then she tentatively stepped back from the window, watching it. The drop cloth stayed attached to the window for a moment, but then its weight pulled it to the floor.

Ellie grabbed the cloth from the floor so quickly that she dropped the tape. Before John could notice the pine needles, she pressed the fabric back over the window, her arms stretched out like a criminal being frisked. She felt John's stare but didn't move.

And still didn't move. The tape lay on the floor just behind her feet. She peered at it over her shoulder, then at John. He was watching her, his head tilted, the sander still lifeless in his hand.

She smiled over at him. "Can you hand me the tape?"

He walked slowly to the window and picked up the tape but didn't hand it to her. He stood close to her, first looking at the window, then at her. "I don't think the tape is sturdy enough to hold that up."

"It'll work if I just put on more tape."

"The drop cloth is too big. How are we going to paint underneath the window?"

"Oh. Um. I'll fold the drop cloth up so it doesn't cover that part."

Then, while trying to hold the fabric against the window, Ellie bent down, grabbed the bottom of the drop cloth, and tried to fold it up. One arm stretched up, the other stretched down, and she lifted one leg for balance. She knew she looked like she was playing a game of wall-Twister, but now that she'd drawn John's attention to the window she didn't dare let him see inside. After several maneuverings, she managed to fold the drop cloth up away from the bottom of the window. Her hair had fallen into her face, and she blew little puffs of air to keep it out of her eyes.

She glanced over her shoulder. He was still standing in the same place, watching her with his head cocked.

"The tape?" she asked sweetly.

"Don't you think you're worrying just a little too much about keeping the window clean?"

She puffed her hair away again. "I didn't give you a bad time when you were stomping around the porch checking for termites."

"Yes, you did."

"Well, I shouldn't have. Give me the tape."

He handed her the roll but didn't move away.

She gripped the tape with one hand while holding the drop cloth up with the other, and she tried to get the end of the tape off the roll with her teeth. It had worked last time, but this time it stayed stubbornly in place.

She tried again.

And again.

All the while John stood a few inches away from her, watching.

She gnawed at the tape for a while before it finally gave way. Then she held the end of the tape between her teeth and tried to rip a piece off. Instead of ripping, it just unraveled more, so that a long strip of tape connected her to the roll. She held it up, like a giant piece of spaghetti, in an attempt to keep it from folding over and sticking to itself.

John's laughter erupted behind her.

Teeth still clenched on the tape, she said, "If you were a gentleman, you'd help me with thith."

"Fine. All you had to do was ask." Instead of taking the tape from her hands, he stepped closer, then reached around her so that he was holding up both corners of the drop cloth and she was nearly in an embrace.

"Um. Thanks."

His chest brushed against her back. She could feel his breath against her cheek. What had she been doing? Oh yes, the tape.

Using two hands she ripped off several pieces of tape and used them to tape the cloth to the window. Then she put more tape on. And more. When she ran out of room on the top she put some along the side. It wasn't because she liked the feel of his arms around her. She just wanted to be really sure the drop cloth stayed put.

She put some tape along the bottom of the window too.

"There," she said at last. "That should keep paint splatters off."

He took his hands from the corner of the drop cloth and they both watched it.

It didn't move.

They didn't move either. Ellie's gaze was on the window, but her mind remained on the fact that John was standing so close behind her that she could smell the scent of his soap—or was it aftershave? Whatever it was, he smelled clean, like the air after a rainstorm.

"It looks like the tape will hold this time," he said. "In fact, you may never be able to scrape that drop cloth off the window again."

"Right. Well. I guess we'd better get on with the sanding then."

"I'll do the sanding. You can tape off the rest of the trim, but try to conserve a little. We only have a few rolls of tape left."

Taking the tape, she left him without saying another word. As she worked she listened to the sander without looking at him. She refused to look at him.

He might be gorgeous, and he might smell like rainwater, and he might have really great biceps—after all, she couldn't help but notice those during the taping incident, but that didn't mean she was attracted to him. She wasn't.

He wouldn't help her defend Bertie to her parents, which meant he was awful, so she wasn't attracted to him, and she wasn't going to waste even one moment staring at him.

She glanced over at him, but it wasn't staring so it didn't count. He was kneeling on the lowest step to the porch, sanding the stairs. In the sunlight his blond hair shone until it looked white. Like an angel. An angel who wouldn't help her when she'd asked him to.

She finished with the tape and picked up a jar of wood filler for nicks and holes in the banister.

The noise of the sander filled the air with its shrill vibration. It moved up the stairs and back onto the porch. But she didn't look. At last the sander quit.

"I think I've taken care of all the peeling paint, but I'd better clean up the mess before we paint over it." He walked toward the front door. "Does Bertie keep her broom in the kitchen?"

The kitchen? Going to the kitchen would take him right past the Christmas tree, the stockings, and a wooden reindeer Bertie had dragged in from her garage and was in the process of repainting.

"No!" Ellie dropped the jar of wood filler and sprinted to the door. "I mean, you don't know where she keeps the broom. I'll get it."

Ellie slipped through the door, careful not to open it far enough that John could get a view inside. She ran in, grabbed the broom from the kitchen closet, and ran back outside. "Here . . ." She handed the broom to John breathlessly.

"Thanks. Does she have a dust pan?"

"Oh. A dust pan. Just a second." Ellie once again opened the door a sliver, shimmied in, and fled to the kitchen. She retrieved the dust pan, then ran back to the porch and gave it to John with a smile.

He took it and swept up shards of peeling paint and dust that had fallen onto the porch. Ellie picked up the jar of wood filler from where she'd dropped it and tried to remember where on the banister she'd left off filling.

"I'm done now," John said. "I'll put the broom away."

The jar dropped to the porch again. "No, I'll do it!"

She dashed back to John and held her hand out for the broom. He kept his grip on it and eyed her suspiciously.

She smiled and grabbed hold of the handle, brushing her fingertips against his. "I know where Bertie keeps it. You know how particular women are about their kitchens."

His eyes remained narrow, but he relinquished the broom to her. He watched her with arms folded as she opened the door a crack and went through.

When she returned to the porch he was still standing there, arms folded.

Ignoring him, she went back to the banister. She picked up the jar of filler, this time tentatively, waiting for his next indoor request. A few moments later it came.

"It's getting hot out here. Do you mind if I go inside for a drink?"

"Yes." She placed the jar down and strolled instead of running back to him. "I mean, what kind of hostess would I be if I made you get your own water? I'll bring out glasses for both of us."

"You're hiding something inside, aren't you?"

"Of course not."

"What are you going to do when either Brother Cromwell or I ask to use the bathroom? That will be a little harder to bring outside for us, won't it?"

She smiled back at him to show she wasn't flustered. "It's just that the house is a mess. It would embarrass Bertie to know you'd been inside."

"I'm a bachelor. I'm used to messes. I don't mind."

"It's no trouble for me to get you water."

From inside, the faint sound of a phone ringing drifted out onto the porch. For a moment Ellie turned to go answer it, then stopped. It was probably her parents calling to talk to John, and it was easier to not answer the phone than to come up with some excuse why they couldn't talk to him. Besides, if John heard her saying things like, "Sorry, he's busy and can't come to the phone right now," it would be an invitation for him to not only come inside, but for him to tell her parents about all the neurological tests he wanted Bertie to have.

"Are you going to get that?" John asked.

"Get what?"

"The phone."

She shrugged. "I don't hear the phone."

"Do you have a hearing problem?"

"No, but you might. How often do you experience ringing in your ears?"

He took a step toward the door, and she stepped in front of him, blocking his way. "Ellie, if you're trying to prove your aunt's sanity by acting crazier in contrast, it won't work."

She held one arm out to block the door. "The phone is for Aunt Bertie, and she's not home. Whoever is calling will just have to call back."

"Have you ever heard of taking messages?"

The phone stopped ringing. "Too late," Ellie said. "Let's get back to work."

Instead of retreating, he took a step closer to her. She took a step backwards and felt the door brush up against her back. She put her hand behind her on the doorknob as though he might try to push her out of the way and go inside anyway.

"Do you know how frustrating it is trying to reason with you?" he asked.

"My parents have told me on occasion."

"Your parents—that was them, wasn't it?"

"I wouldn't know. I'm not about to claim to have psychic powers. You might think I was crazy."

He took a step closer, so close it felt like he was touching her even though he wasn't. "I'm not the bad guy, you know. I don't drive a padded wagon and sneak into people's houses to put them in straitjackets. I'm trying to help your aunt. Why won't you let me help?"

He did look trustworthy, standing so close that she could see the sincerity in his eyes. At least she thought it was sincerity. He was so near that she was getting distracted by all the other things about him and couldn't really catch much of the sincerity.

He had a great jawline. The kind you wanted to reach out and touch. His eyes were cool blue, like he belonged somewhere far away in the sky. And he had such broad shoulders. If he hugged her she'd be lost in them.

What had she been looking for? Oh yes, sincerity.

He slid his hand behind her back, putting it over her hand on the doorknob. "Are you going to let me in?"

"I . . . " I can't think of anything to say when you're standing two inches away. Come a little closer and ask me again.

A creak on the steps saved her from answering. Ellie looked over to see Aunt Bertie and Brother Cromwell coming onto the porch. Bertie clutched hold of the banister with one hand and with the other held a new paintbrush. Her purse swung against her side as she took each step. Brother Cromwell peered over the top of a barrel of paint that he was lugging up the stairs. Ellie hadn't even heard them drive up.

"None of those public displays of affection on my porch," Bertie said, waving the paintbrush in their direction. "I don't want the neighbors talking. They're incurable gossips. They're still going on about that time I slept outside on a lawn chair." She humphed as though the memory burnt. "It was a hot night and my pajamas were very modest. They had no reason to call the ambulance. If I was really going to die somewhere, it wouldn't be on my lawn chair wearing pajamas. How tacky." She motioned for Brother Cromwell to set the paint down by the banister, then turned back to Ellie and John. "So, if you're going to kiss you'd best do it in private."

"We weren't going to kiss," Ellie said.

"I was trying to go inside and Ellie wouldn't let me," John said.

"I explained to him that we hadn't had a chance to clean up

this morning, and it would embarrass us to have people inside," Ellie said.

Bertie collapsed into the sole chair that hadn't been moved off the porch. "Oh *that.* You don't need to worry about the house, Dear." She opened her purse, took out a piece of paper and waved it in John's direction. "Here. Read this."

He stepped over and took it from her hand. "One hundred reasons not to clean. Number one: God made dust mites, too. They have a right to live."

Bertie shut her eyes and nodded as he read on. "Number two: You don't have to worry about seasonal centerpieces if there's always clutter in the middle of your table. Number three: Dirt is organic and therefore healthy."

He turned the paper over in his hands. "You titled it one hundred but you've only numbered to sixty-eight."

"I'm still working on it—oh, I just thought of another one." Bertie held up one hand as though placing the words on a marquee. "Mold. If it's good enough for blue cheese, why not let it grow in the bottom of your fridge?"

Brother Cromwell chuckled. John didn't.

Ellie snatched the paper from his hand, folding it back up and sticking it into her pocket. In a low voice, so only he could hear, she said, "This is just one of Aunt Bertie's games—something to do because she doesn't want to watch *Wheel of Fortune* reruns. It's just a little cluttered inside, but other than that, perfectly normal."

He nodded, appraising her and making the silence stretch out until Ellie had to look away. To Bertie he said, "Before we get started painting, do you mind if I use your bathroom?"

"Of course not," she called from her chair. "It's down the hallway—the first door past the plastic Santa."

It could have been worse. John didn't even mention the Christmas tree when he returned. Nor did he say anything about the Macaulay Culkin *Home Alone* poster taped above the bathroom sink where the mirror was supposed to be. Ellie had put it there. The little boy's hands-on-his-face look of horror was a perfect reflection of how she felt when she dragged herself into the bathroom every morning.

She didn't bother explaining it, though. If she'd explained that, she would have had to explain about Cindy Crawford in Bertie's bathroom, and it was just better not to do that.

Brother Cromwell loaded the sprayer to paint the floor and roof, while John and Ellie took brushes to the banister. Bertie tried to help with the trim, but John insisted she stay off her ankle. He shooed her onto the chairs they'd moved under the shade of a pine tree, and Bertie sat there, calling things up to them every once in a while.

"I still think we should have gone with magenta. Think of what the neighbors would have to talk about then."

They were almost done with the banister when John brought up the subject of Bertie's medical appointments.

"How are you holding up?" he called down to Bertie, as though sitting in the shade in a lawn chair was a strenuous activity that needed a doctor's supervision.

"I'm fine," she said.

"Your ankle is okay?"

"Just fine."

"How's your head? Have you had any symptoms since your fall?"

"No."

He stopped and leaned on the part of the banister that wasn't painted, closer to Bertie so she could see he was giving her his full attention. "You know, sometimes symptoms don't show up until later. I'd really feel better if we knew everything was fine. I'd like you to come back to the hospital for some tests."

"I'm fine. I've had worse falls than that one without any head injuries."

"You've had other falls? All the more reason to come and be checked out."

She tilted her head up at them. "You're acting like you think something is wrong with me."

"A doctor worries about his patients. Come to the hospital. Ellie can drive you."

Bertie chuckled, her shoulders softly jiggling up and down as she sat on the lawn chair. "I understand now. You're looking for an excuse for Ellie to come visit you. Well, she doesn't need to drag me along to see you. She can go on her own. She has my permission."

"No, I just think that it would be better if—" John didn't finish his sentence. He quit speaking directly after Ellie ran her paint brush along his back.

"I'm so sorry," Ellie said, still holding the brush out as if it was a weapon. "Did I get a little paint on you? I'll have to be more careful."

John arched his back and pulled at his T-shirt. "A little? It's running down my jeans."

"Yes, and it's getting on your shoes, too. I hope they weren't expensive." She handed him a rag, and he wiped at his jeans and shirt while he glared at her.

"You can go clean up in the bathroom," she said sweetly. "Don't worry about making a mess. We have sixty-nine reasons not to clean."

CHAPTER 13

From the moment John left Bertie's house and several times during the day, John shook his head and said, "She's crazy. I know she's crazy, but I can't do anything about it." And he wasn't talking about Bertie.

Ellie.

He wanted to strangle her. He wanted to strangle her for thwarting him while he was trying to convince Bertie to come in, for ruining his most comfortable pair of shoes, and for looking so good that he could easily forgive her for the last two offenses.

Because Ellie did look good. She even looked good in that ridiculous oversized T-shirt she wore to paint in and those fraying jean shorts.

It was better not to dwell on the shorts, the ones that showed off Ellie's long legs.

For one thing, she was too young for him. For another thing she was crazy. And besides, since his divorce he'd sworn off women.

At least all women he didn't know completely, thoroughly, and in depth.

If he ever dated again, he wanted to be absolutely sure that the woman in question had no emotional problems, tendencies towards apostasy, or shopping hang-ups.

He would be so careful next time. He'd be sure he didn't make another mistake.

After dinner he went to the library to look at the gardening books. He needed to read something that would tell him why the plants in his front yard kept dying.

He found a few titles on the computer and went down one of the nonfiction rows to look for them. Mid-aisle he realized it was the wrong row. When he turned around he bumped into Suzanne. Literally. The stack of books she'd been holding spilled to the ground with a shower of soft thuds.

She bent down and hurriedly scooped books up. He apologized and bent down to help her. He handed one back to her and couldn't help but notice the title. *What to Expect When You're Expecting.*

She took the book and blushed bright pink. "Thanks."

Then neither of them said anything.

He didn't move because he wanted to say something and wasn't sure what was the right thing to say. Here in the library—he didn't feel like a doctor. Did she even remember him from the ER?

Her hair was pulled back in a ponytail, her face washed clean of makeup, which made her look terribly young. She glanced at him, then the floor, then her books, with more blushing. "Dr.

Flynn." She glanced at him for another moment before her gaze returned to her hands.

So she did remember. It was safe to talk about it. "Suzanne, how have you been? Are you feeling any better?"

"Sometimes. The evenings are the worst."

"Have you seen an obstetrician?"

She clutched the books to her chest and tapped the heel of one foot like an agitated racehorse. Her mouth twitched and she pursed her lips together. "I haven't decided if I'm keeping it. I haven't decided." Then the tears came, puddling in her eyes and overflowing onto her cheeks. She sniffed and wiped her face with the back of her hand.

People often broke down in the ER. When someone walked through his door, it was a given they were having a bad day. He could deal with high-frequency emotion while he wore the protection of his medical scrubs and held his clipboard as though it were a shield. He could rattle off the names and numbers of counselors and support groups with the same proficiency that he wrote prescriptions.

Here, standing by the shelves in the library, he felt completely inadequate. He'd already given her the names and numbers of those support groups, and yet she was standing in front of him, a bundle of pain. "I'm sure it's a very hard decision for you. Have you talked to anyone about it?"

"Just my mother. She says, 'You know you can't keep it. You're too young.' She says it like the baby is a stray dog or something. Like I've brought home a puppy, and we have to take it to the pound. Only she doesn't want me to take this baby to the pound.

She wants me to go to a clinic. Mom thinks if I do it quick enough, none of it will matter." She brushed her hand against her cheek again, and the words came quicker, tumbling out of her mouth as though she couldn't stop them. "But how can it not matter? I already wonder if it's a boy or a girl. I mean it is—it's either a boy or a girl. I just don't know which, but I know I'll wonder about it for the rest of my life. Like, if it's a boy would he have been as tall as Andrew? If it's a girl, would she have looked like me? How can I go to a clinic? How can I kill something that looks like me?"

John put one hand on her shoulder. She trembled under his fingers. "If you don't want an abortion, then don't have one. There are other options."

"I know all about adoption. My best friend was adopted. But I keep thinking, how could I give my baby to strangers? And then I think if I couldn't give my baby away, how in the world could I have an abortion? And I've always told my best friend everything. Everything. But I can't tell her about this because if I do decide to have an abortion, then how will I ever be able to face her again? How can I let her know that although her mother gave her life, I took the life of my baby because I didn't want it?"

"It sounds to me like you want to keep the baby."

"But I can't keep it. My mother's right about that. I'm supposed to go to college. I'm supposed to have a life. I can't have a baby." She bit her lip so hard he thought she would draw blood. "So there isn't a solution. There isn't."

Her countenance, her whole body, seemed to crumple and, half afraid she'd fall, John pulled her into a hug. Her books were still clutched to her chest and they pushed into his ribs while she cried silent, shaking sobs into his shirt. He patted her back almost mechanically while he looked around to see if anyone could hear her and was perhaps coming to see what the problem was.

No one came. They stood alone in the aisle, and he spoke softly to her. "There *are* solutions, just not easy ones."

He thought back to his marriage, back to when Valerie had crumpled this way. Valerie throwing away all the baby things; Valerie nearly sliding down the bathroom wall, beside herself with pain. *Have the baby,* he wanted to tell Suzanne. *Love it and raise it, or give it to someone who will. Just don't throw away such a precious gift.*

He couldn't say it. It was against hospital regulations for him to counsel a patient that way, and Suzanne's mother would have a fit if he did. He could already imagine the woman, eyes blazing, storming into the ER demanding to see him and threatening to sue at the top of her lungs.

But there was Suzanne, right now, trembling in his arms, and a baby in question.

"Children are a precious gift," he said. "Don't throw it away."

Her sniffling subsided. She pulled away from him. "You think I should have the baby?"

"I think you should think about your options, and chose the one you won't regret for the rest of your life."

She swallowed, took a breath as though trying to calm herself. "How could I take care of a baby?"

"Have you talked to Andrew?"

"I haven't seen him since he dumped me. What's the point?"

"He shares the responsibility."

"I don't want him back just because he feels obligated to me. I don't want to trap him into something."

"I'm not talking about romance. I'm talking about child support."

"Oh." She blinked as though the idea was completely new to her. Perhaps it was.

"Do you still have the phone numbers of those support groups I gave you?"

"Yes, but I didn't call any of them because I hadn't decided what to do."

"You can talk to them even if you haven't decided."

"Maybe I will." She took a step back from him and glanced around the aisle as though just remembering where she was. "Thanks for listening to me." She shifted the books in her arms and started down the aisle away from him. After a few steps she turned back. "What do guys usually do when they find out about a pregnancy?"

The nice guys or the jerks? "It depends on the guy."

She nodded and left.

For Suzanne's sake, he hoped Andrew wasn't a jerk.

* * *

While Ellie slept, she dreamt she was back at Sunshine Villa, Grandpa Baxter's nursing home. She walked the white tile hallways, looking down at her shoes to avoid seeing the wheelchairs—or the people sitting in them. When she'd visited before there had been only a few wheelchairs sitting outside of the rooms. Now they lined the hallway, an endless row of wrinkled and vacant faces staring at her as she walked past.

She'd never visited Grandpa Baxter without her parents, but in the dream she was alone. Her footsteps echoed against the tile, at first slowly, and then more quickly the further she went down the hallway. She wanted to find Grandpa Baxter's room, to get out of this hallway, to get away from these faces that were both so like and so unlike her own that they frightened her.

Grandpa Baxter's room. Once she got there it would be all right. Her parents would be there. Grandpa might even know who she was today—he might be better—and she'd tell him about college, her family, and how Mckenna had been voted prom queen and stolen Kirk.

Grandpa always enjoyed a good Mckenna story.

There was his room—number 214. She nearly sprinted the rest of the distance, then pushed open the door but stopped short. It wasn't Grandpa Baxter in bed at all, it was Bertie—looking pale, and vacant, and twisted with age.

Ellie woke, gasping as her room took shape around her.

She sat up in bed, listening to the crickets chirp while she pulled her covers up. It was much colder now than when she'd gone to sleep, and she tried to keep herself from shivering. After hudding under the covers for a moment, she abandoned their warmth to shut her window.

No chance she'd be able to get back to sleep now.

Stupid nightmare.

It was all her parents' fault for putting these ideas in her mind. For insisting there was something wrong with Bertie when there wasn't.

Her parents would call again; Ellie knew that. Maybe tomorrow.

They'd want to know why Ellie hadn't connected them with Dr. Flynn, and she couldn't tell them the truth. She couldn't tell them that John agreed with them.

He was a worrier. And he didn't understand. Or didn't care.

Well, if she couldn't convince John to vouch for Bertie, she'd find a doctor who would.

Like Bertie's regular doctor. Aunt Bertie must have someone she went to when she had a sore throat or a rash. He undoubtedly knew Bertie was eccentric, knew it was normal for her, and best of all, he didn't know of Bertie's off-the-wall answers in the ER.

He'd have no reason to worry about Bertie, or to worry Ellie's parents about Bertie. Ellie really should have contacted him to start with instead of ever hoping John would help.

Over breakfast Ellie feigned a sore wrist and asked Bertie the name of her physician.

"My doctor here in town is Dr. Blair."

"Do you know him well? I mean, is he nice?"

"Oh very nice. Every once in a while I have to call him at home for a prescription or a question, and he's most accommodating." She sprinkled a handful of blueberries across her Cheerios, paused, then dropped another handful on. "But of course you'd want to see Dr. Flynn for your wrist. Dr. Blair's married."

"John and I weren't kissing."

"Of course not, Dear."

After breakfast Ellie looked up Dr. Blair's phone number in the yellow pages, then took the cordless phone into the bathroom so Bertie wouldn't hear her conversation. While the shower water ran, Ellie tried to explain the situation to the receptionist in a coherent manner. "I'm staying with my aunt, Beatrice Goodwin, who's one of Dr. Blair's patients. My parents are quite concerned about her because she lives alone, and I was wondering, if my parents were to call Dr. Blair, could he reassure them that Bertie has a clean bill of health? I mean, just tell them she's not experiencing any health-related problems that would require a nursing home."

Without a trace of emotion the receptionist said, "I'll give Dr. Blair your message and either he or his nurse will give you a call."

"Thank you. I'm going to work but I'll be home around 3:15 or 3:20. Could you have him call me after that?"

"I'll put that on the message."

"Could you make sure it's emphasized? I mean, I really want to talk to Dr. Blair privately."

There was a pause and then the receptionist's voice sounding exasperated. "I'll put it on the message."

When Ellie hung up, her stomach clenched tight with anxiety. This was her parents' fault too. She shouldn't have to hide her conversations from Bertie, to worry that the doctor would call her aunt midday and say, "What's this I hear about your relatives thinking you're senile?"

All she could do was hope the receptionist did a good job of explaining the situation.

Chapter 14

After the morning check-out rush, Diana and Ellie were finally able to talk as they stuffed brochures with the fall rates into envelopes.

"I can't believe Andrew showed up with another woman," Diana whispered. "I've never been so humiliated in my life, and I wasn't even there."

"You don't need to be embarrassed. It was just a miscommunication, that's all."

"He obviously doesn't think I'm good enough to date."

"That's not true. And besides, so what if he thinks of you as a friend? That's a good thing. Friendship can turn into something more."

Diana shook her head. "I'm never asking him out again. I can't. If I did he'd figure out that I asked him out before, and the one saving grace of Saturday night was that he didn't realize he stood me up. Well, that and I got to eat an entire apple pie by myself."

Ellie slipped one brochure and then another into the envelope while she thought. "So don't ask him out. Not exactly. You'll just be somewhere where he is. Where is he all of the time?"

"At the Tour Store or going down a mountainside."

"So take up biking."

"And then I just wait to run into him on the bike trails? I try and make small talk while zooming down the mountain?"

Ellie tried to close the envelope, couldn't, and realized she'd put in two brochures. She took one out. "Go along on one of his bike tours. Tell him that as a resort employee you need to experience the tours you recommend to your guests. It makes sense."

Diana didn't say anything for a moment. The only sound was the rustle of paper. "It does make sense, doesn't it?"

"Yep."

"And I should take the canoe trip too, shouldn't I?"

"Of course."

Diana reached for the phone on the counter, picked it up, fingered the receiver, then set it back down with a click. "What if he's going out with Madison now, though? What if they're a couple?"

Ellie shrugged. "You can sit here and think of excuses all day not to call him, or you can just call him."

Diana picked up the phone, gripping it as though she were trying to strangle it, and punched in the number. Before Ellie could hear any of the conversation, the front desk bell rang. She walked up to take care of a couple who were checking in so Diana could finish her call. Still, as she greeted the guests and checked their names off the list, she half-listened to Diana, judging how the call was going by the inflections in her voice.

Giggling. That was a good sign.

Or at least she hoped it was a good sign. Maybe Diana had reverted to a junior high mentality and was just giggling for no apparent reason.

Here's a map of the resort. Here's a key. Please be on your way so I can check up on the Diana and Andrew soap.

More giggling. Pauses. Diana confirming a day and time.

By the time Ellie made it back to the phone, Diana had hung up and was grinning like the Cheshire cat.

"So that wasn't too terribly painful to set up," Ellie said.

"He's doing an afternoon tour with an older couple this Friday that will work into our schedule perfectly. A short bike trip. A short canoe trip. We leave after work. We'll be back before seven and not only is he going to be our personal guide, he's giving us a discount because we're his friends."

"We're?" Ellie asked. "Us?"

"Right. And he barely knows you, so he must be talking about me when he said he was a friend."

"I'm not supposed to come along on this. You're missing the whole romance angle, Diana."

"I said I was taking the trip because I worked at the front desk and needed to know details about the tours the Tour Store offered, so of course he assumed you were coming too. I couldn't tell him it was just me."

This just went to show why you should never get involved in other people's love lives. Now Ellie was going to be a third wheel on a bike. That made her, what, a tricycle?

"Bring clothes to change into on Friday. He'll pick us up here at the resort right at 3:00." She spun around on her chair once, then tilted backwards so far Ellie was afraid Diana would tip over. "I get to ride in the hunkmobile with Andrew."

* * *

On Tuesday morning Brother White came into the ER with a broken finger. As he was leaving he patted John on the shoulder with his good hand and said, "I saw her at the ward dinner. Good choice."

Later in the morning Julianne Hinz, who did the hospital laundry, paused by him while she wheeled the dirty stuff out and launched into a lecture about how one shouldn't be afraid of remarriage after a divorce. Marriage had its ups and downs, just like a roller coaster. And just because you threw up on Space Mountain once didn't mean Disneyland wasn't still the happiest place on earth.

Uh, yeah.

Hadn't Ellie said she was going to clear up that little misunderstanding with her aunt?

As he got food from the hospital cafeteria, Dr. Parker—who had never let that patient-doctor confidentiality issue stop him from spreading an interesting story—sidled up behind him. As John picked out a sandwich, Dr. Parker smiled and elbowed him. "I hear you've gotten serious with a certain young lady in town."

"Ellie and I are not even dating. We're just acquaintances."

"One of my patients heard it from Ellie's aunt that you were kissing on her porch."

John nearly toppled the water glass on his tray. "We weren't kissing. We were just standing close together."

Dr. Parker nodded with a smile. "I see."

"We're not a couple."

"Of course not. It's perfectly normal for acquaintances to stand so close together that people mistake them for kissing."

"I was trying to get into Ellie's house, and she was blocking the door. It was all on a professional level, really." He grabbed a napkin and flung it on his tray. "I know that didn't make sense, but I can explain."

"You don't have to explain. I caught a glimpse of her when she came in to the ER with her aunt." He winked at John and walked to a table.

Yes, well, Ellie was still too young for him, even if she was pretty. True, she had a warmth about her. She smiled and laughed easily as though life itself amused her. But she was only a junior in college—just twenty-one years old. She wasn't settled in her ways yet. At twenty-one a person was still changing—could change into a person who was on a first name basis with the men down at Helzberg Jewelers. She might buy baby clothes and then throw them all away.

So he was staying away from her even if she did look good in shorts and a T-shirt . . . with those velvety eyes pleading with him while she twisted the sander cord around her finger.

The sander. He'd left it over at Bertie's house. He'd have to go over and get it, even though he fully expected that the next time he got within a ten-foot radius of Ellie people would jump from the bushes and demand to know when their wedding date was.

He should be safe and just call Bertie and ask her to bring it to church with her next Sunday.

He'd do that.

But somehow, throughout the day his mind kept drifting off to Bertie's house. And really, there was no point in waiting until Sunday to get the sander. He might need it before then.

* * *

It was 3:12 when Ellie got home. She rushed into the house as though the phone might ring that moment, then slunk into the kitchen as though it had already rung hours before and Bertie would come storming into the room to yell at her.

Neither happened.

She put her purse on the counter, picked up the cordless phone, and wandered into Bertie's room. Her aunt sat at the easel, one paintbrush gliding across the canvas while she held a second brush in her teeth.

"I'm home," Ellie said.

"Mmmph," Bertie answered.

"Anyone call for me while I was gone?"

"Mmm mmph."

Ellie fingered the phone. "Was that an Mmm mmph—no, or an mmm mmph yes?"

Bertie took the brush from her teeth. "No. Are you expecting a call?"

"No. Not really. Well, sort of." And then she thought of the perfect excuse for privacy, for carrying around the phone so Bertie wouldn't answer it. "I'm hoping to talk to a certain doctor. He should call before 5:00." Because doctors' offices closed at 5:00. It wasn't exactly a lie, and Bertie didn't mention Ellie's extreme attachment to the phone again. As the hour passed and no one called,

Bertie did come out of her room and start making tsking noises as she straightened the kitchen.

5:15, 5:30, and then 5:45 passed. When did doctors leave the office for the day? Had Dr. Blair forgotten? Was he just planning on calling tomorrow? She couldn't keep carting the phone around with her. Would she be able to reach anyone at Dr. Blair's office if she called now?

The doorbell rang. Ellie carried the phone with her to the living room, but her aunt reached the door first.

Bertie opened it, then made a sweeping motion inward. "John, how nice of you to stop by. Come in."

He stepped inside, somehow shrinking the living room as he did. His gaze went to the Christmas tree and stayed there until Bertie spoke again. "Look, Ellie, John's come to see you." She leaned toward him and said, "She's been positively carrying that phone around with her for the last two and a half hours waiting for you to call. I was beginning to get quite angry with you on her behalf."

John's gaze turned to Ellie and the phone in her hand. "Oh, really?"

Ellie opened her mouth, but couldn't find words to put in it.

"But all is forgiven now, isn't it Ellie? You're worth the wait." Then in a lower voice, Bertie added to John, "Roses would have been a nice touch."

"Uh, sorry. I'll try to remember that next time when I don't call." John smiled stiffly at Ellie. "Could I talk to you privately?"

"Oh, don't you two mind me." Bertie went to the tree, picked up a cylindrical package, and shook it. "I'm just about to start dinner. Would you like to eat with us?" With slightly shaking hands she untaped the paper and took out a bottle of spaghetti sauce. "We're either having spaghetti or manicotti, which would you prefer?"

Ellie spoke so John wouldn't have to. "Why don't you make the manicotti—that's the easiest."

"Ellie bought some of the frozen kind," Bertie said, making her way slowly to the kitchen. "You just add sauce on top and throw it in the microwave. Not homemade, but still very good."

John watched Bertie go, then motioned for Ellie to follow him out onto the porch for privacy. They walked out into the evening sunshine, their footsteps making hollow thuds as they stepped across the newly painted wood. She leaned up against the banister. He stood in front of her. "So, how long has Bertie been gift wrapping groceries?"

"It helps her to remember to appreciate her blessings, and it's—" Ellie folded her arms. "Is that why you came here? To check up on my aunt and see if she's doing anything else unusual?"

"No, actually I came by to get my sander, and hey—by the way, thanks for clearing up that little matter with Bertie about you and me not being a couple. I can tell you've done your best to dispel *that* rumor."

Ellie fingered the phone and felt a blush creep into her cheeks. "I can explain about the phone call."

But how could she? She didn't want to tell him she was trying to get another doctor to do what he wouldn't—testify to Bertie's mental health.

"Well?" he asked.

"I said I could explain, not that I was going to."

"But you did tell Bertie you were expecting a call from me?"

If she said no, he'd think Bertie was conjuring up false realities. If she said yes, then she'd have to explain why. "Sort of," she said.

"I see." He stepped toward her, smiling at her discomfort. "And what was I sort-of going to say to you?"

"I'm not sure. What do you want to say to me?"

"Oh, I can think of several things."

He moved closer, and she wished she could step backward but she was up against the banister already. "Are they things I want to hear—or am I going to hang up on you halfway through our conversation?"

"Why are you letting your aunt think there's something going on between us? Do you *wish* there was something going on between us?"

"No." She said it too quickly and realized she'd insulted him. With her free hand she fidgeted with a knot of wood on the banister, pushing it like it was a button. "I didn't mean it that way. I'm sure you're very nice, that is, when you're not trying to commit innocent old ladies into nursing homes."

He leaned forward, placing his hands on either side of her. "But only when I'm not trying to commit innocent old ladies into nursing homes."

"And you're very handsome. I'm sure a lot of women go for that smoldering eyes look."

"Are my eyes smoldering?"

"They are."

"Do you know why?"

She didn't answer. The phone rang, startling Ellie. She'd forgotten she was holding it.

John straightened, nodding in the phone's direction. "Oh. That must be me calling now."

She fumbled with the on button, then pushed her way away from him, walking a few steps from the banister to let John know she wanted privacy. "Hello?"

"Hello, Miss Baxter?"

"Speaking."

"This is Dr. Blair. I just read the message you left me about your aunt. It seems you wanted me to talk to your parents about Bertie?"

"That's right."

John moved toward her side, and she turned again, walking another step away from him. It was annoying how the more she tried to ignore him, the more solid his presence felt. Dr. Blair. She was supposed to be concentrating on what he was saying.

"—so I really can't discuss a patient's medical record with another party unless my patient agrees or signs a medical release form allowing me to discuss the case."

She didn't want to let John hear any part of her conversation and yet she couldn't let Dr. Blair hang up without making him understand. She lowered her voice. "But I'm not asking you to release medical records. You don't have to tell my parents the results of her last strep culture. I just want you to reassure them, speaking as one of Bertie's friends, that they don't need to be looking at brochures for nursing homes. You can just talk to them, can't you?"

Before he could answer, John took the phone from Ellie's grasp.

She turned in time to see him putting it to his face. "This is Dr. Flynn. Who am I speaking to?"

"Hey!" Ellie grabbed for the phone, but John caught her hand and held it tightly. She reached up with her other hand, and John casually held the phone between his cheek and shoulder, while restraining her other hand too.

"Oh—hello, Roger. Listen, before you talk to Ellie's parents, I think you should know that Bertie had an unexplained neurological episode in the ER, and she's refusing to have the testing I've recommended to rule out problems."

"You can't do this." Ellie pulled at her hands, yanking one free. She reached for the phone again, and not only had her hand recaptured, but John spun her around so that her arms were crossed in front of her and her back was pressed up against his chest. She tried to stomp on his foot, but he moved it before she could, and her foot thunked against the porch floor.

"I'm not sure," John continued into the phone in an even voice. "That's why I want testing done. Perhaps you could encourage Bertie to follow my counsel, recommend she have a physical."

Ellie stomped again, this time hitting John's right foot. He winced, but went on with his conversation. "No, you don't need to talk to Ellie again. I'll tell her your answer for you. She's too busy to talk on the phone just now."

"Give me the phone or I'll scream."

He held onto her wrists, and she twisted at them but didn't scream. Screaming would bring Aunt Bertie outside, and how would she explain all this to her aunt? Instead she hissed out, "I'm sure you're breaking several doctors' codes of ethics by doing this, and I'm going to report you to the medical board."

"Maybe you could give Bertie a call and talk to her about coming in for an exam," John continued into the phone. Then after a pause added, "I'm just here at Bertie's house to pick up my sander. Really. No, we're not a couple."

"I hope they take your license away!"

"Thanks. I appreciate it. Talk to you later."

And then Bertie swung open the front door.

All of Ellie's struggling instantly fell away, and she stood silent and unbreathing in John's grasp.

How could she explain this? How could she tell Bertie why she and John were fighting over the phone? Her mouth opened, forming a silent "O."

Bertie shook her head. "What did I tell you about public displays of affection on my porch? Honestly, I can't turn my back on you two for a minute." But then she did. She turned around, letting the screen door gently sway back and forth. "Dinner's just about ready." Her footsteps slowly padded off in the direction of the kitchen.

John released Ellie, taking the phone from his ear as he did. She grabbed it out of his hand, held it up as though she was going to throw it, then shook it at him instead. "I can't believe you did that! You're not allowed to interfere that way. Doctors can't just commandeer your phone conversations."

"You were speaking to Dr. Blair as a friend, not a doctor. You said so yourself."

Ellie gripped the phone so hard the buttons beeped in protest. "That still doesn't make it right."

"And I suppose it's right for you to ask Dr. Blair to make assurances to your parents while you withhold information from both of them."

"She's fine. They want to put her in a home, and I'm not going to let you, or them, or anyone do it."

He shoved his hands in his pockets, rattling his keys, clanking them together in an angry rumble. In his voice there wasn't a drop of sympathy. "I see people like you every day, Ellie. Heart attack victims that ignored the warning signs. Cancer patients who put out their cigarettes before they walk into the hospital. People who don't take their medicine because it's inconvenient. Everyone's convinced they'll be just fine if they pretend things are normal. Well, I'm where people end up when they discover they're not immortal after all. You're not doing Bertie any favors. You're keeping her from getting help."

"I'm keeping her from getting assisted living."

"Dr. Blair will call Bertie and tell her she's overdue for a physical. Make sure she keeps her appointment, and make sure you're the one who takes her there. Her driving might be impaired."

"Her driving is not impaired." Ellie hadn't actually seen Bertie drive this summer, but that didn't mean Bertie couldn't do it. She'd done it just fine for almost fifty years.

"I'll check back with Dr. Blair tomorrow." He walked across the porch and down the stairs, taking them two at time and yet still not seeming in a hurry.

Bertie didn't really matter to him. He was just one of those people who couldn't stand to have his instructions ignored.

She watched him go, wishing she could hurl some retort at his back but was unable to think of a single thing to say. Finally, after he'd pulled away in his car, she found the words. "Hey, Dr. Flynn, looks like your memory is failing you. You forgot your sander."

Chapter 15

John tapped the steering wheel with his thumb and then forced himself to stop. He wasn't going to let Ellie get under his skin. He'd spent too much time dealing with the head-in-the-sand approach to health care to let it bother him now.

The forty-year-old woman he'd seen during residency with stage-four breast cancer. "Did you do regular breast self exams?" he asked her when he was giving her a diagnostic work up.

"No," she said quietly. "I knew I was supposed to. But I was always afraid I might find something."

He had stopped writing in midstream, the pen stiff between his fingers. Finding something was the whole point. If she'd found something earlier she'd have a fighting chance. Now . . .

As she left the room, she pulled a picture key chain from her purse. She had three children. Three. And none of them looked very old. That day he'd gone to the break room absolutely sick. Baffled. He'd sat in front of his lunch unable to eat.

Since then he'd seen the same thing happen in a hundred different ways. It hardly fazed him now, so he shouldn't be frustrated by Ellie's attitude.

John tapped his fingers against the steering wheel again. He couldn't believe he'd actually confiscated Ellie's phone.

Well, that's what happened to doctors after having their instructions repeatedly ignored. They snapped. They took things into their own hands.

Tap. Tap. Tap. John shook his fingers, then stretched out his hands in an attempt to relax them.

Maybe it was just Ellie. Maybe when you were around her you did crazy things. For all he knew, Bertie had been a perfectly normal individual until Ellie appeared on the scene.

He pictured Ellie clutching the phone in her hand, warning him: *They want to put her in a home, and I'm not going to let you, or them, or anyone do it.*

That was the thing about doctors. People either saw them as medical fairy godmothers who used pills and shots to grant all wishes or employees of the grim reaper—only there to deliver bad news.

Apparently Ellie belonged to the latter category. Too bad. If she belonged to the first category she'd be following his advice, hanging on his every word and looking up at him with awed admiration . . .

Tap. Tap.

She was still too young for him.

* * *

Ellie walked back into the house, shutting the screen door with a clang.

Fine. Let Dr. Blair call. Let Bertie go in for a physical. Then they'd see there was nothing wrong with her. After Dr. Blair gave her a clean bill of health, Ellie would insist that not only he, but John Flynn too, call Ellie's parents and assure them of Bertie's mental capabilities.

In fact, Ellie would pester every M.D. in Colton to call her parents. It would be her new hobby. By the end of the summer Ellie's parents would be so sick of hearing from physicians that they'd hang up the phone at the first mention of the word *doctor*.

Only Ellie wasn't going to be the one to suggest the physical to Bertie. She wouldn't hurt her aunt in that way.

Bertie had never thought Ellie was crazy when she was eleven and angry at her parents because they wouldn't let her dig up her floorboards and plant a cherry tree in her bedroom. Ellie liked cherries. They wouldn't grow outside in Las Cruces. It had made perfect sense to Bertie.

When Ellie reached the kitchen, Bertie looked at her and then looked behind her. "Where's John?"

"He couldn't stay for dinner after all."

"You're not fighting again, are you?"

"No. Yes. Sort of." No, because she didn't want to explain why. Yes, because she wanted to let Bertie know she and John were not a couple. And sort of, because she couldn't decide between the two.

Bertie picked up the third plate on the table, returning it to the cupboard with slow steps. "That's all right. We'll have him over after you make up. That way we'll have time to prepare something more elaborate than frozen manicotti." She set the plate on the shelf then came back for the silverware. "Do you know how to cook any really elaborate meals?"

"No."

"Neither do I. Perhaps we'll order out and pretend we cooked it."

"He doesn't want to eat dinner with us. He just came by to pick up his sander."

"Did he? Then it's funny that he didn't take it. It's still in the laundry room, isn't it?"

"Well, yes."

Bertie smiled and sat down at the table. Ellie sat beside her, slowly picking up her fork and feeling defeated.

"Don't worry, Dear," Bertie said. "If he goes too long without calling you, I'll fake an injury so you can see him at work."

The phone rang, jangling noisily from where Ellie had placed it on the table.

Bertie didn't reach for it. "That might be him now. He has a cell phone, you know. I saw it at the ward social."

"It isn't John."

Bertie sighed then picked up the phone, clicking it on as she brought it to her mouth. "Hello? Oh, Roger, it's nice to hear from you." To Ellie she mouthed the words, "It's Dr. Blair."

Silence. Ellie twirled her fork between her fingers and waited for Bertie's response.

"But I'm fine, really. John has just taken to worrying about me since he started seeing my niece. The two of them positively hover over me looking for ailments—that is, when they aren't wrapped up in each other. You should have seen them at the church social we had last Saturday; they were—"

Another moment of silence.

"I'm fine, honestly, and you know how I feel about doctors prodding around my body. No offense, Roger, but you prod with the best of them."

Silence.

"Why in heavens would I need a neurological exam?"

Ellie clenched her fork so hard her fingernails dug into the palms of her hand.

"My memory is just fine."

Silence.

"You're not serious. Roger, I couldn't count backwards by sevens from one hundred when I was in school and actually paying attention to math. You want to judge my memory by that now?"

Another silence. Bertie gripped the phone, the rippled veins in her hand contrasting starkly with her pale skin.

"I'll tell you what I *do* remember. I remember every swear word I've heard since I was in the second grade. Do you want me to repeat *those* back to you? Well, we'll just consider this conversation completed then."

She hung up the phone, setting it down so hard Ellie's spoon and knife jumped.

"Impertinence. The man is only ten years younger than me and suddenly I'm so old I'm on Alzheimer's watch."

Ellie took a bite of her manicotti so she wouldn't have to say anything.

"My memory is fine. Well, it's as good as it's ever been anyway. You forget one appointment and you're branded for life."

"You forgot an appointment? Recently?"

"Now don't you start in on me, too. I go in for an annual physical every April, and I just never made the appointment this year. That doesn't mean my memory is going. I can still name all fifty capitals, can you?"

"No."

"Olympia, Washington. Salt Lake City, Utah. Boise, Idaho." She picked up her knife from the table. "Rupertsville, Georgia—"

"Bertie, there's no such place as Rupertsville. You're making that up."

"Well, what do I care what the capital of Georgia is? When am I ever going to Georgia?" She cut into her manicotti and stabbed it with her fork. "I bet Dr. Blair doesn't know the capital of Georgia. I have half a mind to call and ask him." She took a bite and chewed angrily. "Except if I call him with that question, he'll really think I have half a mind." Another bite. "Charleston, South Carolina, and Helena . . . Well, Helena is the capital of *some place*."

Bertie went on for the rest of the night, flinging out capitals as though they were exclamations. Sacramento, California! Phoenix, Arizona! Tapioca, Kansas! Some of them were wrong, Ellie knew, but she couldn't be certain about all of them. And if Ellie herself didn't know, then Bertie's lack of knowledge certainly couldn't be considered a memory lapse.

Bertie was fine, but apparently Ellie would have to come up with another way to prove it. Dr. Blair and Dr. Flynn would not be calling her parents.

* * *

John made it through all of Wednesday and Thursday without thinking about Ellie. Unless one counted the times he thought about setting up a home teaching appointment, which really didn't count since it was his priesthood duty. Even if it did cross his mind on an hourly basis.

Thursday evening Chris knocked on John's door. Chris was the same age as Diana—eighteen—although he looked younger. His wispy blond hair and choir boy features made him seem more like he was entering high school than college. Still, he seemed to grow taller on a daily basis, and his glasses gave him a contemplative look, which John liked. It made him feel that Chris would never do anything stupid because he'd contemplated everything beforehand—like the fact that John would hurt Chris if he touched Diana the wrong way.

John opened his front door wide when he saw him. "Chris, hi."

Chris nodded, swallowed, and tapped his hands against his leg. "Hi, John. Can I talk to you for a few minutes?"

"Sure. Come in." Chris followed John back into his living room and sat on a brown leather recliner. John sat on its matching counterpart. The room was western, tasteful, and done completely in Pine Top resort cast-off furniture his mother insisted he have when he moved back to Colton. Valerie had taken all of their stuff when she left.

"It's about Diana," Chris said. "You know that she broke up with me?"

"I heard."

"I think she's making a big mistake. I mean, she didn't even give me a reason. She just called me and told me our relationship had grown stale. She wanted to experience more out of life. It's like she's going through some sort of post-high-school midlife crisis."

Mid life? Diana was midway through thirty-six years. In Chris's mind, John was three years away from his final demise. How nice.

Chris went on waving his hands in front of him in an uncharacteristic show of emotion. "Stale? What exactly is that supposed to mean? Bread gets stale. People get to know each other. I always thought that was a good thing. I mean, I didn't have to ask what kind of shake Diana wanted when we went to the Ice Cream Shack. I knew she wanted the large Oreo, just like I knew she wanted curly fries instead of the regular ones. Now I'm stale. What am I supposed to do—pretend I don't know her anymore?"

He obviously didn't know about Andrew. Diana had left her new crush out of the break-up equation. John couldn't decide whether that was a cowardly or kind move on his sister's part. "Have you talked to Diana about all this?"

"I want you to talk to her about it. You can tell her how unreasonable she's being."

"I'm not sure she'd listen to me."

"Well, I can't talk to her. She's avoiding me. She won't return my calls, and she didn't come to the ward social. I waited for her in the parking lot of the resort today. She said she was in too much of a hurry to talk to me, so I asked her if I could talk to her after work tomorrow. Get this, she said she couldn't because she's going mountain biking and canoeing. Since when has she liked to do either one of those? I mean, this is the girl who wouldn't ride the

Ferris wheel at the state fair because it was too scary, but she's going to plunge down a mountainside on a bike? I tell you, it's some sort of midlife crisis."

It was Andrew. "She's taking a tour from the Tour Store?"

"Yeah, I think that's what Diana said. She and another girl at the front desk."

Ellie. He should have known. Ellie would be there tomorrow, cupid on wheels, doing all in her power to bring Andrew and Diana together.

Well, two could play the manipulating game. John rubbed his hands together. "Do you know how to ride a bike, Chris?"

"Of course I do."

"Ever go mountain biking?"

"A long time ago."

"Well, it's time to go again. Diana wants fresh and exciting and you're going to show her you can be both."

"You think I should barge in on her biking tour?"

"You're not going to barge. You're going as my guest."

CHAPTER 16

The shift at the resort dragged on. This was mostly because every half hour Diana asked what time it was, whether her hair and makeup still looked okay, or what would happen if she did something to make a fool of herself, like crash her bike.

"Well, if you end up crashing, swoon about so Andrew has to carry you down the mountainside."

"Do you think he would?"

"I have no idea."

"With my luck he'd just call the paramedics, then they'd come and take me to the emergency room, where my brother would set all of my bones without anesthesia while lecturing me on what a fool I was."

"Better not risk it; stay firmly on your bike."

"Does my hair look all right?"

When 3:00 came Diana was beside herself with nervousness. She went into the lobby restroom and, taking three times as long as it actually takes to change clothes, switched from her Pine Top Resort uniform into some khaki shorts and a T-shirt. Ellie took considerably less care as to her appearance. She threw on faded jean shorts and a bright pink T-shirt then pulled her hair into a ponytail. When she emerged from the restroom she saw Andrew walking toward the front desk with a smile.

Diana returned his smile. "Hey, Bikerboy, I guess I finally get to see you in action. Are you going to turn on the charm like you do for the little old ladies, or is charm an extra fee?"

"No use trying to charm you," he said. "You know the real me."

"I'm not sure about that. But maybe I'd like to."

It was the perfect let's-be-more-than-friends line, and as Ellie walked up she held her breath waiting for Andrew's response.

He raised both eyebrows, said, "Oh?" then laughed.

A casual response. One that didn't show anything, and yet Ellie could see it in his eyes—she could see a flicker of calculation. He knew. He knew Diana was interested in him now, and his response today would mean everything.

Andrew glanced in Ellie's direction. "You ready for your big adventure?"

"I think so."

"Are the others here yet?"

"Others?" Diana asked.

Just then the resort door swung open and John walked in with a younger man. The stranger was tall and lanky and somehow gave the appearance that his jeans and T-shirt had been ironed before he put them on.

"Chris," Diana said with a stiff smile. "What are you doing here?"

"I invited him," John said. "I figured if I was going to make the trip I'd better do it with someone who wasn't afraid to take his feet off the brakes. You two women will probably still be halfway up the mountain, puttering down the trail, when Chris and I reach the bottom."

"You're making the trip?" Diana said.

"Sure. I've wanted to go mountain biking for a long time, so I called Andrew, and he mentioned you had already set up a time with him. It only seemed natural that we all go together. Sorry I didn't tell you before now. I guess it slipped my mind."

Diana continued to look at her brother with the same fixed smile on her face, but her hand gripped her purse so tight that her knuckles turned white.

"Well, I guess we're ready to start then," Andrew said, as he handed them each two waivers. "You can sign these in the van. The Smiths are already there waiting."

The group walked to the van without speaking. In the front seat were the driver and a guy who, judging from his tight black biking shorts and Tour Store T-shirt, was another tour guide. The driver looked considerably less athletic. His stomach protruded out almost to his knees, and his meaty arms lay casually against the steering wheel.

Andrew introduced the other guide as Kevin and the driver as Mr. O'Brien. He was there to drive them up the mountainside, and, as he added cryptically, to pick up any pieces of them that fell off during the ride down.

An older couple sat in the back of the van, both tan, wrinkly, and dressed in matching Lycra exercise pants. They waved at the newcomers, then turned their attention to checking over supplies of bottled water and suntan lotion.

As Andrew sat in a seat, Diana plunked down next to him. Chris sat on the other side of Diana, which left John and Ellie to share the only other available bench seat.

She sat next to the window, and he sat beside her, tucking a backpack underneath the seat.

She hadn't brought anything on this venture but her wallet, and he'd thought of a whole backpack of things to bring?

"Let me guess," she said. "A first-aid kit?"

"Nope. I'm sure they have one of those on the van. It's sunscreen, sunglasses, powerbars, bottled water, and a book."

"You're going to read while you ride your bike?"

"No, I'm going to read while I wait for the rest of you at the bottom. I've seen Diana on a bike, and she couldn't go fast if she were falling off a cliff."

"You think she's going to ride her brakes the whole way?"

"The girl didn't get her training wheels off her bike until she was eight-and-a-half, and that's only because I took them off and hid them."

Diana leaned over the back of the seat. "Are you talking about me?"

"No, I'm just telling Ellie what's in my backpack." He stretched out and flicked Diana's hair.

"He was telling me how slow you are," Ellie said.

"And you should see how the girl skis. She snowplows down the entire mountain."

"I do not." Diana leaned back in her own seat and turned to Andrew. "I love to ski. I just haven't ever figured out how to do moguls. Do you know how to do those?"

"I can give you a few pointers next season."

"Great." She smiled at him. "That would be wonderful."

"I tried to get you to do moguls," Chris said. "You never wanted to do them last season."

"Now I do."

"I bet after a few times of eating snow, you'll be back to cross country again," John said.

Diana lifted her chin. "Eating a little snow never hurt anyone. You've got to take risks. You've got to embrace your fear if you want to live a full life. Don't you think so, Andrew?"

Ellie didn't hear his response. John leaned close to Ellie and in a low voice said, "This is your doing, isn't it?"

"What?"

"A few days with you and suddenly the girl who wouldn't take off her training wheels is espousing the benefits of eating snow."

"I've just given her a little encouragement."

"Encouragement? You set up this whole trip, didn't you? You just couldn't leave her love life alone. You had to manipulate things."

"Me?" Ellie's voice dropped to a whisper and she leaned closer to him. "You're trying to commandeer this trip just like you commandeered my phone conversation. You're the one who brought her ex along."

"That's not manipulation. That's wisdom in action."

"Manipulator."

He was so close to her that their faces were almost touching. "I have wisdom, and you have stupid theories on embracing your fear and eating snow. You don't know what you're doing."

She smiled at the challenge. "Yeah, well I don't need wisdom. I have feminine charm, and that's been controlling relationships since Eve batted her eyelashes at Adam and said, 'Hungry, Dear?' "

Diana leaned forward in her seat again. "What are you guys whispering about up there?"

"Nothing," John said. "We're just discussing the Garden of Eden and who the snake was."

After that neither of them spoke. John pulled his book out of his backpack, and Ellie wasn't about to try and talk with him while he was reading. In fact, she didn't want to talk to him at all. She turned and stared out the window while listening to Diana chatter to Andrew.

The pine trees grew thicker up here, crowding the road, making it impossible to see past the next bend. Patches of blue sky appeared and disappeared overhead like an ever-changing jigsaw puzzle.

At last the driver pulled over onto a pine-needle–covered dirt patch by the side of the road. Andrew left his seat and walked to the van door. "This is where the fun begins. Put on your helmets while I get the bikes down."

One by one the passengers spilled out of the van, stretching while they strapped their helmets on. Andrew hefted the bikes down from the rack on top of the roof, and Diana watched him, absorbed as the muscles in his arms flexed.

Ellie wasn't sure whether it was cute or pathetic that Diana was so mesmerized by him.

John walked up to Ellie, snapping his chin strap in place. "You've got your helmet on wrong."

She reached up and felt the helmet on her head, patting at its ridges to make sure it was facing the right direction. "It's on the right way, isn't it?"

"It's facing the right direction but it's too loose. It wouldn't stay put in an accident." He stepped closer, fiddling with her strap.

What should she do with her hands? If she put them in front of her, she'd touch him. She put them on her hips and tilted her face up toward him to make it easier for him to see the strap. A scant few inches separated their faces. His fingers were brushing the skin under her chin.

He was flirting with her, wasn't he? This meant something, and she shouldn't allow it. She should show him he couldn't keep interfering with her life and then expect it to be all right if he flirted with her. Instead she leaned closer to him.

He finished fiddling with the strap and rebuckled the helmet. "There. That should keep you safe." Then he turned to walk away.

Well, she sure showed him.

Ellie rubbed her neck, feeling the place his finger had just left. It was definitely pathetic that she was so mesmerized by him.

* * *

Before the group started the downward descent, Andrew stood in front of them and lectured them on safety. Gone were his quick smile and offhand jokes. He was as serious as a professor here, telling them to stay in the bike lane, to give fair and clear warning if they needed to pass someone, and to look behind them before they crossed into traffic. "I'll be leading the way so no one gets lost. Kevin will follow the group to make sure no one has any problems. Everybody ready?"

Andrew pedaled off, and John went next. No point in waiting for Diana or Chris. Despite all of her talk, Diana would be the last one down the mountain. Chris would ride close to her, and Ellie would most likely stay by her, too. The Smiths would ride somewhere in the middle.

Andrew looked over his shoulder to check on the group, casually keeping one hand on the handle bars. "Don't worry about keeping up with me," he called back. "Go at your own pace."

As if he couldn't keep up with Andrew.

John released his grip on the handle bars, easing up on the brakes. His bike rushed forward, dashing by trees and bushes. The wind felt good against his skin, made him feel alive. He gulped in big breaths of air as if he were eating it.

How long had it been since he'd done something like this?

Too long.

He glided down the mountainside, taking in the vibrant green of the trees as though he hadn't seen them before. The bike made a whirring sound that almost drowned out the chirping of the birds.

He didn't seem to be traveling as fast now, even though he knew he was. This is when accidents happen, he told himself. Don't get too comfortable with this speed, because if you fall now it won't be snow you're eating. Still, he didn't slow down, didn't let Andrew gain any ground on him.

That would be his goal for this trip. Keep next to Andrew so Diana couldn't be alone with him. It was easy enough now but might get tricky during the canoe ride.

Ellie had already said she'd pit her feminine charm against his wisdom. But then, she didn't realize how much wisdom she was up against.

He'd find a way around her.

CHAPTER 17

An hour later, Andrew stopped at a parking lot at the bottom of the mountain, rested his bike against a tree in full view of the road, and motioned John to come over. John knew where they were. It was an entrance to a picnic area and dock that boaters used to sail on the lake.

Andrew continued to wait in full view of the road, ready to motion the next biker over. It wouldn't take the rest long to get here.

John dismounted from his bike, took off his helmet, and ran a hand through his matted hair. He hadn't planned on saying anything to Andrew about Suzanne. Legally, ethically, he couldn't. Doctors were only supposed to know things about personal lives when they were on the clock. Anything else wasn't their business.

But the scene in the library was still fresh in his mind. Suzanne shaking, crying. The words, "There is no solution," tumbling from her lips. He was supposed to help people, wasn't he? Wasn't that the whole point of being a doctor?

Besides, there was that moment on the top of the mountain when he'd seen Andrew give Diana the once-over. She had been awkwardly getting on her bike and Andrew had watched her, running his gaze over every inch of her, stopping where his eyes had no business stopping.

Andrew took a water bottle from the side of his bike, opened it, and took a gulp. The water trickled down his chin and he wiped it away with the back of his hand, then nodded at John.

"Do you need some water? We have cold bottles over there on the picnic table."

"That's okay. I still have some left." John pulled a bottle from his backpack and twisted off the lid. Tilting the bottle quickly, he let water slide down his throat, quenching his thirst. He might have only one opportunity to talk to Andrew alone. He twisted the lid back on, closing his water bottle. "It will probably be a while until we see Diana. I think she's taking it slow so she can talk to Chris."

Andrew nodded.

"You know how it is when you break up with someone. There are still things left to say. Things to discuss." John nonchalantly waved his bottle in Andrew's direction. "But you probably know about that. It hasn't been that long since you broke up with your girlfriend."

Andrew's head cocked. "How did you know I broke up with my girlfriend?"

"Diana told me." It was probably the wrong thing to say. It

implied that Diana cared enough to discuss Andrew's dating status with her brother. "Besides, I used to see the two of you around town. Pretty girl. Long brown hair. Big smile."

"Yeah, that's Suzanne."

"She seems nice."

"She is." Andrew took another drink of water, finishing off the bottle.

"Have you talked to her recently?"

"Not really. Why?"

John shrugged. "I just think it's a good thing to do. Like Diana and Chris. Clear the air."

"I don't think Suzanne wants to clear any air with me."

John waited for Andrew to say something more, but he didn't. John tried to draw him out. "She was mad at you when you broke up?"

"She was mad at me before we broke up."

"Oh. A fight."

Andrew took another sip of water then screwed the lid back on his bottle. "No. She was just mad. That was the problem. I couldn't do anything right. When that happens in a relationship, you know it's time to move on."

That was it? That's why he'd dumped Suzanne? The girl was pregnant at the time. She had a truckload of hormones running through her system, of course she was emotional

How did he explain this to Andrew without saying too much? John fingered his water bottle, moving it from one hand to the other. "Do you have any sisters?"

"No."

"I have three of them. Diana's the youngest but there are two others between us, so I know what women can be like. Sometimes, in some situations, they get very emotional. Very hormonal. It doesn't matter what you do, you won't be able to do it right. Do you understand what I'm saying?"

Andrew's brows furrowed together. "Diana has PMS?"

"No." And then because it might keep him away from his sister: "Yes. Yes, she can get real moody at times. Just awful."

"Bummer. Don't they make medication for that?"

"Yes, but try and tell a hormonal woman she needs medication."

Andrew nodded. "I see what you mean. Thanks for the warning."

This was not going in the direction he wanted. "Actually, what I meant was that you really ought to talk to Suzanne because for all you know she might just have been having one of those times before you broke up. She might feel differently now."

Andrew didn't answer. The Smiths had turned the last bend and were gliding towards them, breathless and laughing. Andrew stepped out in the street and waved at them. They guided their bikes to the parking lot, chatting as they dismounted, both talking at once about how much fun they'd had. Diana, Chris, and Ellie joined the group a few minutes later, and then the van pulled in. John hadn't had nearly enough time to talk to Andrew, but he hoped it was enough.

* * *

While Kevin passed out life preservers and Andrew gave the safety lecture, Ellie eyed the canoes.

Three boats and eight people. That meant two boats would

carry three people and one boat would launch with two people. How would the guides split them up? Would they get to chose their own canoes?

Diana chomped down on a piece of apple from the cooler of snacks the Tour Store had provided, but her gaze was also on the boats. Ellie knew what she was thinking.

She knew because Chris had stuck to Diana the entire way down the mountain, making one-sided conversation to her, trying to—what?—wear down her insistence that they no longer had a relationship?

"Nice weather we're having today. Do you remember that weather we had when we went to my little brother's last soccer game? The wind blew so hard the kids could barely kick the ball into the goal. The thing kept flying off like one of those nannies on the Mary Poppins video. Mary Poppins. Hey, that would be a good Halloween costume, don't you think? You could dress up as one of those nannies and carry around an umbrella that was bent backwards. I bet all the kids would laugh. Well, the ones who got it, anyway."

He was just chatting with no apparent purpose. Ellie hadn't known whether to feel sorry for him or whether to try and slash his tires.

When they all dismounted from their bikes in the picnic area, Diana took Ellie aside and whispered, "You have to help me."

"How?"

"I don't know, but Chris is ruining everything. He's acting like we're still a couple, and Andrew is bound to think we are."

Ellie shrugged. "What do you want me to do? Make a pass at Chris?"

"No, just . . . I don't know."

Well, now as Ellie looked at the boats, she knew.

Andrew finished his lecture, and everyone strapped on their life preservers as they walked to the dock. Ellie held hers in her hand so she could walk faster. She sidled up next to Andrew, smiling. "Diana and I want to go together in a boat, but we're going to need someone with us who's strong enough to actually row. Will you be in our boat?"

"Sure. That'll work. We'll put the Smiths and Kevin in the first boat, John and Chris can handle the second, and I'll go with you in the third."

As John walked along the dock beside them, Ellie couldn't help herself. She sent him a triumphant smile.

He glared back at her.

Diana finished strapping on her preserver and stepped into a boat.

"I'd better sit in the stern," Andrew told her. "That way I'll be able to steer better. He walked around her and as he did the boat swayed in the water. She giggled as he passed and held onto one of his arms for balance.

Ellie stepped into the boat and slid her preserver around her neck. While Andrew and Diana seated themselves, she remained standing. "You know, actually, I need to talk to John about my aunt. Maybe I should go in his boat."

She stepped from the boat back onto the dock, then walked

over to John and Chris's boat. "You don't mind if I come with you, do you?"

John stood, and the boat swayed. The side clunked into the dock. "Don't mind at all. You can have my seat."

She stepped down into their boat, went past Chris, and switched places with John. She was about to sit down when John spoke. "Of course, I can't discuss your aunt's medical conditions with Chris here. Chris, why don't you go with Diana and Andrew?"

Chris stood without another word.

Ellie leaned forward, waving a hand to get his attention. "Wait, you don't have to leave. I didn't mean I wanted to speak to him as a *doctor*. I just wanted to speak to him as a . . . um . . . home teacher."

Chris hesitated at the end of the boat. It was clear he wanted to go but wasn't sure if he still had a mandate.

"Home teachers should also keep their conversations private," John said, and Chris nearly leapt from the boat onto the dock.

Ellie stood. "Maybe this wasn't such a good idea. I don't want to chase Chris away. I didn't mean to be rude."

She took two steps toward the end of the boat but John stood and wouldn't let her pass. "You weren't being rude. Chris doesn't mind."

"I don't mind," Chris agreed as he headed toward Diana's boat.

"No, really." Ellie waved one hand in Chris's direction. "I've changed my mind." When she tried to step around John, he moved to block her. She stepped the other way and almost made it around him. Almost. The boat rocked on its side, and for a moment they both stood waving their arms to try and regain balance. But only for a moment. The boat tilted, slid out from underneath them, and dumped both of them into the water.

The lake engulfed Ellie with a sting of cold. She was able to gasp in a breath of air before she went under. The water was unexpectedly deep here at the dock, and she couldn't see the bottom of the lake, only the tendrils of long, slimy plants growing upward. They brushed against her arms and legs, seeming to grasp onto her. A stream of sunlight lightened the murky green water above her, and she swam towards it, her feet feeling heavy and awkward because of her tennis shoes. If she kicked them off, she'd lose them. She left them on.

John was already at the surface, treading water. She could see him twisting in the lake, looking for something. Probably her. She could also see an orange object floating in the water nearby. Her life preserver. She hadn't fastened it, and it had popped off as soon as she hit the water.

She pushed her way through the surface of the water with a gasp.

"There she is!" Diana called.

They were all hovering at the sides of their boats except for Andrew and Kevin, who were on the dock, their shoes already off. They had been about to come in looking for her.

Ellie wiped the hair out of her face as she swam for the dock. "I wasn't under for that long."

"You didn't have your life preserver on," John said. "And none of us knew if you could swim."

"Well, I can." She reached the dock and held her hand up to

Andrew. He heaved her onto the dock. The lake water had been cold, and now the evening air felt even colder. She stood on the deck with her arms wrapped around her body, dripping water and shivering.

Andrew held down his hand to help John up. "We've got towels in the van. I'll get you some."

Ellie didn't want to wait for Andrew to come back. She followed after him, and John followed after her. Each step felt squishy and slimy as she walked. Lakes were full of decaying plants. Bugs. Fish poop. Now that lovely concoction had soaked into her shoes.

She should have kicked them off while she was in the lake. After this she wasn't going to bother keeping them anyway. It was all she could stand to walk in them now.

Ellie hurried as quickly as she could to the van. The driver sat in the front seat reading *Sports Illustrated* but looked up when Andrew opened the side door. "Well, I see we've already had a mishap."

John held the front of his shirt away from his body and rung out water. "Ellie tipped the boat over."

"*I* tipped it over? *You* were the one who wouldn't let me pass."

"Yeah, and a normal person would sit down, not tip the boat over. And while we're discussing it, a normal person would have buckled on her life preserver instead of draping it around her neck like a feather boa. You worried the rest of us to death."

Andrew handed each of them a towel. Ellie wrapped hers around her shoulders. It didn't keep her from shivering. "I wouldn't have gotten in the boat without my life preserver buckled on if I didn't know how to swim, and I would have had time to buckle it on if you hadn't refused to let me pass, thus virtually throwing me into the lake."

"Don't tempt me."

Andrew pulled out two blankets from underneath the van seats. "You're still shivering. Why don't you try the blankets?"

Ellie poked a shaking hand out from underneath the towel to grab the blanket. She wrapped it around her tightly. It helped, but she was still numb everywhere her wet clothes clung to her.

Andrew looked back and forth between John and Ellie. "Do you want us to wait for you to dry out so you can come, or do you want to stay here?"

"Don't wait for us," John said.

Ellie nodded.

"I can turn the heat on in the van and let you sit in here," the driver said.

Ellie nodded again, this time climbing into the van. John followed her, stopping to take off his shoes before he did. "That's another pair of my shoes you've ruined. Is it some sort of tradition you have?"

"Don't talk to me about shoes. I think something swam into mine and died there, and it's all your fault, Mr. Wisdom."

The driver turned the ignition then flipped on the heat. "I, uh, better get the food ready for when the others come back. So I'll just, um, leave now."

It was obvious he didn't want to be trapped in the van with them while they fought. Not only was Ellie drenched and shivering, now people were fleeing from her. This was just one more humiliation of the day. And it was John's fault too.

The air coming from the heating vent felt cool against Ellie's skin, and she tightened the blanket against her shoulders. "Why don't we ask the driver to take us home?"

"He's here in case of emergencies. If he took us home and there was some sort of boat crash while he was gone—"

"A boat crash? What are the chances of that happening with two canoes?"

"Well, normally I'd say pretty low, but who knows now that you've convinced Diana to embrace her fear. Anything could happen. She might try to water-ski upside down on the back of her boat." He tugged his blanket tighter around him. "What harebrained scheme are you going to try next? Maybe Andrew could take you sky diving."

"And if we did, we'd be okay because you'd find some way to come along." She changed her voice, inflecting it with melodrama. "Is there a doctor in the house? Why yes, there's one in the house, and at work, and at church, and on the bike ride. You're like some medical version of Sam-I-Am. The only time you're not there to help me is when I ask you to help me, and then you won't help me because you think my aunt is crazy!"

The van fell quiet as she ended her monologue. Seconds passed by with nothing but the heater humming to fill the silence.

"She's not crazy," Ellie said.

More silence.

When he spoke it was with the professional calming tone he'd used when she first came into the ER. It was almost as though now that she'd reminded him he was a doctor, he'd fallen back into that role. "I know that's what you think, and I hope you're right. I don't want anything to be wrong with your aunt. I don't want her to have to go to a nursing home. Do you believe that?"

She took her now-soaked towel from underneath the blanket and laid it on the seat next to her. "Yes."

"Are you willing to believe a doctor might know more about a patient's health than the patient?"

"Are you willing to believe a doctor might know less?"

He sighed and ran a hand through his hair. "You're determined to make me out as the bad guy, aren't you?"

She didn't answer. It was probably a rhetorical question.

Silence again. The air from the heater was finally warming the car. She let the blanket slide from her shoulders and looked out of the window. In the distance she could see the lake but no sign of the boats.

John leaned over to her. "Some of your feminine charm is running down your cheeks." He picked up her towel from off the seat and wiped her face with the edge of it. The towel was soft against her skin, almost as soft as his fingers.

He was close enough she could have easily reached out and touched him, run her fingers across his cheek the same way he was caressing hers.

He leaned back. "There. Now you're as charming as ever."

"Right. I'm wet, makeup-less, and have whatever was growing in that lake saturated into my hair." She lifted her chin and smiled despite herself. "Or was that your point all along? I'm as charming as something that smells like fish?"

He smiled, his eyes softer than they'd been before. "You try to find things to argue with me about, don't you?"

With that one phrase, with that one note of teasing, the space between them seemed very small. They were here. Together. Alone. How long would it be until the others came back?

She pulled the blanket around her again.

"Are you still cold?" he asked.

"No."

He let his blanket sag onto the seat and leaned forward with his elbows on his knees. Why had she thought his eyes were soft before? They weren't that way at all. They were dark and intense, and just like Bertie had told her—smoldering. "So do you distrust all doctors or is it just me?"

"I don't—" I don't distrust doctors, she almost said, and then wondered if it was the truth. Did she? Her mind was drawn back to the Sunshine Villa, back to a heavyset, balding doctor whose name she could no longer remember. He'd cared for Grandpa Baxter and then Grandma Baxter when it was her turn. As a child she'd been suspicious of his medical skills. How was it that he could be a real doctor, yet not be able to help either of her grandparents? He didn't even seem to try. She saw it in the brisk way he came into the room. The way he looked at her parents instead of her grandparents when he spoke.

And then most egregious of all, he'd predicted the amount of time her grandparents had left, to the month, and been right both times.

There was something wrong about that. Only God was supposed to know how much time a person had left.

Almost before Ellie realized what she was doing, she told John about the doctor, her grandparents, and the Sunshine Villa. She wasn't sure what she hoped to accomplish. It wouldn't change his mind about Bertie. Still she told him everything, right down to the smell of sterilized decay that permeated the hallways, and how even all these years later she felt a cold, sick ball form in her stomach when she drove by any nursing home.

He listened without criticizing and didn't contradict her once, not even to point out that it wasn't the doctor's fault that both her grandparents had contracted Alzheimer's.

When she was done he reached over and put one hand on her knee. His voice was low, a gentle hum like the heater. "I'm sorry, Ellie. I know it's awful to see someone go like that and be powerless to do anything to help."

"You're sorry? Why wasn't our doctor sorry?"

"He probably was. Death, for doctors, is an inevitable failure. We see too much of it, are constantly reminded of it. If we had to think of what it meant, the sorrow foisted on each family, we'd all be broken before we got out of med school. It helps to have the gospel perspective. It helps to know that angels are waiting to receive each person that passes out of this life, but it isn't much comfort for the loneliness that the loved ones inherit. For the years left to walk alone." He dropped his hand from her knee, but it was still beside her on the seat. A strong hand. She wanted to reach out and put her hand on top of it, to intertwine her fingers with his.

"Diana was just a baby when our father died. I was fifteen. I've never really been certain whether I was the lucky one because I knew him, or whether Diana was lucky because she never realized what she lost."

A tightness crept into his lips and he clenched and unclenched the hand beside her.

Here Ellie had been complaining about the trauma of losing her grandparents when he'd lost his father at fifteen. So young to suddenly become an adult. "I'm sorry, John. It must have been devastating. Especially being the oldest."

"I learned how to feed, change, and put a baby to sleep awfully fast. When I got home from school I put Diana in one of those baby backpacks and lugged her around while my mother made dinner, helped the other kids with their homework, and did the things she needed to do at the resort. Until I left on my mission, Diana probably thought I was her father. I guess I've always thought it myself."

"That's sweet."

He raised an eyebrow. "You didn't think it was so sweet when I was trying to keep Andrew away from her."

"Poor Andrew. You must think a guy needs references from angels to date Diana."

"It would help." The humor left his voice. His brows drew together, and she knew he was no longer in the van. Not really. His thoughts were far away. Probably somewhere in the past, in a timeline where instead of having a father he had to be one.

She reached out and laid her hand on his arm. His skin still felt chilled from his wet shirt. "I'm really sorry, John."

"It's fine."

It wasn't. It couldn't be. He had missed so many things growing up. She wished she could comfort him, could show him she cared.

She wanted to let her hand slide down his arm, to take his hand in hers.

It was Kirk all over.

Except that suddenly she didn't care about Kirk. He was far away, a memory it seemed, from a long time ago.

And John was sitting next to her. His strength of character seemed to overshadow everything and everyone else.

I'm in love, she realized, I'm in love and sitting alone with John in the van. If I don't do anything about it, he'll never know how I feel.

Seconds ticked by.

She took a breath and let her hand slide down his arm and then wound her fingers together with his. His hand felt strong and callused, and she wondered how a doctor managed to get calluses on his hands. Maybe she would ask him. She wanted to find out everything there was to know about him. But then again, she didn't really want to talk right now. She wanted him to hold her close, to bend down and kiss her, to—

He pulled his hand away from her and ran it through his hair, then leaned against the door and away from her. He looked out the window. "I wonder how long the others will be?"

She couldn't answer, couldn't think to speak for several moments. She felt as though she'd been dunked in chilly water a second time.

How could she have been so stupid as to touch him? He wasn't interested in her, far from it. He'd made that perfectly clear in the library. Why had she forgotten it?

She scooted farther away from him on the seat, embarrassment battling with anger.

She hadn't spurned him when he'd put his hand on her knee. Why had he given her the brush-off when she'd touched him? Did he really find her so repulsive?

"I have no idea how long the others will be. I suppose that all depends on how fast Diana can row."

He pulled his gaze from the window and looked at her, no, not at her—through her. "There were six of us children. It was hard on my mother to have so many to take care of, but the opposite would have been just as hard—if she hadn't had any children at all. You just never know what trials life is going to throw at you."

"I suppose not." Ellie leaned against her side of the van, away from him. Why was he bringing this up now?

"What would happen if you couldn't have children?" he asked.

"I guess I'd have a clean house."

"I'm being serious."

"Oh, well seriously then, I'd probably still have a dirty house. I just wouldn't be able to blame it on my children."

"Are you saying you don't care if you can have children or not?"

"No, of course I care. I was just joking." He didn't say anything and so she added, "I want lots of children. I'd be devastated if I couldn't have any."

"Then why joke about it?"

"Because whether I joke about it or not won't change the future, and I might as well have a sense of humor, don't you think?"

Again he said nothing.

"Besides, maybe I would get a really neat niece who was as good as a daughter. That worked for Bertie."

Still nothing. Not only had he rebuffed her, now he wasn't even going to attempt to make polite conversation. There would be long awkward pauses until the others returned. Great.

She looked out the window and saw the driver walking toward the van. He opened the door but didn't get in. "The food is set up at the picnic table if you're hungry. The others should be back any minute, but I thought you might want a head start."

John and Ellie climbed out of the van, walked slowly to the picnic table, and made submarine sandwiches. She wasn't sure if he even once glanced at her. She refused to look at him.

They finished eating in silence until the others came back from the lake.

Diana didn't say much while she made her sandwich, but as she ate, she and Ellie drifted off toward the van by themselves.

"The whole thing has been awful," Diana muttered. "Chris kept asking me things. Did I want a drink? Did I need more sunscreen? Did I see that fish that went by? What kind of fish did I think that was? Did I still hate to fish? I couldn't say two sentences to Andrew. So then Chris asked me if I needed a rest from paddling, and I just snapped at him. I told him I was perfectly capable of handling the paddles, that I didn't need his help, and if he asked me one more question I'd scream. Chris looked at me like I'd suddenly grown fangs, and Andrew leaned over and said, 'You know, they make medication for your hormonal times. Your brother just told me about it. I'm sure he could prescribe you something.'" Diana gripped her sandwich so hard, mustard squeezed out one end. "This is all John's fault. I'll never forgive him for today."

That made two of them.

Chapter 18

John still wasn't completely dry when he got home. He peeled off his clothes and stood in the shower, letting the hot water pelt his skin. He'd achieved his goal of keeping Diana away from Andrew. On the drive back they'd barely spoken to each other. Diana had sat next to Ellie and the two of them had ignored everyone else. Especially him.

Well, it was okay if Diana was mad at him. One day she'd realize that Andrew wasn't right for her and then she'd thank him. And as for Ellie . . . well, maybe it was for the best that she was angry at him too. Anger would keep her at a distance, and that's where she needed to stay.

He could still feel her hand on his arm, her fingertips sliding down his skin until her hand rested on his. It would have been so easy for him to have returned her caress, to pull her closer to him. Too easy. That was just the sort of impulsive thing he needed to avoid.

So he was attracted to Ellie. He'd once been attracted to Valerie.

He needed to think about love logically. For one thing, he didn't know enough about Ellie to guarantee she would do well in a long-term relationship. Second, even if he had wanted a relationship with her, by the time he started to figure her out, she'd be leaving. She was only here for the summer.

So anything between them was impossible, and he was going to stop thinking about her hand running down his arm. And the way her eyes shone when she spoke of sad things. And how her clothes clung to her when they were wet.

He turned off the shower and grabbed a towel. He should have felt tired; instead he felt restless. He would fill up the rest of the night working on some of the never-ending home improvements he'd signed up for when he bought a forty-year-old house.

In retrospect, the house had been a mistake, but when he first moved to Colton he liked the idea of redoing floors and cabinets. He had wanted something to keep him occupied. Something to rip up, tear down, and then rebuild. Now months later he found himself surrounded by a half-finished kitchen and laundry room, a never-ending list of landscaping, and a church calling that took all his free time.

Tonight, though, he would wield a hammer like Thor in judgment.

He'd been meaning to put cabinets in the laundry room and—Dang. He'd gone over to Bertie's house to get the sander and then forgotten to get it.

Now he'd have to go back there again, and when he did, Bertie would take one look at him and order the wedding invitations. Of all the people in town, Bertie seemed to be the most insistent that he and Ellie were a couple, which was odd because she lived with Ellie and should know better.

He stopped toweling himself and let this thought sink in. Bertie should know better. She shouldn't think they were a couple at all.

Okay. So they had been standing close together last Monday, and perhaps their struggling over the phone on Tuesday could be interpreted in romantic terms. Perhaps Bertie had even caught him once or twice looking at Ellie in, well, an admiring sort of way. But to be so convinced they were a couple when he'd never even asked Ellie out on a date—a normal person wouldn't think that way, would she? A normal person wouldn't tell everyone in town they were a couple.

Was Ellie somehow encouraging Bertie's fantasies?

Nah.

Even that moment today had only been brought on by Ellie's sympathy. She wouldn't have reached over and touched his arm if he hadn't just been telling her about his father.

But there had been that business about Ellie pretending to expect a call from him so her aunt wouldn't know she was getting a call from Dr. Blair. Had Ellie done other things like that—using their supposed romance as a way to manipulate Bertie?

Or perhaps Bertie's ideas stemmed from something more serious. Could it be another symptom of psychosis? During his residency he'd seen many patients with delusions. The CIA was having them followed. The President was really an alien. Animals spoke to them.

Schizophrenia. Porphyria. Alzheimer's.

He let out a slow sigh. Please don't let it be that. For Bertie's sake, don't let it be that. Let it be that Ellie wasn't honest with her. That would be so much easier to treat.

Now that he was worrying about it, he'd have to bring the subject up with Ellie the next time he saw her, and that was a conversation he wasn't looking forward to.

* * *

The next morning while Ellie got dressed for work, she heard a thump in Bertie's room.

"Ellie . . ." came Bertie's voice. "Ellie!"

Ellie sprinted to Bertie's room, nearly pummeling into the plastic Santa on the way. Inside, Ellie found her aunt on her back, her arms and legs splayed as if she were trying to make a snow angel on the carpet.

"Bertie! What happened?" Ellie knelt down beside her aunt, tugging on her arm to help her sit up.

"I fell. My legs just went out from underneath me. I was walking to my dresser and I fell."

"Did you hurt anything?"

"I think so. My leg is throbbing. You'd better take me to the doctor."

"All right." Ellie wiped her hands on her pants, looking around the room as she gathered her thoughts.

She'd have to call the resort and tell them she couldn't come in today. But there wasn't time for that now. She'd call once they reached the doctor's office.

Ellie put her arm around her aunt's waist. "If I help you, do you think you can make it to the car?"

Bertie nodded, and with a bit of tugging Ellie was able to pull her to her feet.

Two falls in as many weeks. Ellie could almost hear her mother—the ominous tone of her voice repeating the words, "She's started falling." Now her mother had all the proof she needed, and it wouldn't matter what sort of doctors Ellie dug up to vouch for Bertie's health.

They wouldn't listen to Ellie's opinion after two falls.

So Ellie just wouldn't tell them. They didn't need to know. Anyone could fall twice in two weeks. It was just bad luck. Ellie had probably done it herself, only she was young and strong, so she hadn't hurt herself.

Ellie would just make sure Bertie went to see a foot and ankle specialist, someone who could pinpoint the problem, and make sure Bertie did whatever it took to fully recover. That's all Bertie needed. Time to recover.

Ellie managed to help Bertie out of her room and down the hallway. She paused by the coat closet. "Let me get our purses. Where is Dr. Blair's office?"

"Not Dr. Blair. I won't go to him anymore. Take me to the ER. I want to see Dr. Flynn."

"Dr. Flynn?" Ellie's gaze shot back to her aunt. "You're not faking this just so I'll see John again, are you?"

"I'm most certainly not. If I was going to fake a medical

problem, I would have picked something less painful than throwing myself on the floor. A stomachache, perhaps. As it is, I'm probably bruised all over." She pulled her pink muumuu above her knees to check her legs. "No bruises yet but—oh my heavens, look how my legs have swollen up! Oh wait, that's just weight gain. I remember that now. You see, I'm not forgetting things." She held onto Ellie's arm and took lumbering steps to the door. "Detroit, Michigan. Rupertsville, Alabama."

"Rupertsville isn't the capital of anything, Aunt Bertie."

"I know that. I'm just not planning to go to Alabama either."

They walked across the porch and down the stairs to the carport, Ellie shouldering as much of Bertie's weight as she could. "Shouldn't you see Dr. Blair about this? He's your regular doctor. Perhaps he could recommend a podiatrist."

"He's not my regular doctor anymore. I've fired him. He thinks I need a neurological exam. I want to see John."

"Isn't there anyone else you could see besides Dr. Flynn?"

"I know you two are fighting, but this is an emergency and for emergencies you go to the emergency room. You'll just have to put your feelings aside for the day."

As if Ellie's feelings were nothing more than clutter that could be tucked somewhere out of sight.

Well, she'd do it. She'd approach John—Dr. Flynn—as professionally as the next patient.

Ten minutes later they were at the ER.

* * *

John counted off the seconds as he held a small laceration together. Ten seconds. That ought to do it. He slowly released his grasp on the boy's forehead, examining the liquid stitches. Beautiful. This was so much easier than suturing a wound. So much less painful for seven-year-olds.

Two brown eyes looked up at him seriously. "Am I going to have a scar?"

"Just a cool one. Probably like Harry Potter."

"Like Harry Potter?" The boy grinned over at his mother. "Just wait until I show Aaron. He's going to want one too."

His mother shook her head at him. "Aaron's mother will be thrilled to hear that."

John helped the boy down from the bed. "Remember, Luke, you're just allowed *one* forehead scar. I don't want to see you in here again."

His mother grunted. "Between the bike, the trampoline, and the skateboard, we're regulars." She moved aside her son's bangs, examining the wound with a sigh.

"I'm gonna look like Harry Potter," he said.

"Yes, and if your scar starts to hurt, it means the jungle gym is after you again."

As they left, Marsha, the shift nurse, stuck her head into the room. "A patient in the waiting room is requesting you. Bertie Goodwin. Do you want to see her?"

"Bertie's here? Yes, I'll take her." Marsha turned to leave but he called her back. "Can you give Roger Blair a ring and tell him she's here? He wanted to talk to her."

"All right." She turned and was almost out of the room before he called her again.

"Marsha, is Bertie's niece with her?"

"Her niece?"

"A young woman. Shoulder-length brown hair."

Marsha nodded and smiled. "Oh yes. I saw her. A pretty girl. She's here too."

Marsha kept smiling.

"I was just curious," he said.

She gave him a wink, and as she left called back, "I'll put them in bed three."

Okay. He wasn't just curious. He wanted to see Ellie again, although he wasn't sure why.

Well, if he thought about it for long enough he probably knew why.

Marsha popped her head back into the room. "They're waiting for you."

He grabbed his clipboard and glanced at the nurse's notes as he walked. *The patient fell and is now complaining of pain in her left leg. Tender to the touch. No swelling. Patient was able to walk assisted across the waiting room.*

Another fall. Didn't appear to be serious. It could be a muscle spasm or an inner ear problem. Then again, it could be a symptom of hydrocephalus.

Or . . . it could be Bertie's next attempt to bring him and Ellie together.

He held the clipboard down at his side. Why did this suddenly seem like the most likely diagnosis?

Well, whatever her reason for being there, he'd use this visit to once again press for a neurological exam.

He opened the partition. Bertie sat propped up in bed while Ellie stood beside her, fussing with the ties on her hospital gown.

"These things are indecent," Bertie said. "I don't care what they say, one size does not fit all."

"Hello, Bertie. I hear you had another fall."

"I was just walking along and the floor came up and smacked me."

"And now your left leg hurts?"

"Throbs."

He walked to the bed and, starting with her lower left leg, felt for any abnormalities. "I'm going to ask you some questions while I examine your leg, and then we'll send you to X ray to make sure nothing is broken."

"All right."

"Can you tell me your address?"

Bertie huffed. "And that's another thing—Why does the hospital keep asking me the same questions? I filled out all the paperwork telling my address and Medicare number when I was here last time. I come in today, and they want to know the same stuff. Don't you people keep your records on a computer? Besides, you know where I live. You were just at my house."

"I'm not asking for directions, Bertie. I'm checking you for head injuries." As he prodded her leg, he moved further down Bertie's side, and Ellie left her place beside Bertie to make room for him. She sat down on the chair by the partition door.

"My head is fine."

"Can you tell me today's date?"

Bertie's eyes narrowed. "That depends. Can you tell me the capital of Georgia?"

"The country or the state?"

Bertie nodded at Ellie. "Oh—he's good. Very smart. Your children will be brilliant."

Ellie blushed and wouldn't look at him.

"Today's date?" he asked again.

"Today is May . . ." Bertie looked over at her niece and John turned in time to see Ellie holding up three fingers on one hand and making the shape of a zero in the other.

"May thirtieth," Bertie said.

"Can you tell me the name of the Relief Society president and her counselors?"

"Well, there's Sister Pike. She's the president and her first counselor is Sister Grossman. No, wait. Sister Grossman is a teacher. There are so many people who stand up every week in Relief Society"—Bertie folded her arms and lowered her head, a double chin suddenly forming above her neck. "I don't have Alzheimer's."

"I didn't say you did."

"My memory is just fine."

"Head injuries are serious business, and you've had two falls in a short time. I want to be certain you don't have any bleeding or leakage of spinal fluid." Or anything else. "I'm going to schedule a CAT scan for you at the hospital in Spokane. Promise me you'll go." He turned to Ellie. "And I want you to promise you'll drive her there. Agreed?"

Bertie humphed again. "I'll try to remember it."

"Ellie will help you remember. Won't you, Ellie?"

"Yes," Ellie said.

"Good. And by the way it's the thirty-first, not the thirtieth."

Ellie rolled her eyes at him.

A smiling technician opened the curtain door. "Are you ready for X rays?"

"She's ready," John said.

The technician took the end of Bertie's bed and rolled it toward the door. "We're going to see how photogenic your bones are."

"I know the capitals of all fifty states," she answered.

Ellie started to follow Bertie, but John reached out and took her arm. "I want to talk to you."

CHAPTER 19

Ellie walked back into the room, decided she wasn't going to look at John, and then realized she had to. There wasn't any place else to look, really.

All right. She'd look at him, but she was not going to find him attractive. She was not going to be mesmerized by those blue eyes and start spouting off unintelligible things. He was just a doctor, and an arrogant one at that. *And by the way, it's the thirty-first, not the thirtieth.*

As if she wouldn't have realized that eventually.

He tapped his thumb against his clipboard. "You're going to drive Bertie to her appointment?"

"I said I would."

"Good."

She turned to leave.

"That's not what I wanted to talk to you about."

She turned back to him.

"It's about the things Bertie keeps saying about us. The 'Won't you have beautiful children' comments. Half the town thinks we're on our way to engagement, and it's beginning to concern me."

He spoke so calmly, so unemotionally, as though this, too, were part of his job. Women, apparently, threw themselves at him at such a constant rate that it no longer fazed him. She was just one of the many unwanted intrusions in his life. Like junk mail. And spam. Gold-digging women trying to trap him into marriage.

"I asked you to tell Bertie that we weren't a couple and you said you'd do it. The fact that she still thinks we're on our way to the altar leads me to one of two conclusions." He tapped his pen against his clipboard. "How do I put this?"

'How' was not the question. 'Where' was a better question.

It was really too humiliating that he was making her stand here and listen to this. How many times did she need to hear that he wasn't interested in her?

She held up one hand to stop the lecture. "Look. I know what you think of me, but you don't need to say it. I'm not interested in marrying you." She meant to say more. She meant to say, "Does that make you feel better? Do you feel safe from my clutches now?" But at the very moment she was forming these words she heard someone clear his throat.

Ellie turned and saw an older man standing behind them. He looked from John to Ellie, his mouth hanging slightly open. "I'm sorry to interrupt. They told me Bertie was in here."

"They just took her for X rays." John held one hand out in Ellie's direction. "This is Bertie's niece, Ellie Baxter. Ellie, this Dr. Blair."

"I'm sorry to interrupt," Dr. Blair repeated. "I'll just wait outside for her."

Ellie forced a smile. "It's all right. We're through talking."

John shot her a dark look. Apparently he wasn't through talking, but she wasn't about to stick around and listen to a detailed list of why he wasn't interested in her.

She smiled at Dr. Blair again, and this time it was easier. "I'm sorry you had to hear that. It's just that John keeps proposing to me at the most inopportune times." She looked back at John. "I hope you'll believe me now when I tell you it will never work out between us."

She didn't wait for his response. She slipped out of the room and walked back to the foyer. Anything else Dr. Flynn had to say about Bertie's condition he could say to Bertie. Ellie was staying as far away from him as possible from now on.

She sat on a vinyl seat, picked up a *Time* magazine, and flipped through the pages without seeing anything that was written on them. Minutes went by. She put down one magazine and picked up another.

John Flynn.

Annoying.

Presumptuous.

And walking right towards her.

What was he doing in the waiting room? Wasn't there some unspoken rule that doctors couldn't pass through the door that separated the treatment rooms from the waiting room?

Every patient in the waiting room looked up. Every patient watched him as he strode over and sat beside Ellie.

He wouldn't have come out here just to yell at her about the scene with Dr. Blair. It must be something about Bertie. He'd found something very wrong and now had come out to tell her.

She clutched the magazine. "What's wrong with Bertie?"

"Nothing. The X rays were fine. The nurse is going over some instructions for taking care of her leg with her, but I need to finish talking to you."

She lowered her voice so the other patients wouldn't hear. "I don't think there's anything left to say on that matter."

"Look, I wasn't trying to offend you. I was just trying to figure out if there was a reason Bertie believes we're a couple. Does she have any other delusions?"

"Yes. She thinks you're a nice guy."

"Ellie, I'm not trying to insult you. I'm trying to understand your aunt's mindset."

"You think the idea of you and me as a couple is delusional."

"I didn't say that."

"You did too."

He took a glance around the room at the other patients and leaned in closer to her. "I'm just saying that the fact your aunt thinks we're a couple with so little evidence is unusual."

"You think you're too good for me, don't you?"

His head snapped back, surprised. "No, of course not."

"Yes, you do, or it wouldn't bother you so much that people think we're a couple. Some men would be flattered, you know."

"This is a medical issue. It has nothing to do with you."

She opened the magazine again and flipped the page with such force she nearly ripped it. "You don't think I'm pretty enough, do you?"

"I happen to think you're gorgeous. That's beside the point."

She stopped flipping pages midway through a turn, and the magazine page fluttered to rest on her lap. "You think I'm gorgeous?"

"We're talking about your aunt, Ellie. Does she have any other unusual views—does she think the FBI has tapped her phones, or that somebody is out to get her?"

"When you say 'gorgeous', exactly what do you mean? Are you one of those men who just throws adjectives around loosely?"

He took her hand and clasped it between his. "Focus for a moment, Ellie. Does Bertie have any other unusual views?"

"No, Bertie doesn't have any delusions."

"Nothing odd comes to mind?"

"No, nothing."

The door to the treatment rooms swung open, and a nurse pushed Bertie in a wheelchair toward them. Dr. Blair trailed behind them. He wore a tired frown, which probably meant his conversation with Bertie hadn't gone well.

"Of course, who really cares what the capital of Arkansas is anyway," Bertie told him. "I'd never go there myself. I might run into Bill Clinton, and you know what a womanizer he is." Bertie put her hand across her chest. "I positively wouldn't feel safe around him. He might try to grope me."

John raised one eyebrow, but Ellie stood up, took the handles of the wheelchair from the nurse, and began pushing it to the door before he could comment. Over her shoulder she called back to him, "It's a perfectly normal opinion. A lot of women feel that way about Bill Clinton."

As soon as Bertie was situated in the car—her muumuu straightened and her seat belt snapped snugly over her hips—she turned to Ellie. "I noticed you and John were sitting very close together talking. Did the two of you make up?"

Ellie put her foot down on the gas, backing the car out of its parking space with a jerk. "There was nothing to make up, because we weren't—well, all right we *were* fighting, but not in the way a couple fights. We were fighting in the way two disinterested people who are not dating fight."

"Then you're saying you didn't make up?"

Ellie wound her way through the parking lot, keeping an eye out for patients walking toward the hospital. "Why do you keep telling people we're a couple? That 'won't your children be brilliant' comment really bothered him."

"I suppose I shouldn't have said that. I forget some men don't like to think of children right off."

"And some men don't like to think of children until they have a wife picked out."

"He'll pick you, Dear. You don't have to worry about that."

Ellie took the turn out of the parking lot too sharply and ran over the end of the curb with one tire. "He won't—I mean, he hasn't even—why are you so certain we're going to get married?"

"Some things you just know. You feel them in your bones."

"I see. And have you ever wondered if the FBI is tapping your phones?"

"Why would they need to, when they have all those surveillance cameras scattered throughout the house?"

Ellie didn't laugh. She sat at a four-way stop while the other cars around her waited. "You're not serious, are you?"

Bertie sighed, heaving her shoulders as she did. "Oh, Ellie, when did you lose your sense of humor?"

And then Ellie felt like an idiot. Of course Bertie had been joking.

The driver behind them honked his horn, and Ellie pulled through the intersection. "Sorry. I'm just worried about you."

"Yes, that's exactly what the doctors told me while urging me to get a CAT scan. I know what they think. They think I've gone senile. Well, I can forgive people who don't know me very well for that—but now *you're* asking me whether I think the FBI has surveillance cameras planted around my house? Honestly, Ellie, of all people, I never thought *you'd* agree with them."

"I don't. Of course I don't. John just got me worried with all of his questions and insisting I drive you to your appointment."

They drove in heavy silence past prim painted houses, pine trees, and children roller-skating on sidewalks.

"I'm not going, you know," Bertie said.

"You promised John you'd get a CAT scan."

"I'm not crazy, and I didn't hit my head. There's no reason for me to go."

"But that's exactly the reason you should go. That way John will have the proof that there's nothing wrong with you, and he'll stop bothering me about it. I mean you. He'll stop bothering you about it."

"Has he been bothering you about taking me in for a CAT scan?"

"Yes." She let out a sigh. It was all out in the open now. "I bet you don't want him for a nephew-in-law now, do you?"

"So if I don't go in for a CAT scan, he'll keep bothering you?"

"Yes." And then she understood. "Oh no you don't. No more of your matchmaking attempts. You're not going to refuse a CAT scan as a way to lure John to me."

"I have many reasons to refuse a CAT scan. Luring John is just one of them."

Ellie pulled up into the driveway and turned off the car. "Get the CAT scan, Aunt Bertie. You said you would."

"Enough of this arguing." Bertie pulled the latch on the door and hefted himself out of the car. "The FBI may have bugged the car and we don't want them listening to our petty squabbles." As she swung the door shut she yelled, "We're going inside now, Officer Birkenstock."

Bertie limped into her room to rest and didn't even come out for lunch, but every once in awhile Ellie heard her in her room, noisily talking to the FBI agents and telling them all her woes.

At 4:00 Ellie's parent's called. They wanted to know why Bertie's doctor hadn't called them.

"Patient-doctor confidentiality rules," Ellie told them. "Apparently they have to have a signed medical release from the patient before they discuss someone's medical condition."

"But we're her only family," her mother said.

"I know. In fact you have no idea how hard I've tried to get her doctor to be reasonable about this. But apparently doctors are an unreasonable bunch."

There was a pause on the line, and then her father's voice. "You said her doctor is also her home teacher?"

"Yes. Right. We painted the porch last Monday. White instead of chartreuse, by the way."

"Then we'll talk to him as her home teacher."

"Um . . ." Um what? Um you can't because he's . . . deaf, insane, died suddenly.

"What's his phone number?"

"I don't know."

"He's the home teacher and you don't know his phone number? Doesn't Bertie have a ward list somewhere?"

"Um . . . I'm sure she does, but I don't know where, and she's resting so I can't ask her. Besides he's at work right now."

Her father's voice sounded tight. "Make sure you get the phone number and then call us."

After she hung up, Ellie made her way into Bertie's room. She should say something to her aunt. Ellie couldn't keep putting her parents off indefinitely. She should break the news to Bertie that her parents were, how would she phrase it—concerned? Worried? Plotting?

Bertie was propped up in bed with a stack of Christmas cards on one side and her address book on the other. One card sat in her lap, but she twirled the pen in her hand instead of writing. Bing Crosby's rendition of "White Christmas" played softly in the background.

"Don't tell me you're actually sending out Christmas cards," Ellie said.

"Apparently I'm not. I can't think of anything to say."

"What will people think if they get a Christmas card from you in June?"

"They'll think I have an incredibly boring life because I can't think of anything to say."

Ellie sat on the edge of Bertie's bed. "You can always lie. That's what you do in your letters to me."

Bertie smiled, but only for a moment. "I wanted my cards to be special this year. I thought if I started now I'd have plenty of time to make each one special." She picked up the card from her lap, looked at the snow-covered scene on the front, then spread it open. "This one will be for your parents. What should we write to make it really memorable?"

Stop trying to kick me out of my house, you conniving bunch of hypocrites.

Well, at least that way it would be memorable.

Ellie shrugged. "They don't pay much attention to cards. Why don't you start with someone else?"

Bertie flipped through her address book, murmuring comments about the names written there, until she at last found someone to write to. And after another minute Ellie left the room without mentioning her parents' phone call at all.

CHAPTER 20

John was getting ready for bed when his mother called.

"John, I wanted to talk to you about something." She sounded breathless, unsure, the way she always sounded when she was worried. Probably Diana was embracing her fear again and wanted to buy a motorcycle and tattoo "Harley Babe" on her forearm.

He sat down on his bed. "What is it?"

"Tonight I ran into Delsa Rohner in the grocery store, and she asked me how I liked Ellie Baxter. Well, people have been asking me that question over the last week, and I always thought it was a little odd that everyone was so concerned about how my new desk clerk was working out, but I told her I thought Ellie was a nice girl. Then she said, 'Yes, she and John make such a lovely couple. Everyone at church thinks so.'"

There was a pause on the line. His mother expected him to either confess or deny the claim. For some reason he didn't feel like doing either.

"Well?" she asked. "Are you a couple?"

"Not necessarily."

"Not necessarily? What does that mean? Why do the people at church think you are?"

"Maybe you should come to church and find out."

He heard her exasperated sigh. "What kind of answer is that?"

"The only one you're going to get from me."

"John—"

"Goodnight, Mom."

He hung up the phone, then finished the business of undressing and putting on his pajamas. He couldn't help his smile. If there was ever a way to convince his mother to show up to church, he'd just stumbled upon it.

* * *

Ellie didn't go to church. She stayed home to take care of Bertie. Bertie grumbled about this, insisting that she was well enough to go. After all, church was mostly just sitting.

"Dr. Flynn told you to rest for a couple of days. Do you want him to know you're ignoring his orders?"

So Bertie consented, retreating to her room to paint. Ellie checked on her several times during the day, but Bertie never let her come very far into the room. She didn't want Ellie to see what she was painting. This was unusual in and of itself; Bertie had never been secretive about her work before, but even more worrisome was the way Bertie's hands shook while she painted. Ellie had never noticed that before. And she had to work very hard to shake the fear that John might be right about Bertie after all.

* * *

On Tuesday during the morning rush, Diana didn't. Rush, that was. She mumbled her hellos, tossed keys, and typed with two fingers. She also sighed and slouched. When the stream of people coming in slowed down, she told Ellie the story. "My friend Crystal called me before work, and guess what? Andrew and Suzanne are back together. They were at Ricco's last night. Everyone saw them eating dinner. She looked absolutely dowdy, but he kept holding her hand anyway."

"Oh . . ." What else could Ellie say?

"I never had a chance with him. He didn't even know I liked him. Chris and John ruined my only opportunity."

"I'm sorry."

"I hate them both," Diana said, sniffling. I'm never speaking to John again. Ever."

Ellie crossed names off the check-in list that lay by the computer. "He's only so overprotective because he cares about you. He feels like your father."

"I don't need a father. I want to live my own life without John interfering whenever the mood strikes him—and let me tell you, the mood strikes him frequently."

"When you were a baby, he took care of you every day after school."

Diana shut the key drawer so quickly that all the keys jangled noisily inside. "Why are you sticking up for him?"

Ellie didn't have a chance to answer. Lauren Flynn opened the door from the lobby and walked behind the desk. "Good morning, ladies."

They both mumbled good-mornings back at her while she breezed around, looking at things. Ellie went to a pile of restaurant coupons and started stapling them together.

Usually if Lauren came back to the desk it was to pick up something, and then she immediately left. She never stayed around to make small talk. Ellie wasn't sure Lauren even remembered her name, which was why it was so disconcerting that the older woman now stood by the desk staring at her with a wide smile. "So . . . how are you today, Ellie?"

"Fine."

"I didn't see you at church on Sunday."

"I stayed home to take care of my aunt." And then before Ellie could stop herself the words slipped out, "You went to church?"

"I'm usually too busy with the resort to go, but I decided it was time to reconnect with my old friends. See what's new. Catch up on the gossip." Lauren didn't leave the desk. In fact she fiddled with items on the counter while she continued to look at Ellie. "John doesn't really tell me much about his social life, but I hear you two are a couple. Is that right?"

The stapler nearly slipped from Ellie's hands. "No, not really." She fumbled for a moment, nearly stapling her hand. "It's just that people have seen us together, and my aunt thought that we were kissing once, and she sort of told some people about it, but we weren't, and we're not a couple."

"Oh." Lauren picked up a stack of papers, straightened them, then set them down again. "And he didn't propose to you?"

The stapler dropped from Ellie's hands, hit the countertop, and fell to the floor. She felt herself blush bright red as she retrieved it.

Diana's gaze had moved to Ellie, and Lauren's eyes were brimming with questions.

"No. No. Of course not," Ellie said.

"But Sister Henricksen heard it from Mrs. Blair that John proposed to you at the ER and you turned him down."

Ellie set the stapler down on the counter so she wouldn't drop it again. "That was just a misunderstanding. He didn't really propose to me."

"Dr. Blair didn't hear him propose?"

"No, he just heard me turn him down, but you see, that doesn't mean John *asked* me. I was just saying I wouldn't marry him as a sort of . . . general statement."

Diana walked up beside her mother, eyeing Ellie skeptically. "As in: It looks like rain, they're serving ham for lunch, and oh, by the way, in case you're wondering, I won't marry you."

Ellie flet herself blush. "Right. Exactly."

Diana put her hand on her hip. "I can't believe you didn't tell me you were involved with my brother. That's why you're sticking up for him." The hand went from her hip to the air. "That's why the two of you were always off together whispering on the bike trip. You've been on his side all along, haven't you?"

"No," Ellie said.

Lauren leaned toward her daughter. "Stop being so selfish, Diana. Your brother and his girlfriend are trying to decide whether to get engaged, and all you can think about is your crush on Andrew. Try to think about someone else for once."

"I'm not his girlfriend," Ellie said.

Diana bit her lip, tears pooling in her eyes. "So how I feel towards Andrew doesn't matter? All that matters is if John is in love?"

"Not," Ellie said. "He's not in love with me."

Lauren reached out and patted Ellie's arm. "He wouldn't have proposed if he wasn't." Her voice took on a soft motherly tone. "Of course, you've only known each other a short time—I can't say I blame you for turning him down. I can't even blame you for being scared off, but he really is a wonderful man. He ought to know there's no need to rush into things."

Diana crossed her arms. "I see how it is. If someone rejects John then you care about it. Then you come down here and talk to his girlfriend. But if someone rejects me, you're happy about it. You were happy this morning when I told you about Andrew." She didn't wait for a reply. With a gulp that was already leading to tears, she turned and rushed from the room.

Lauren watched her go, let out a sigh, then turned back to Ellie. "I'd better go try and reason with her. But I do want to talk with you some more." She walked toward the door then looked back at Ellie. "Why don't you come to dinner at my house on Friday night? John isn't working then, and we can spend time getting to know each other."

"I'm not sure that would be—I mean . . ." How did she go about explaining this, when she'd already told Lauren she wasn't his girlfriend and Lauren hadn't listened?

"We'll say six-ish. John will pick you up. See you then."

Ellie didn't say anything else as Lauren left. But as she worked through the rest of the shift alone—Diana never did come back—a knot of dread grew in her stomach.

After Theresa relieved her at 3:00, Ellie drove home with a stomach full of dread. How in the world was she going to get out of this situation gracefully? She had to see John's sister and mother every day at work. When they found out John and she weren't a couple, that he was annoyed about all of the rumors regarding the two of them—and that he thought she was partially responsible for them—how would she ever face his family?

And how could she tell John about all of this? *Your mom invited me over for dinner on Friday night. She wants to get to know me so she can see what kind of daughter-in-law material I am.*

He already thought Ellie was hitting on him. This new event would not be reassuring.

She pulled up in front of Bertie's house, turned off the car, and dragged herself through the door. "I'm home."

No answer.

She went to Bertie's room, then, when she couldn't find her aunt, she walked around the house. Bertie wasn't home.

There wasn't a note from her anywhere, and Bertie didn't have the car. She couldn't have gone far. She probably went to one of her friends' houses and would be back soon.

Ellie dug through the clutter on the kitchen counter until she found the coupon with John's home phone number. She dialed it before she could grow too afraid.

One ring. Two rings. She waited, knowing he was going to be unhappy. *Why didn't you put a stop to these rumors when they first started?* he would say.

I tried, she would answer.

Well you obviously didn't try hard enough—or is it just that your aunt is crazy and you're a gold digger? he would say.

That's it, she'd tell him. *I'm starting a new rumor and in this one I dump you for good.*

The phone clicked onto the answering machine, and hesitatingly she spoke.

*   *   *

John got home at 6:30, after stopping by Andre's for dinner. He sipped down the last of a bottled water, then walked to the kitchen and dropped the container in the trash. As he did he noticed the message light on his answering machine blinking. He hit it, then walked to the dishwasher to unload it.

"Um, hi, John. It's Ellie. I need to talk to you about something so can you give me a call?" A moment's pause. "And, probably you should talk to me before you talk to either your mother or your sister, because you see there's been this little bit of confusion that I *tried* to clear up, but it's still not cleared up, and I think it would be best if you cleared it up. I won't go into all the details because your answering machine will probably cut me off, but it involves your mother thinking that you want to marry me. Bye."

He stood by the dishwasher holding a plate mid-air while the answering machine beeped.

Well. Yes. That probably did merit a phone call on his part. He put the plate down and walked back to the phone. What in the world had his mother said to Ellie?

It was a long way from, "If you want to know what people at church are saying about us you should come," to, "Ellie is my fiancé." Why would his mother think—and then he remembered the scene in the ER room with Dr. Blair.

Apparently Dr. Blair had found that proposal scene far too interesting to keep to himself and it was now the latest Colton news.

John ran his hand through his hair and leaned against the countertop. He and Ellie were going to have to do something about these rumors, but how did one go about letting an entire town know they weren't a couple? Did they start pulling people aside to straighten them out, make an announcement in church, or take out an ad in the paper? Perhaps it would just be easier if they started dating.

The thought made him smile. He would go over to Ellie's house and tell her, "I'm tired of running against popular opinion. Let's go out." Then he would take her hand, pull her toward him until he could feel the warmth of her body close to his, and—

Man, he had to stop thinking those types of things. He was being careful.

He picked up the phone, then set it back on its cradle. Ellie wanted to talk to him, and he needed to pick up his sander. Why not do both at the same time?

* * *

Ellie hung up the phone with Margaret. Bertie wasn't there and Margaret hadn't talked with her all day. Neither Lucille, Delsa, nor her visiting teachers knew where Bertie was. Ellie couldn't remember her aunt mentioning the names of any other friends. She'd already asked all the neighbors if they'd seen her. No one had.

Ellie leaned against the counter and surveyed the kitchen. The chicken and rice dish she'd prepared for dinner was getting cold. She dished a little up on a plate and ate it while standing.

It was silly for her to be worried about her aunt. Bertie was a grown woman and had been taking care of herself, by herself, for a long time.

Just because Bertie had been here every other time Ellie had come home didn't mean there was a problem. And just because Bertie hadn't left the house by herself since Ellie came to Colton didn't mean it was reason to worry. Bertie probably had a perfectly sensible reason for disappearing and not leaving a note.

But there had been those falls. Two of them. What if Bertie had fallen somewhere and needed help, and Ellie was standing here eating chicken and rice as if nothing was wrong?

She put her plate down on the counter and walked through the house again, looking in every possible corner. Under the bed. In Bertie's bathtub. She went out in the yard and checked under all of the trees and in the bushes.

Nothing. Not a clue as to her aunt's whereabouts. The sun was low in the sky. There was probably only a half an hour left of daylight and Bertie was missing.

Ellie went back inside and surveyed the phone list again. Would it be obsessive to call everyone? Would it be paranoid to call the police?

She opened the coat closet. Bertie's purse was sitting on the shelf above the coat rack where it always was. The rack of brightly colored sweaters and jackets appeared unchanged.

Ellie walked into Bertie's bedroom—again—not even sure what she was looking for. Perhaps a note that Bertie had forgotten to put up somewhere visible. Bertie's art supplies laid scattered in front of the easel. Beside the easel was a stack of canvas sketches Ellie hadn't seen before. The first one caught her eye—it was a drawing of Ellie wearing a wedding dress. She was smiling, reaching out to touch—well, Bertie hadn't completed who it was Ellie was touching. He was just a few unfinished lines. Surprising really, since Bertie seemed so determined about who'd be standing next to Ellie.

The next sketch was also of Ellie. This time holding a baby peeking out of a blanket. The third was Ellie with a small child riding piggy back on her shoulders. The fourth was a self-portrait of Bertie—complete with muumuu—finger-painting with the same small child. The fifth was a banner, falling to the ground, with the words, "Moments Missed."

Moments missed? Were these the moments Bertie was afraid Ellie would miss if she didn't marry John? Honestly. They needed to have a talk about Bertie's expectations. Bertie was far too—

It was then that Ellie noticed the painting on the easel. The field with the wild flowers Bertie had been working on before had become a cemetery. Gray headstones stuck out from the wildflowers. There was something familiar about the trees, the field—and then Ellie realized what. It was an actual cemetery, the one Ellie had accidentally gone to when she'd gotten lost on her way to the resort. And sketched in the center of the painting stood a headstone which read: Bertie Goodwin.

Ellie pick up the painting, the canvas shaking in her hands. Why had Bertie done this? Why had she drawn her own tombstone?

The doorbell rang. Hurriedly, she laid the canvas back on the easel and ran to get it. She flung open the door. John stood in front of her, hands tucked in his pockets.

His gaze moved to her casually, then stopped suddenly. "What's wrong?"

She took his hand and pulled him inside, pulled him down the hallway toward Bertie's room. "Bertie's not home. I don't know where she is, and I just found this."

He looked at the painting, stepping up to the easel for closer inspection. "That's a bit morbid. Has she been feeling depressed lately?"

"I don't think so. She was concerned that she didn't have anything to write on her Christmas cards. That's not the same as depression is it?"

"Do you know how long she's been gone?"

"She was here when I left this morning."

"She didn't leave a note?"

"No."

"Did you check the calendar to see if she had an appointment listed?"

"She never writes anything on the calendar. It wasn't even turned to the right month when I came."

"Did she take her purse?"

"No."

"Did you call her friends?"

The way he was asking questions reminded her of a policeman, taking notes at the scene of a crime. Her voice caught in her throat. "The ones I know."

He put his hand on her shoulder. "We'll find her. Don't worry. She's probably just out for a walk or something."

Ellie nodded. He was right. Of course he was right. Bertie had most likely taken a sketch pad and was off some place drawing something more cheerful than tombstones.

"I'll call Brother Cromwell and a few of the high priests, and we'll make some phone calls to see if anyone knows where she went. You and I can go out and look for her. Write her a note and tell her to call my cell phone number if she comes home while we're out. If she doesn't turn up, we'll organize a search party."

Ellie nodded, getting a piece of paper and pencil from a drawer. She scribbled a note and taped it to the refrigerator door. The casserole dish with the chicken still sat on the table, and Ellie mechanically put it into the fridge, then was almost stabbed with guilt. How could she worry about the mundane details of food when Bertie was missing?

After John had given Brother Cromwell his cell phone number, he hung up and they walked out the door. "We'll take my car."

"Shouldn't we split up so we'll have a better chance of finding her?"

"If she's all right it won't matter if we find her. If she's not all right it will take both of us to lift her into the car. Besides, you don't know the way to the cemetery."

"The cemetery? You think she's there?"

"It's close and it's a good place to start looking."

They followed a narrow road that led up the hill. They had barely left the rows of houses that made up the neighborhood when there it was, a spread of land, a park that wasn't a park. Trees and grass and lines of stones. Birds warbling as though they didn't know better. It only took Ellie a moment to spot her aunt. Bertie wasn't seated in a chair, sketching. She sat on the grass, among the crosses, faded plastic flowers, and the worn stones pitted from time and weather. She sat staring at nothing at all and not moving.

"Bertie!" Ellie called. She flung the car door open and ran across graves toward her aunt. "Bertie, are you all right?"

Bertie turned and looked at Ellie, her expression so unlike the one she usually wore. This face was flushed, puffy, with glassy eyes that didn't seem to see Ellie at all.

"I couldn't paint it," she said. "Because you can't paint cold. And that's how it felt. It's not supposed to. So what kind of artist does that make me?"

"What are you talking about?"

"The stone."

John came and stood beside Ellie. "Bertie, are you all right?"

"I'm not a very good artist."

"How long have you been here?"

"Long enough I suppose." She broke out laughing then, heaving her shoulders as though it were hard to breathe. "God would say I've been here long enough."

John knelt beside her, slipping his arm around her back. "I'm going to help you get up, then we'll drive down to my office. Okay?"

"Okay." She let him help her as though she were a little child, and all the while Ellie stood frozen, watching them as though she weren't really here. This wasn't really happening. That wasn't really her aunt.

As they stood, Bertie wobbled and John steadied her. "How are you feeling? Dizzy?"

"Yes, dizzy."

"Anything else?"

"Disconnected. Quite disconnected. That's what they do with your phone, isn't it? If you can't pay your bill you're cut off from the rest of the world. Disconnected."

They walked slowly back to the car. John kept his arm around Bertie's waist, and she leaned into him. Ellie trailed them.

"Have you taken any medication recently?" John asked.

"Vicodin," Bertie said.

"How many?"

She shook her head. "I don't remember."

"Why did you take them?"

"Because I was in pain."

"What kind of pain?"

"The kind that starts in your mind and pushes it's way into your heart. The pills weren't working, you know, so I had to take more."

He nodded. "Who prescribed them for you?"

"A doctor. He wasn't as handsome as you, but I'm a fair woman and I don't hold that against him."

John continued to ask questions as he put Bertie in the front seat of his car, his voice matter-of-fact, as though he were asking her what she thought of the weather. When did she take the pills? What did she take them with? Was she feeling depressed? Bertie didn't answer the last question, just started laughing, and kept laughing as they drove to hospital. "Do you think I was trying to kill myself, is that it? You look at my life and think I have nothing left to live for? No reason to be here? So my taking pills must be a suicide attempt. How very funny."

Ellie didn't say anything. She couldn't say anything at all—she'd stopped functioning some time ago.

Chapter 21

When they got to the hospital John parked in front of the building but didn't turn off the engine. He turned to Ellie. "I'll take Bertie in. I want you to go back to the house and gather up every prescription bottle you can find. Look for one marked Vicodin. Then call me on my cell phone. We need to know how much was prescribed and how much she took. I want the name of the doctor who prescribed it for her."

Ellie nodded, and the next moment John was out of the car. He helped Bertie out, his arm around her waist, holding her up as they walked through the hospital doors.

Ellie drove away from the hospital numb, hardly seeing the traffic around her. There would be no more pretenses that Bertie was all right, that Bertie could live alone. That hope was gone. Ellie had been a fool for not seeing it, for insisting it wasn't so. Her parents had known the truth, and they hadn't even seen Bertie. John had known after the first time he'd talked to her.

Why had Ellie been so blind?

She parked John's car in front of Bertie's house, slipped his keys into her pocket, and ran up the porch steps. As she opened the door, the Christmas tree greeted her. This time when she saw it she winced. A Christmas tree in June. She should have known there was something wrong when she first walked in and saw it. Instead she had thought it was a good idea. How sweet that Bertie wanted to keep the spirit of Christmas alive.

Tears stung her eyes as she walked. She let them roll down her cheeks without bothering to wipe them away. She didn't look at the poster of Cindy Crawford in Bertie's bathroom, just pulled open the medicine cabinet. A toothbrush, toothpaste, and an entire row of prescription bottles. Ambien. Oxycontin. Fenatnyl. She didn't know what any of this stuff was, hadn't ever seen her aunt take medication. Dilantin, Zofran. What was wrong with Bertie that she took so much medicine? Vicodin. That was the one John wanted.

She gathered up all the bottles and dropped them onto Bertie's bed. With shaking hands, she dialed John's number from the phone on Bertie's night stand. He picked up after the first ring.

"Ellie?"

"I found the Vicodin, and a lot of other bottles."

"Read the drug names to me."

She did, along with the other information. The prescribing doctor was always Dr. Joseph Russell. The pharmacy was one listed in Boise.

Ellie clutched the last bottle in her hand. "Is Bertie going to be all right?"

"She's on an IV and resting. There was no point in flushing her stomach because the medicine is already in her system. I ordered some blood work to make sure her electrolytes are fine, but I don't think she took enough Vicodin to do any serious harm."

"The Vicodin, is that what made her act so funny?"

There was a pause on the line. He didn't answer. Ellie tried to clarify herself. "Bertie wasn't making any sense. She acted like she was drunk or something, but that was only because she took too much medication, right?"

"That's not a common side effect of Vicodin. Too much Vicodin represses breathing. It makes a person flaccid. Bertie hadn't reached that point yet."

"But then why was she acting that way? And why was she taking Vicodin in the first place? What's wrong with her?"

Another pause. "Ellie, I want you to come down to the hospital and then we'll talk."

She gripped the phone harder. "Why can't you tell me right now? I want to talk about this now."

"We shouldn't talk about this over the phone. Come to the hospital."

The phone suddenly felt cold in her hand. He knew. He knew what was wrong with Bertie, and he wasn't telling her. He didn't want to tell her over the phone because it was something very bad, and you didn't give a person very bad news over the phone. She slumped against the pillows, shutting her eyes. "It's Alzheimer's, isn't it?"

"No. Listen, Ellie, you need to come down here. I'll call Dr. Russell and then I'll know more about what is happening."

Mechanically, Ellie got up, left the house, and climbed back into John's car. It didn't take long for her to reach the hospital. She tried to comfort herself with the thought that Bertie didn't have Alzheimer's. John had said so. Perhaps it wasn't so bad after all. Only her eyes seemed to know otherwise. She couldn't keep herself from crying.

When she walked into the ER foyer, John stood waiting for her by the front desk. He looked out of place. Without his scrubs on, he looked like just another person waiting for treatment.

He walked over, took her by the arm, and propelled her through a door in the back of the lobby. They went down the hall away from the ER and toward the main section of the hospital. She glanced over her shoulder at the door they'd just gone through. "Where are we going? Isn't Bertie in the ER?"

"Bertie's sleeping right now. I think it's best if we let her rest for a while. Have you had anything to eat tonight?"

"I'm not hungry. What did the other doctor tell you? What's wrong with her?"

He paused, as though not sure whether to take her to the cafeteria, and at last just led her into an empty treatment room. She sat on a plastic chair, and he pulled another chair around in front of her for himself. Their knees were touching. He took her hand in his. His eyes didn't waver from her face. He was already offering her sympathy, which meant it was already severe. She wanted to shake his hand loose, to push his chair away. It was hard to breathe.

"Ellie, Dr. Russell diagnosed Bertie with a brain tumor three months ago. It's in the stem. That means they can't operate."

Tears pinched at Ellie's eyes. Her throat felt tight. "But there must be something they can do. Chemo. Radiation."

He shook his head. "That won't get rid of the tumor, and as long as there are any cells left, it will just grow back."

She stood up, smacking her chair into the wall as she did. "Don't tell me you're not going to do anything. You were the one who kept telling me she needed help. Now when you know the problem you're not going to do anything?"

"There's nothing to do, Ellie. I'm sorry."

"You're not sorry." She knew he was. He had pain in his eyes, but she still said the words. She wanted to hurt something. It was irrational but she didn't care.

He stood and without another word pulled her into an embrace, and then she fell apart, sobbing so hard she couldn't speak. She leaned into him, holding onto his shirt as though it were a life raft.

He rubbed her back and murmured into her hair. "I am sorry, Ellie. I am so sorry."

* * *

They stood together that way for a long time, Ellie crying into his shirt, and John feeling utterly useless. He couldn't help Bertie. He couldn't do anything.

At last Ellie's sobs subsided and she turned her face up to look at him. "Why didn't Bertie tell me?"

His arms tightened around her. "She was going to eventually. She was afraid you'd drop out of school to take care of her."

"You talked to her about it?"

"Yes. Before I called Dr. Russell she told me everything."

In fact, once he had helped Bertie into the ER she'd grown calm, limply resigned. She lay on the bed, blanket tucked under her arms, and told him everything. In March while she was in Boise for an art convention she'd blacked out and gone to the hospital. They had found the tumor then. She'd been on medication ever since.

"Why didn't you tell Dr. Blair about it when you got home?" he'd asked.

Bertie had simply shrugged. "I didn't want everyone treating me differently. I didn't want to become Poor-Old-Dying-Bertie. When one is struggling with such a big issue, one wants to do it in private, without everyone tip-toeing and tongue-tied around you."

He had nodded in response. She had the right to feel any way she wanted to about her own death.

Now Ellie blinked and another set of tears rolled onto her cheeks. "How long does she have left?"

"Somewhere between two and five months."

She let her face fall back against his chest. "It isn't long enough."

"I know."

Her shoulders heaved. She shut her eyes, still leaning against him.

It wasn't an appropriate time to notice the way her hair lay against her shoulders in unruly auburn curls. Or to feel the heat of her body next to his. It wasn't the right time, and yet as they stood together this seemed to be the only time left in the universe.

It isn't long enough, she'd said. Well, it was never long enough. Time was a limited resource, and then it was gone. His arms tightened around Ellie. He knew it, and yet he'd forgotten. He and his attempts to be careful. It wasn't *careful* he wanted, it was control. Only it could never be that way. The tumor could have just as easily happened to him, to Ellie. And then what would his caution have gained him?

He wanted to bend down and kiss her. But he couldn't. Not when she was shocked with grief. It was a poor time to realize he was in love with her.

She lifted her face from his shirt. "Was it the tumor? Is that why Bertie keeps falling?"

"People fall for a lot of reasons. She needs to be careful, but she knows that. She hasn't driven since her blackout. She's used her ankle as an excuse to get people to drive her places. So she didn't have to tell them the truth."

Ellie let out a sigh. "I'll have to tell my parents eventually."

"Let Bertie decide when."

She nodded, then rested her head back against his chest. "Will her mind deteriorate? Has it started to already? Is that why she has the Christmas tree up?"

He wasn't sure which question to answer first, and she didn't give him time to answer.

"I walked around the house singing carols. I made eggnog. I thought Christmas every day was a good idea."

"It is a good idea, Ellie. It's a sweet thing to do."

Her voice caught in her throat. "I'm a selfish person."

"No, you're not."

"Yes I am, because all I can think about is: Who will understand me when she's gone?"

* * *

Eventually Ellie let John take her to the hospital cafeteria. She ordered apple juice. It was all her stomach could handle. He said many things to her. Some of them informative. Some of them comforting. She couldn't remember any of it. When Bertie woke up they walked back to the ER.

"I'll let you have some time alone with her," John said. "I'll take you home whenever she's ready."

Ellie did her best to put on a smile before she walked into Bertie's room. It didn't work. Bertie took one look at her and said, "He told you, didn't he?"

"Yes, he told me. I wish *you* had."

"I was going to do it before you went home. There was no point in ruining your whole summer."

Ellie sat on the end of the bed. "I'm not leaving, you know. You need someone to take care of you."

"Yes, but it won't be you. I won't have you missing school just to take care of me." Then Bertie let out a sigh. "I had hoped that you'd want to stay for other reasons, but my matchmaking attempts didn't work. It seems you and John have done nothing but fight since you got here."

Ellie was going to stay, she was determined about that. The other things she'd been so eager to get back home for didn't seem important now. And with that one comment from Bertie, Ellie knew how to convince her aunt to let her stay. She leaned closer to Bertie. "We're not fighting now. In fact, his mother wants me to come over for dinner on Friday so she can get to know me better."

"Really?"

"Really. I . . ." She lowered her voice to a whisper because there were no walls here, just curtains, and she didn't know where John was. "I think he's wonderful." It felt like a lie to say it, even though it wasn't. "I think I'm in love."

Bertie smiled. "Good. Maybe I'll be able to finish your wedding portrait after all."

It was 9:30 when they made it back to the house. Bertie, having napped in the ER, wasn't tired, and Ellie knew she wouldn't be able to sleep.

They stayed up until 2:00 A.M. talking about everything. Bertie's feelings. Ellie's feelings. Bertie's funeral wishes. Her plan not to tell anyone about her illness until it was evident. The gospel. The afterlife.

"I was just feeling sorry for myself today," Bertie said over her third cup of hot chocolate. "Most of the time I concentrate on how nice it will be to see my loved ones again. My sweetheart, Floyd, my parents, my Aunt Lavina, and of course I'm going to look up Elvis once I get there."

"Only you could joke about the afterlife."

"I hope they have chocolate there." Bertie took another sip of her drink. "I think I'll start eating it for every meal just in case they don't."

"Why don't we travel this summer? We'll go to the Grand Canyon. Niagara Falls. The Great Wall of China."

"How would we afford all of that?"

"I'll put it on my credit card."

"I couldn't let you do that."

Ellie took a sip of her own hot chocolate. "All right then, we'll put it on your credit card."

Bertie leaned back in her chair, smiling. "You see, I knew I could get you to joke about death."

"I want to make this summer special, Aunt Bertie."

"You already have, Dear. You're here. That's all I want. To stay here with my friends and have my favorite niece with me."

Chapter 22

When John returned home, he got ready for bed mechanically, thinking of all the things he should have done. He should have offered to give Bertie a blessing. He'd do that tomorrow. He'd talk to Bertie and see if he could tell Brother Cromwell about her situation so he could help John administer. He also should have told Ellie not to go in to the resort tomorrow. She needed time to adjust, time to be with her aunt, probably time to sleep. He should have told her to stay home, doctor's orders.

Well, he'd find a way to remedy that.

It didn't take long to change his schedule at the ER. The next morning, instead of heading to the hospital, he drove to the resort.

Diana was already at the front desk when he got there. Ellie was in the back room, just putting her purse on a shelf. She looked pale, and her face was without its usual smile. There was no grace in her movements. He wanted to go squeeze her hand; instead he waited until she noticed him. She turned and raised an eyebrow. "What are you doing here?"

"I came to relieve you. I thought you could use the day off."

"You want to work the front desk for me?"

"Trust me, I know how."

"Well I . . ." Her gaze went to Diana and then back to him. "I guess I could use a nap." Then a quick smile. "Thanks."

"I'll be over after my shift for a home teaching visit."

"Okay. Thanks again." She took her purse, and without looking back, walked out of the resort.

He didn't take his gaze off of her until she disappeared into the parking lot.

Diana sidled up next to him. "So what was that all about?"

He shrugged and took a stack of reservation slips to the computer. "Ellie had a long night. I thought she could use the time off."

"Weren't you supposed to work at the ER today?"

He typed without looking at his sister. "I swapped a shift."

"Why did Ellie have a long night? What were you two doing?"

"I'm not going to tell you."

"A fight?"

He didn't answer.

"Was she mad at me for walking out yesterday?"

He finished one card and started another. "She didn't mention it."

"Is she going to be okay?"

"I hope so."

Diana printed out the check-in list while he glanced over the check-out list. "That's sweet of you to take her shift," she said.

He grunted a reply as his eyes scanned over the names on the list. Not many check-outs today. It wouldn't take housekeeping long to have the rooms ready.

Diana rolled her list into a tube and tapped it on her hand. "Do you think Andrew would have ever done something sweet like that for me?"

The guy who broke up with Suzanne because she was hormonal? He shrugged. "Probably not."

"Chris would have though."

"Chris already *did.* He went on the embrace-your-fear bike tour."

"Yeah, that was kind of sweet of him."

Diana unrolled the check-in list but didn't look at it. "You think I made a mistake when I broke up with him, don't you?"

"No. I think your mistake was not appreciating him in the first place. You were right to break up with him when you did. You couldn't chase after Andrew while you were still dating Chris."

For a minute Diana didn't say anything else, and he thought the conversation was over. Then she said, "Crystal called me last night. She said there's some rumors going around about Andrew and Suzanne."

He opened the key drawer, checking to make sure they had all the keys they needed for the morning's check-ins. They were missing keys for cabins 4 and 13. Housekeeping would probably bring those keys by before the guests showed up, but if not he could move cabin 4 to . . . He scanned over the reservation list to see which cabins were empty.

"Don't you even want to know what the rumors are?"

"Nope."

"Even if it meant you were right about Andrew and could gloat and everything?"

"I never gloat."

"You gloat all the time."

He could move cabin 4 to cabin 6, and cabin 13 to cabin 12. Easy. He penciled in a notation on the list.

"Will you gloat if I go crawling back to Chris?"

"Maybe a little."

"I yelled at him during the canoe trip. He might not want me back."

"He might not. You're a real pain most of the time."

She pointed a finger at him. "You're gloating."

"Okay. I'm gloating. Go call him."

She walked in to the back room to use the phone there and didn't emerge again for some time. He could hear her giggling, though. It was a good sign.

When the shift ended at 3:00 John went back to his house and dug through the boxes in his garage until he found the Christmas decorations. Or rather, his half of the Christmas decorations. The things Valerie hadn't taken. It was still a considerable haul. Valerie had liked to shop the after-Christmas sales and every year bought enough stuff to trim a small forest. He found several brand new angel ornaments still in the boxes. He wrapped them and drove over to Bertie's house.

Once on the doorstep, he felt suddenly awkward. He wasn't sure whether he was a doctor now or a home teacher, or perhaps something else. He wanted to be something else.

Ellie answered the door. Sadness showed in her eyes, but she did her best to hide it with a smile. Before he even had a chance to explain why he'd come, she turned her head and called, "John's here!"

Bertie appeared from the kitchen holding two glasses of eggnog. "Of course he is." She shuffled over, handed one glass to him and the other to Ellie. "You came just in time for New Year's resolutions. I'll get myself another glass and be right back."

John waited until Bertie was in the kitchen to speak to Ellie. "How are you holding up?"

"All right, I guess. Sometimes it doesn't seem real."

"That's normal."

Bertie came out of the kitchen, holding her glass of eggnog in the air. "Time for resolutions. I'll go first." She came and stood within toasting range. "I'm going to clean out my closets."

Ellie held her glass up. "I'm going to write home more."

John raised his glass. "I'm going to check on my home teaching families every day. At least one of them, anyway."

Bertie didn't toast. Instead she looked over at Ellie. "We should have explained to him that we only resolve to do things we're not actually going to do." She patted John's arm. "It's Christmas every day so the New Year never comes."

"Oh." John raised his glass again. "In that case I'm going to finish remodeling the kitchen."

They clinked glasses together, and John laughed. He wasn't sure why.

Bertie took a sip, then glanced at the packages in his hand. "You've brought something to put under the tree?"

"Actually, they're for you."

He handed her the presents, and she opened them, her eyes shining with excitement.

"Ohhh," she said, and then, "Ahhhh!"

She placed the ornaments gently on the tree, oohhing and ahhing several more times. "Thank you. They're beautiful."

"They're exquisite," Ellie said.

And they were. The angels' crystal wings glistened in the tree lights. As Bertie ran her fingers over them in admiration, he—for once—thanked Valerie's shopping habit.

Amid the glow of lights from the tree, Ellie shot him a smile. He smiled back at her, willing the moment to last, wanting to connect with her through his gaze. She turned away.

He was a fool, really, for reading things into simple gestures. Her smile was a simple thank you, that was all. She'd already made her feelings for him clear. The second time she'd come into the ER she had said she had no interest in marrying him.

It would take time to change her opinion. He'd be patient. He'd be subtle. He'd give her all the time she needed.

He talked with Bertie about a blessing, set up a time to come over with Brother Cromwell the next night, and then asked her if she needed help with anything else.

Finally he left. He walked away from Christmas and back into the stark June afternoon.

As he drove home he found himself setting up a mental schedule for his relationship with Ellie. He would check in on her every day. He'd give her a shoulder to cry on if she needed it and, if she seemed glad to see him, he'd ask her out to dinner. From there, well, he'd take it one step at a time without pushing her. The whole thing needed to be handled delicately.

Chapter 23

The whole thing needed to be handled as quickly as possible, Ellie realized. She stood in the hallway listening to Bertie talk to Lucille on the phone in her bedroom.

"John just left," her aunt crooned. "He brought me the most beautiful angel ornaments. Of course that was just an excuse to see Ellie, really. He couldn't keep his eyes off of her. Makes one wonder what he'll bring next. I think I should tell Ellie to put in a plug for Almond Joys. I'm quite addicted, you know."

Bertie was silent for a moment, then said, "They looked so cute standing in front of the tree. I want to sketch them that way. I'll have to ask John when he comes over next time if I can take some pictures of Ellie and him together." There was mischievous laughter on Bertie's part. "I'll tell him to put his arm around her."

Ellie put her hand across her eyes. She could already imagine the look of discomfort on John's face.

"No, they're not fighting anymore," Bertie said. "Ellie's going over to Lauren's house for dinner on Friday." She lowered her voice, but Ellie could still hear her whispering. "Ellie told me she's in love."

Well, okay, she did tell Bertie that, but she didn't want everyone else to hear about it. She especially didn't want John to hear about it. What would he say?

Now Ellie put both hands across her face. She knew what he'd say. He'd say, "We have to put a stop to these rumors once and for all." Then he'd march in and tell Bertie that they weren't a couple, they weren't in love, and his only feelings toward Ellie were professional ones—unless he was being really truthful, in which case he might admit to annoyance, frustration, and the time he threatened to throw her into the lake again.

And then what would Bertie think?

Ellie bit her lip and stared at Bertie's closed bedroom door. How long would this Ellie-told-me-she-was-in-love-with-John story take to get back to him? Probably not long. Which meant she'd have to talk to him before he could deny the story and try to set people straight.

She walked slowly to the pantry and picked up John's sander from the shelf. Bertie still needed a cell phone. Ellie could go get one and, while she was out, she could stop by John's house, return the sander to him and . . .

And tell John that the being-in-love story was just an excuse so she could stay and take care of Bertie. That way he wouldn't contradict it. But what if he told his mother and sister about her reasoning? He might. After all, they were his family. His mother was planning a Friday dinner date—and who knew how many other events she would shove Ellie and John together for if she thought they were a couple. Yes, he might tell his family the truth, and then they would know about Bertie's illness. They might tell someone else. This wasn't a good town for keeping secrets.

She lugged the sander to the kitchen, picked up her purse and car keys from the table, then stood in the doorway debating.

The easiest thing to do would be to tell John she loved him. He'd most likely avoid her for the rest of her time in Colton, but at least she would have a viable alibi for staying. She wouldn't have to worry about who knew which story or keep them all straight. So everything Bertie had told Lucille was the truth, and if he told everyone in town he didn't return Ellie's affections, well, when people saw her they'd shake their heads sadly and murmur about the tragedy of a broken heart.

She could live with that.

The hardest part would be telling John she was in love with him, which meant she should get it over with as quickly as possible.

She hesitated for a minute longer, then called out to Bertie, "I'm going to take the sander back to John!"

"Tell him you like Almond Joys!" Bertie yelled back.

Ellie didn't have to drive around much to find John's house. Bertie had told Ellie the general direction during one of their conversations, and Ellie got his address from the ward list. When she pulled up to the small brick house, he was standing in the yard by a tree that had approximately three leaves still clinging to its branches. He held a rake in his hands, and a bag of mulch lay at his feet amongst the dead leaves.

She climbed from the car, looking at the tree instead of him. "Did fall come early this year?"

"No. Just my usual black thumb at work." He stopped raking, kicked at a couple of leaves, and set the rake against the tree trunk. "Is everything all right with Bertie?"

"Yes. I was just on my way to pick up a cell phone for her and thought I'd return your sander on the way . . ."

She should have planned exactly what to say so it would sound natural. Now she was stuck trying to figure something out on the spot. "Well you see, I thought you might hear some new rumors, and I didn't want you to think Bertie was just making things up, so I thought I'd tell you right off . . ." She hadn't even realized she'd brought her purse with her, and now noticed that her fingers were wound up in its strap. She shook them free, put her purse back squarely on her shoulder, and took a deep breath. "I just thought you ought to know I'm in love with you. I understand you don't feel the same way, and that's fine. I mean, you're not obligated to me or anything. Well," she took her keys out of her purse, flipping through them until she found the car key, "I've got to get to the phone store before it closes, so I'll see you around."

John's eyes had grown wide during her confession, but now they narrowed.

"Ellie, why are you doing this?"

"Doing what?"

He let the sander drop down onto the bag of mulch and then put his hands on his hips. "Telling me you're in love with me when you're not."

"But I am." She took one step backwards toward her car.

"You drop by to tell something like that and then you rush off to the store?"

"Well, it's unrequited love. What's the point of sticking around and making us both uncomfortable?"

He took off his gloves and slapped them on one of the lower branches of the tree. "I don't know what bothers me more: that you're lying to me, or that you're not taking into account how you're manipulating my emotions."

"Manipulating your emotions?" She wanted to take another step backwards but held her ground. "What are you talking about?"

His jaw was clenched, his lips were pressed tight, his eyes were, well, smoldering. "Think about it."

She might if he hadn't taken several more steps to diminish the space between them. How could she think about anything with him standing so close to her? He smelled of sunshine and dirt, and there was sheen of sweat along his collarbone.

"I'm not manipulating you, I . . . I'm really in love with you." Somehow, even though it was the truth, with him glaring down at her she gulped anyway.

"Oh really? Then you won't mind proving it."

"What?"

"Prove it. If you're in love with me, prove it."

She glanced away from him. "Do you want me to carve our names together on your tree? I've heard that's bad for trees, but in this case . . ."

"Kiss me."

"What?"

"If you were really in love with me, you'd want to kiss me."

With his hands still on his hips, he looked like a boxer taking a breather before the bell rang. Her heart rate had doubled in speed, and she wasn't sure if it was fear or excitement that made her blood race. She took a step toward him, and then another step. They were only inches apart. She could smell traces of soap from his clothes. "I'll kiss you," she said. "Don't think I can't do it, because I can."

He bent his head down, smiling at the challenge. "All right. Let's see you then."

"All right." She put her hands against his shirt then nervously wound her arms around his neck while he stood stiff and unrelenting. She shut her eyes, then opened them again. What would he think if she missed his lips and accidentally kissed him on the chin? On her tiptoes, she leaned into him, kissing him quickly on the mouth.

"There. I kissed you." She loosened her arms from his neck.

"And you proved my point. That was not the kiss of a woman in love."

Which just went to show what he knew. "Oh, and how should I have kissed you?"

"Like this." He leaned down, gathering her into a tight embrace. His lips came down on hers quickly, intently, and she stood at once overwhelmed and lost in his arms. He felt so warm, and this felt so right. How could this feel so right when he was just trying to prove a point?

When the kiss ended she looked up at him, feeling dizzy. He dropped his arms from around her, and let out a deep breath.

"That's what I meant about manipulating my emotions. Don't tell me you're in love with me again until you mean it."

She stood in front of him, trying to process everything he'd just said, while her mind was simultaneously going through kiss withdrawal. His arms had felt so comforting and strong around her, and now he was putting on his gloves as though none of it had happened. Who was manipulating whose emotions?

She folded her arms. "Are you accusing me of toying with your affections because I said I loved you?"

"Yes."

"You're the one who's rebuffed me every time I've shown you any sort of attention. When I put my hand on yours in the van you nearly crawled out of the window to get away from me."

He took hold of the rake but didn't move any leaves. "We were alone, and you were wearing wet, clingy clothes."

"Only because I'd just fallen in a lake."

"Right. I tend to be cautious when I'm alone with women in wet, clingy clothes."

"Well fine, think whatever you want to. I only told you all of this so you wouldn't be surprised when you heard rumors that I was in love with you."

"Rumors that—wait a minute." The rake went back against the tree. "You told Bertie you were in love with me because she's sick, and now you'll tell her whatever she wants to hear. That's it, isn't it?"

She felt herself blush. "No."

"Yes, Ellie. This is just like your phone call to Dr. Blair. You're pretending to have feelings for me to hide your true motives from your aunt, and you haven't taken into consideration how I'll react to any of it. Well, what would you have done when you put on this performance if I had told you I was in love with you too?"

She refused to turn her gaze. "I would have been thrilled, of course."

His eyes narrowed. "Okay then, I call your bluff. Be thrilled. I'm in love with you."

She shrugged her shoulders. "Fine. I'm thrilled."

"We'll be a couple for the entire summer. Everyone will know about us, make predictions about our engagement date, and no other guys will ever ask you out."

Ellie shrugged again. "Bertie will be ecstatic. She's painting a wedding portrait of us in case she doesn't live to see the real event."

"Great. I'll show it to my mother once it's done. Maybe she'll want to hang it in the resort. And, by the way, Mom's expecting you for dinner on Friday. Since we're in love I will of course hold your hand all evening and kiss you during any private interludes."

"Perfect. I love romance. I'll spend the rest of evening trying to think of endearing nicknames for you."

"Fine. I'll pick you up at 6:00."

"Fine. I'll be waiting." She turned and walked back to the car, thinking how strange it felt to tell the truth like it was a lie.

Ellie's shifts on Thursday and Friday went by slowly. She didn't know what to say to Diana, who had apologized for being "so emotional the other day," and who had assured her, "I really hope things work out between you and John. You'd be a totally cool sister-in-law." She also didn't know how to act around Sister Flynn, who dropped by the desk several times to get Ellie's opinion on menu items for dinner.

When John picked her up that night, was she supposed to act like she was in love with him, or was she supposed to act like John thought she was—someone who wasn't in love with him pretending to be in love with him? Or just the plain truth—she would act like someone who was in love with him pretending to be someone who wasn't in love with him pretending to be someone who was in love with him.

When she got home from work she changed clothes and spent extra time touching up her hair and makeup, which was probably foolish since she'd just spent all day working with the people she was meeting for dinner. They knew what she looked like.

John rang the doorbell at ten to six. Bertie let him in, all smiles. Ellie was afraid John would say or do something—would let some vestige of sarcasm show, that would alert Bertie that his feelings were counterfeit. But he didn't. He was all smiles back. He put his hand on Ellie's back, gently massaging her shoulder. "Ready to meet my family?"

"I've already met your family."

"But you met them as an employee before. Now you're meeting them as my girlfriend."

"I'm ready."

Bertie picked up her camera from the coffee table. "I want to get a few pictures of the two of you together. You don't mind posing for a minute, do you?"

"Not at all," John said. "We'll pose for as long as you want."

He slid his arm from Ellie's shoulder to her waist and pulled her closer to him. She tried to smile as the flash went off repeatedly.

John pulled her even closer. "How about one of us kissing?" Before Bertie could answer, he bent down and kissed Ellie on the lips.

Well, if he was trying to embarrass her, it wouldn't work. She kissed him back. And perhaps the fact that she was blushing wouldn't show in the photograph.

Bertie snapped the picture, then held the camera down and sighed happily. "You make such a darling couple, but I suppose you had better be off. We don't want to keep your mother waiting."

They said their good-byes, then went out the door and down the porch steps. The warm summer evening surrounded them. Ellie fiddled with her purse strap as she walked. She could still feel the way John's lips had come down so casually on hers. Her lips almost tingled. But he was walking, taking in the scenery, as though he hadn't given the event a second thought. How easy was it for him to kiss women he had no interest in?

He turned to her with a half smile. "So, did you come up with any endearing names for me yet?"

"Endearing ones? No."

"I was considering Elle for you. What do you think?"

"I think it sounds dangerously close to a swear word."

"Just out of curiosity, what's going to happen to our love affair when the summer ends? Will we be having one of those long-distance romances?" They reached his car and he walked around to the passenger door. "I need to know since I'm Bertie's home teacher, and she'll no doubt ask me about it when you leave."

"I'm not leaving after the summer. I'm taking a break from college."

He put his hand on the door latch but didn't open it. "You're dropping out of school to take care of her? I thought she didn't want you to do that."

"She doesn't, but she understands because . . ."

He let go of the door latch and crossed his arms. "Because you're in love with me. Of course. You don't want to leave your boyfriend. It's so convenient to have me around, isn't it?"

She tilted her head at him in an appeal for understanding. "She needs someone to take care of her, someone who loves her."

"And that makes it okay to use me, I suppose. What if I had believed you, Ellie? What if I proposed to you before she died? What would you do then—marry me just to make her happy?"

"I don't think there's much chance of your proposing, do you?"

His eyes narrowed. "I'm going to propose to you the next time Bertie's with us. So help me, I will."

"You're threatening me with a marriage proposal?"

He took a step closer. "And I'll push for a short engagement so Bertie can see the event. What will you do then?"

Her hands went on her hips. "Is this a proposal? Because I don't think I should be required to answer that question unless you're prepared to get down on one knee while you're asking."

"And I don't think I should be required to play this game anymore." He took hold of her hand and pulled her a step away from the car. "Ellie, you're going to come clean with your real feelings right now or, so help me, I'll march you back to your aunt's house and propose."

He didn't let go of her hand. She didn't let go of his.

"Well?" he asked.

"When you propose, will you be giving me a flashy engagement ring?"

He dropped her hand. "Do you joke about everything?"

"No, not everything." And then she couldn't meet his gaze anymore. She looked at his shoes and noticed that they were new. Probably because she'd ruined his last two pairs. Her voice lowered. "I wasn't joking when I told you I loved you."

Silence.

She kept her gaze on his shoes. He tilted her chin upwards so she had to meet his eyes. "What did you just say?"

"I wasn't joking."

There was no clock around, but still she heard the seconds tick by in her mind. He wasn't saying anything, which obviously meant he didn't feel the same way and now was about to come up with some awkward apology for accusing her of toying with his emotions.

Dinner was going to be *so* uncomfortable.

His hand moved from her chin to her shoulder. "Do you know what I kept thinking while I held you that day in the ER?"

She shook her head.

"I kept thinking that it could have been you with the tumor, and how devastating it would be if I never saw you again. I knew you were leaving after the summer, and I wondered how I was going to stop that from happening because I didn't want to lose you that way either. I love you, Ellie."

The clock in her mind stopped. All time stopped. There was

only him standing in front of her. "Why didn't you tell me how you felt?" she asked.

"I was getting around to it. I was giving you time without pushing you. I was being cautious."

"Oh. So you were giving me time two days ago, but today you're threatening to propose in front of Bertie so I'll have to say yes?"

"Right. And I'm still going to do that."

"What happened to caution?"

He pulled her closer. "Caution has its time and place and this is no longer it." He bent down with a kiss, enveloping her with his embrace. She wound her arms around his neck, holding on to him the way she'd wanted to for so long.

They stayed that way until Bertie's voice called out to them from the porch. "How many times have I told you—none of that on my front lawn. People will talk!"

John let Ellie go, smiling as he waved good-bye to Bertie. He opened the car door for Ellie and she slid in.

"People have been talking for a long time," he said. "Now they'll finally be right."

About the Author

Sierra St. James lives in Chandler, Arizona. As a mother of five, she's spent far too much time stuck in doctors' offices trying to entertain sick children with nothing but tongue depressors and the middle-ear-infection chart. Although she likes doctors individually, as a profession they drive her crazy, and she has a theory that when a doctor goes to heaven, he is required to wait outside the pearly gates the accumulative amount of time he made his patients stay in his waiting room. If heaven is really fair, he will also have to keep small children from crawling under coffee tables, ripping pages out of magazines, and emptying the water machine at the same time.

Sierra loves Christmas and generally keeps her decorations up far too long. (Although for reasons of procrastination, not philosophy.) She is currently working on her own reasons-not-to-clean list.